Sue Minix is a member of Sisters in Crime, and when she isn't writing, you can find her reading, watching old movies, or hiking the New Mexico desert with her furry best friend.

Sentenced *to* Murder

SUE MINIX

avon.

Published by AVON
A division of HarperCollins*Publishers*
1 London Bridge Street
London SE1 9GF

www.harpercollins.co.uk

HarperCollins*Publishers*
Macken House
39/40 Mayor Street Upper
Dublin 1
D01 C9W8
Ireland

A Paperback Original 2024

24 25 26 27 28 LBC 7 6 5 4 3
First published in Great Britain by HarperCollins*Publishers* 2024

A catalogue copy of this book is available from the British Library.

ISBN: 978-0-00-865982-0

This novel is entirely a work of fiction. The names, characters and incidents
portrayed in it are the work of the author's imagination. Any resemblance to
actual persons, living or dead, events or localities is entirely coincidental.

Typeset in Sabon Lt Std by Palimpsest Book Production Limited,
Falkirk, Stirlingshire

Printed and Bound in the United States

To Dawn Dowdle, a wonderful agent
and an even better friend.
We miss you.
R.I.P.

CHAPTER ONE

Silence blanketed Riddleton Park at this hour on a February Saturday morning, and my senses reveled in the lack of input. In a few months, the ball fields would buzz with kids trying to get their games in before the sun rose too high and the temperatures vaulted into the nineties. Right now, the picnic shelters stood empty, too, although they'd likely fill up this afternoon with birthday parties and folks enjoying a moment in the sun. Pine trees dotting the landscape remained the only constant from one season to the next. Tall and majestic, their needles turned brown and fell, only to be replaced by fresh green ones.

Tiny water droplets plastered my face as my running buddy, Angus Halliburton, and I trotted laboriously through the early-morning fog. The rest of the Riddleton Runners were on the other side of the mile-long track around the park. Not for long, however. They'd already lapped us twice, and we were only finishing our first trip around. Needless to say, we didn't run out of a need for speed.

I'd never asked Angus why he'd joined the group, but I suspected it had more to do with camaraderie than exercise. The forty-seven-year-old New Hampshire transplant opened the Dandy Diner over ten years ago, but making friends in a small southern town like Riddleton, South Carolina, could be a challenge, even for a gregarious soul like Angus. Especially since he moved here from northern New England. Yankee distrust still ran deep down south, where the Civil War had never really ended.

I glanced over at him as he puffed along, face the color of an overripe apple, his black combover plastered to his scalp by moist air and sweat. The wet "V" extending down from the neck of his plain gray sweatshirt offset the circles under his armpits, and his matching gray sweatpants seemed to stick to his legs as he ran. Poor guy had to be miserable, but he never complained and never broke stride.

"You okay?" I asked. "You're awfully quiet today."

As the general manager of the Riddleton Rumor Mill, Angus typically regaled me with all the juicy tidbits he'd picked up in the diner during the week. Not that I had a particular interest in the intimate details of my neighbors' lives, but it made him happy to share them, so I uh-huhed and laughed in all the appropriate places. And his information had come in handy more than once when I was investigating the rash of murders that had struck Riddleton since I'd moved back home two years ago. Sometimes, it felt like I played a character in one of my mystery novels.

"I'm fine, Jen. You didn't seem interested in talking, so I'm giving you your space."

"My space?" I looked down at my German shepherd cantering along beside me. "You hear that, Savannah? He's giving me space."

She pricked her ears and forged ahead, falling drops of saliva marking her trail. We might have to cut our run short today. The wet air made it difficult for my dog to dissipate heat since the liquid wouldn't evaporate from her tongue. Fortunately, the sun still hung near the horizon, the temperature only in the fifties; otherwise, she might already be in trouble.

I turned to Angus. "See? She doesn't believe you either. What's up?"

He lifted the bottom of his sweatshirt, exposing his T-shirt-covered midsection to wipe perspiration off his face. "I'm trying to decide whether to decorate the diner for Valentine's Day."

"There's no contest for this holiday, right?" The town council often conducted a decoration contest for major holidays during the year, Valentine's Day not usually being one of them. The townsfolk went nuts over the competitions despite the rewards for victory mostly being symbolic. Bragging rights went a long way in a small town.

"No, no contest, but I'm still considering it. Love needs to be celebrated, in my opinion. It's so difficult to find."

Difficult to find? Is Angus lonely? He'd always seemed so happy to me, but the more I thought about it, the more sense it made. There weren't very many eligible women over forty in town. And being tied to the diner all day didn't give him much opportunity to meet any of them.

"What's the problem then? You should do whatever makes you happy."

"Spoken like a true friend." His plump lips spread into a smile. "What about *your* plans for Valentine's Day? Eric taking you someplace special?"

3

Eric O'Malley was my boyfriend, a rookie detective with the Riddleton Police Department, and the former high school track star about to lap us for the third time. We'd been friends since my return to town and only started dating last summer. The relationship had stumbled over some rocky places the last few months, making us question the wisdom of it at times. However, we'd finally settled into something we both found comfortable. For now.

"I don't know. We haven't discussed it yet."

Angus sidestepped over to poke me in the ribs. "Well, you better start dropping some hints. He might forget about it. You know how us guys are."

"Ha! No chance with all the promotion going on. It's like the whole world turns pink in February. Besides, Eric's not like that. He'd never forget." I brushed sweat off my face with my shoulder. "Personally, I think this holiday puts too much pressure on relationships. I don't need a box of candy and flowers to know that he loves me. He shows me every day."

"That's sweet, but you never know. He might do something exciting this year."

I glanced at him and caught a twinkle in his eye. Was he insinuating Eric might propose? An extra layer of perspiration appeared on my palms, and my heart sped into a staccato beat, accompanying the cloud of dread accumulating in my chest. I loved him, but I was nowhere near ready to get married. To anyone. "Why do you say that? What have you heard?"

Savannah looked up at me, feeling my tension through her leash. I scratched behind her ears, soothing her. Her head bobbed at mid-thigh level, making it easy to reach without concerns about falling over if I stepped on a pinecone.

4

"I haven't heard anything. It's your first Valentine's Day as a couple. I just figured he might go all out."

"Well, I hope not. It isn't necessary. I think a low-key dinner would be perfect for us."

"You mean like every other night?"

I narrowed my eyes at him, but he never looked back at me. *Smart man.* "We enjoy each other's company. What's wrong with that?"

"Not a thing. There's nothing wrong with a little romance, either. Except it makes you uncomfortable for some reason. Why?"

How did he know? Was I that obvious? My brain searched for an answer to his question, coming up empty. "Beats me."

"Could it be you have a fear of commitment?"

The sound of footfalls behind us told me we were about to be passed again. "What? No, that's not it at all."

"Then what is it? I can see how tense you are, even discussing it now. You'd think I told you he was planning to propose when all I said was he might do something interesting."

Unfortunately, in my mind, the two were the same. I'd never tell him that, though. Besides, wasn't that what guys usually did on Valentine's Day? Propose to their girlfriends? Eric had already mentioned marriage once or twice before. The dread moved from my chest to my head and rearranged the furniture. "Can we change the subject, please? I don't want to talk about this anymore."

He shot me a knowing look. "Okay, what are you getting *him*, then?"

I curled my fingers into fists as I ran. Savannah's

leash bounced against my leg. "I don't know. I haven't decided yet."

"You'd better decide in a hurry. It's less than two weeks away."

Gritted teeth joined my clenched hands. Why couldn't he let this go? Was he living vicariously through us? Or did he enjoy watching me squirm? Probably a little of both. "Don't worry. I'll figure something out."

"Do you need some help? I've been told I'm pretty adept at picking out gifts."

"Oh yeah? By who?"

"A gentleman never tells."

My hands relaxed, and I tapped his ribs with my elbow. "Okay, but what does that have to do with you?"

"You never know," he replied with a sly grin.

Angus had a secret love life? Nah. Secrets like that were impossible to keep in a small town like Riddleton. Of course, I'd be thrilled to be wrong. He deserved to be happy. "I'll let you know if I get stuck. I haven't given up yet."

We jogged in silence as the rest of the runners flew by us, smiling and waving. Eric turned around, running backward to give me a double thumbs up. His green running shorts and red Riddleton HS Track tank top were darkened with moisture, lending a more funereal appearance to his Christmas colors. A wide grin and crinkling eyes more than made up for it, though.

I waved back, focusing on the pine scent in the crisp air and the brown needles crunching under my feet. On days like this, I almost enjoyed running. I did it the rest of the time because it sparked my creativity. A necessity given I had to write the next two books in my mystery series by the end of the year, and writer's block tended to be more than a passing acquaintance.

Once we were on our own again, Angus asked, "How are things at the bookstore?"

I'd inherited Ravenous Readers a year and a half ago when the previous owner died unexpectedly in an explosion. With no experience running a business, the challenge had seemed overwhelming at times, but an infusion of cash from a new business partner had things looking better. Financially, anyway.

"Pretty well, I'd say. Sales have picked up some, and we're also beginning to get online orders. I think we might be okay." *Fingers and toes crossed.*

"How are the new arrangements working out?"

"It's only been a few weeks, so nothing's changed so far. I'm sure we'll hit some bumps in the road eventually. When we do, we'll deal with it. We've come this far together, right?"

"True. Have you ever thought about selling?"

Selling the bookstore? "No, never. What makes you ask?"

"I just wondered. It was only a few weeks ago that you thought the store might go under. You never considered selling even then?"

"Strangely enough, no. Not even then." I turned to look at him. "What's this all about, Angus? Are you thinking of putting the diner up for sale?"

He suddenly found the dusty tops of his running shoes fascinating.

"Angus?"

Still staring at his feet, he said, "I got an offer the other day. A really good one."

I stopped and gawked at him, open-mouthed.

7

Savannah didn't notice and almost jerked my shoulder out of its socket. Pain flashed down my arm, and I rubbed it as she coughed.

Angus caught on and turned back toward me. "That guy came in and said he'd pay me a ton of money if I'd sell him the diner."

"What guy?"

"You know, the developer. The one who wants to turn Riddleton into a tourist town."

Simeon Kirby. "What did you tell him?"

"I told him I needed to think about it. Riddleton is my home. What would I do without the diner? Where would I go?"

"How much money are we talking about?"

"Enough that I could do whatever I wanted, I suppose. But I'm happy where I am. It's tempting, though." He lifted his gaze from his shoes to me. "He hasn't approached you yet?"

"No, I haven't seen him."

"I'm surprised. I got the impression he wanted to replace all the existing businesses with shops of his choosing. Stores to support the resort he's building out by the lake."

"Well, he can't have Ravenous Readers. He's just going to have to change his plans. Of course, a bookstore could be part of his strategy, so maybe he doesn't need mine."

Angus arched his eyebrows. "Maybe, but what if he makes you an offer you can't refuse?"

I rolled my eyes. "He's not the godfather. He can't kill me if I say no."

"If you say so. It wasn't that long ago that you thought he was a hitman, remember?"

My face heated. "I remember. And I was wrong." When a woman was murdered a few weeks ago, I believed Kirby might've been a mob enforcer sent to make her husband repay a loan. I was way off base with that one. Not for the first time and probably not the last.

Footfalls behind us meant the group had caught up again. More smiles. More waves. Except for this time, Ingrid Kensington, Riddleton's town doctor and part-time pathologist, dropped out of the crowd. Ingrid had moved to South Carolina from London when the state offered to pay her way through medical school in exchange for five years of service in a small town. We were happy to have her. After all, who doesn't love a British accent? PBS had always been my favorite channel on Sunday nights.

"Hello, you two. Giving up already?"

Savannah pushed in to nuzzle Ingrid, who squatted to give her a good scratch. The dog closed her eyes and arched her back to get the most out of the experience. No, she wasn't spoiled at all.

"We only stopped to talk for a minute," I said, shaking my head and laughing. "We can get back on the road whenever her highness is done with you."

Ingrid stood and shook the dog hair out from between her fingers. "I think that'll do for now." She gestured toward the path. "Shall we?"

We took off down the track, Ingrid holding herself back to stay with us. "I hope I didn't interrupt something important," she said.

Angus shook his head. "Not at all. We were discussing the new development out by the lake. I think it'll be great for business. What do you think, Ingrid?"

She twisted her lips. "I imagine I'll also have more business, but I'm not sure that's a good thing. It's considered bad form for a doctor to wish for more patients."

"I can see that," I said, turning my head from side to side to loosen my shoulder muscles. Specifically the one Savannah'd tried to pull out of joint. "Frankly, what's good for business isn't necessarily good for Riddleton. I've been to Myrtle Beach in the summertime. The crowds are awful. You can't walk on the sidewalk, and there's always bumper-to-bumper traffic in the street. Even at midnight! I don't want to live that way. Do you?"

"Not when you put it that way," Angus said. "Still, wouldn't it be nice not to have money worries all the time?"

I had to concede that point. Money, or the lack of it, had been an issue for me since I left home for college twelve years ago. "Maybe, but I still don't think it'll be worth the price we have to pay."

"Actually, Angus," Ingrid began. "You'd need a lot more help at the diner to accommodate the crowds. Would you ever be able to find enough workers? I can't imagine too many people are lining up to wait tables in Riddleton. Not that there's anything wrong with it."

"I hadn't considered that. I might have to give the whole thing a little more thought."

Did Ingrid just give Angus the excuse he needed to sell the diner? I hoped not. I would miss him. And the new owner might not keep the current staff, which would put Ingrid's boyfriend, Marcus, out of work. However, Angus obviously didn't want to mention the prospective sale, so I wouldn't either. It wasn't my secret to tell.

"Ingrid, what does Marcus think about the new resort?"

"We haven't talked about it much. He's been a bit distracted lately."

"With what?" Angus asked. "He's not unhappy at work, is he?"

Ingrid rested her hand on his shoulder. "Not at all. He loves his job. He got an odd telephone call the other day. It's been bothering him."

"Did he say who it was from?"

"No, only that it was from a chap he met in the Sutton County Jail. Whatever the man said, it upset him greatly. He hasn't been himself since."

11

CHAPTER TWO

After a shower, I donned clean jeans and a Gamecocks sweatshirt. The pants hugged my hips a bit more than they used to, reminding me I needed to lay off the chocolate chip muffins that had become the core of my daily breakfast. On second thought, I'd probably left them in the dryer too long, and they shrank. Yup, I'd go with that.

I parked myself at my desk to take advantage of the influx of oxygen my brain had received during my morning run. While waiting for my work in progress to load, I took a few deep inhalations of the stale apartment atmosphere. I couldn't wait for the weather to warm up so I could open the balcony doors and windows for air exchange.

A few more deep breaths topped off my tank. Sometimes, it worked; sometimes, it didn't. With the deadline for the third book in my Davenport Twins Mystery series only a few months away, I needed today to be a good day. So far, though, I'd only succeeded in making myself light-headed.

The stars of my series, teenage twins Dana and Daniel, had been my constant companions for almost a decade, though they'd only aged a couple of years in the process. I, however, felt forty years older than the college junior who'd begun the journey with them. The stress of trying to duplicate the success of my first book, *Double Trouble*, and the trail of failed relationships I'd left behind me had contributed greatly to my rapid aging. Not to mention the four murder investigations in less than two years, in which most, if not all, fingers pointed at me as the culprit.

I stared at the flashing cursor camped out beneath the *Chapter Four* scrawled across the screen's top. My "Creativity Begins with Coffee" mug warmed my hands as I valiantly willed the words to be true. Writer's block always seemed to have the last say, however. I longed for those carefree college days when the words flew from my brain out my fingertips onto the screen so fast I couldn't keep up. That seemed like a lifetime ago.

My fingers rested in the correct position on the keyboard, and I waited for the magic prose to appear in my mind. What I got was: what's Savannah doing? Napping on the couch. I watched until her ribcage rose, then tried again. Nope, nothing. Nicht, nix, nada. Multiple languages all amounting to the same result: I'd never finish this book.

I scrolled back to the end of chapter three and reread the last paragraph. Daniel had just entered the old Underground Railroad tunnel where he and the rest of the fraternity pledges were being blindfolded and taken, one at a time at thirty-minute intervals, to find their way out again. I needed only to describe his journey until he found the murdered pledge so he and his sister would have something to investigate. How hard could it be? I'd been in the same situation only a few weeks ago while investigating the murder of a guy left on my doorstep.

I put myself back in those tunnels, pictured the scene in my mind, and began describing what I saw. Then I added in the smells and the sounds and the gut-wrenching fear that threatened to paralyze me the whole time I was down there. Once I got started, a stream of words flowed through my fingers, just like the old days. Before I knew it, a thousand of them flooded the pages, two hours had passed, and my brain was as dry and empty as the Sahara Desert. I rested my head on my forearms crossed on the desk, drained. Good enough for now. I'd try again later.

An hour remained before I had to meet Eric at the diner for lunch, so I roused my sleeping German shepherd, and we headed for the bookstore. After Savannah's pit stop at the oak tree at the bottom of the steps, we strolled down Main Street past the Dollar General and crossed Oak Street to the Goodwill, where I stopped for a minute to admire the old Remington manual typewriter on display. Who was I kidding? As much time as I spent backspacing and deleting, I'd have to retype every manuscript fifty times.

The fog had lifted, and we now enjoyed a mild, sunny late morning, the blue sky dotted with puffs of clouds I failed to find any interesting shapes in. Punxsutawney Phil had seen his shadow the other day, but winter seemed to be on hiatus for the moment. Maybe I'd be able to get those windows open today after all.

I waved at Angus through the still-undecorated window of the Dandy Diner, then traversed Pine to cover the last block, which housed the town hall, police station, and Ravenous Readers. Having the cops right next door had always been a source of comfort, except when it was me they were after. As a rule, though, Riddleton had little crime to speak of.

Unless you counted murder.

Downtown had been fashioned into a rectangle divided into sections by seven streets—three across and four down. While the official population pushed the ten thousand mark, most residents lived in the surrounding farms and housing developments and on the shore of Lake Dester. Only a few hundred people called Riddleton itself home, giving it a quaint, small-town feel. I'd hated the cloying everybody's-always-in-your-business atmosphere growing up and left at the first opportunity, but had come to love it since my return a couple of years ago.

When we entered the bookstore, an older couple browsed the Biography section, two teenage girls hung out on the brown-and-gold-striped couch surfing their phones, and a middle-aged blonde stirred sugar into her cup at the coffee bar. Not too bad for a Saturday, when most town residents preferred exploring the shopping malls in the nearby cities of Blackburn and Sutton. Hard for us to compete with the vast selections found in the major chain stores.

Charlie Nichols, our barista-in-chief, as he liked to call himself, handed the blonde a muffin to go with the coffee she held in her other hand. She smiled and made herself comfortable at one of the butcher-block tables by the Mystery section to flip through a romance while she ate. With luck, she didn't have sticky fingers. As my mother liked to say, "Napkins are our friends." Especially in a bookstore.

Charlie was a thirty-six-year-old computer geek who'd offered to help out for next to nothing when I inherited the store and had no idea what to do with it. When he'd moved into the apartment below mine, his mission had been to convince me to go out with him. *My* mission at the time was to get him to leave me alone. The war had ended in an awkward truce.

I had concerns about working with him, but he'd been on his best behavior ever since I convinced him I'd undo all his expensive dental work if he asked me to dinner one more time. In exchange for his concessions, I agreed to let him dress however he chose rather than insist he wear the standard uniform of khaki pants and a red Ravenous Readers polo shirt. And allow him to keep all his teeth.

Today, he decided to be Zorro—leather pants, a silk long-sleeve shirt, a cape tied around his neck, and the hat with a feather tucked into the band I'd given him for Christmas last year. All black. Still no sword or mask, though. The mask might be his next birthday present. The blade, however, he'd have to live without.

I reached under the coffee bar for my "Writer in Residence" mug and filled it with coffee from the urn. Charlie whipped out his invisible sword and carved the famous "Z" on my chest with a flourish.

After sending him a super-sized eye roll, I said, "Really, Charlie?"

He sheathed his blade and stood with arms akimbo. "What? I'm placing you under my protection. Now everyone knows not to mess with you."

Terrific, but who would protect me from him? "Thank you, kind sir." I gripped the sides of my imaginary skirt and curtseyed, banging my forehead on the pastry case glass. I rubbed the sore spot, feeling for the lump soon to follow. "Ow! Some protector you are."

16

He shook his head, the feather waving. "Even Zorro can't protect you from yourself. That's a full-time job."

I squinted and wrinkled my nose at him. "Where's Lacey?"

He eyeballed the store. "I don't know. She was here a minute ago. She must be hunting for something in the back."

Lacey Stanley—brown-haired, mid-thirties, mother of two and one on the way—was my store manager and business partner. She and her husband, Ben, had recently bought a 50 percent stake in Ravenous Readers, giving us enough cash to stay open until sales picked up and the store became self-sustaining. We worked well together but still had to adjust to our new roles. Well, I had to adjust to *my* new role, anyway. Lacey pretty much did what she always had—run the store with an expert, loving hand.

She came out of the stockroom, carrying a biography to the older couple. Savannah charged to the cash register counter, knowing Lacey had stashed the bacon treats underneath. She waited patiently, decorating the glass case containing bookmarks and booklights for our more considerate nighttime readers, with nose-print art and wagging her entire rear end.

Lacey noticed the dog and smiled. "Hold on, little girl. I'm coming."

Savannah leaped to her feet and pranced in a tight circle.

I sipped my coffee and headed in that direction, laughing. "Poor starving baby. You'd think she hadn't eaten in a month. Although she did have a pretty good workout this morning."

"You really should try feeding her once in a while."

Lacey offered her a snack, which Savannah nibbled out of her palm using only her lips.

"I don't know what you're talking about. She ate the day before yesterday. She's not due for another two days. How much more does she need?"

Lacey wiped her hand on her polo shirt. "Yeah, right. I'll bet she eats more in a day than you do."

"I'll bet you're right. A pound of kibble, plus leftovers and treats. And she still thinks she's a famine victim." I scratched her neck as she begged for another snack.

"She's a growing girl."

"Are you kidding? She weighs eighty-five pounds! She's grown quite enough as far as I'm concerned. Any more, and I'll have to feed her with a snow shovel."

"Good luck finding one around here."

"I'm just happy we almost never *need* one around here."

Savannah gave up on conning any more treats out of Aunt Lacey and trotted to the coffee bar to sniff out crumbs dropped by Uncle Charlie. The older couple carried three books to the cash register. As Lacey dealt with them, I retreated to the stockroom for glass cleaner and paper towels. While I appreciated my dog's ingenuity and creativity, I doubted our customers would feel the same way about the streaks and swirls obscuring the merchandise.

When the front door closed behind the biography buffs, I said, "What have you been up to this morning?"

"Other than helping customers, reading to kids, and throwing up? Not much."

Lacey was near the end of her first trimester, struggling with morning sickness. "I'm so sorry. Why didn't you call me?"

18

"No need. I'm used to it. This is my third time around, you know."

She had a son, Ben Jr., who we called Benny, and a daughter, Brianna, six and nine, respectively. "I know, but I'm still happy to help if you need me. You must be miserable."

"I can handle it." She pulled a half-sleeve of unsalted crackers and a bottle of ginger ale from under the counter. "See? I've got it covered. And you have two books to write by the end of the year." After swapping the snacks for a spiral notebook, she said, "Look at what I've been working on. I think it'll make a great window display, don't you?"

I accepted the book and studied the first drawing. Cupid on the right-side window, bow cocked, ready to fire an arrow. I flipped to the next one of an arrow traveling across the front door. The left-side window had a group of people reading romance novels, with more arrows headed straight toward them. "This is great, but are you sure you want to take all this on in your current condition? It's not like there's a contest for this one."

"What do you mean, my current condition? I'm pregnant, not wasting away on my deathbed. It's a baby, not consumption."

My ears burned, and I shuffled my feet in discomfort. I hadn't intended to upset her. "I only meant the paint smell might bother you or something. You've also been having dizzy spells, remember? I don't want you passing out and falling through the glass, either."

"I'll be fine. Stop being such a worrywart." She collected her notebook. "I'm also going to take a few of the small bookcases we pulled out of the children's

19

section, fill them with romances, and station them around the store."

"Will you let us help you with that, at least? Those bookcases are heavy since Eric bolted them together in stacks of two, and you need to take it easy."

"Jennifer Marie Dawson! It's 2024, not 1824. Stop treating me like some magnolia blossom that's going to wilt in the sun."

"Hey! Only my mother's allowed to use my middle name when she's mad. You might be a mother, but it doesn't make you mine."

She crossed her arms. "Fine, but you got the point, right?"

I replied, "Yes, ma'am," but anxiety danced through my belly. Not long ago, I'd have had the right to insist she listen to me. But we were partners now. Fifty-fifty. They'd only asked for 30 percent of the business, but I didn't think that was fair, given how much money they offered. Perhaps I should've kept 51 percent instead. Then, I'd still be in charge.

However, Lacey was the heart and soul of the bookstore. She knew how to run it, what the customers would respond to, what would make us successful in the long term. I knew how to write books, not sell them. I had no experience managing any kind of business, let alone a bookstore. In truth, I should've given *her* 51 percent.

But I didn't; now, I'd have to learn to live with it. It never occurred to me how difficult it would be to give up the illusion of control. Lacey had always been in charge of the store. The only difference now was she no longer had to run her decisions by me first. Why did it matter? I almost never disagreed with her. Guess I liked having the option more than I'd realized.

The clock on the wall showed eleven fifty-eight. I had two minutes to meet Eric at the diner for lunch. And my propensity to be late made him unhappy. I'd been working hard lately to be more considerate of his feelings. The least I could do was be on time for lunch.

CHAPTER THREE

I left Savannah at the bookstore with Aunt Lacey and Uncle Charlie since the diner was likely crowded on a Saturday afternoon. The locals would never complain as my German shepherd was the closest thing to a town mascot Riddleton had, unless you included the Riddleton High School Jackrabbit who patrolled the sidelines during Friday night football games in the fall.

However, there was no telling how many strangers traveling the back roads between Blackburn and Sutton or guests from the resort might stop by for lunch. The last thing I'd want is to bring negative attention to Angus's diner. On the selfish side, though, enough bad press might make Kirby withdraw his offer, and Angus would have to stay. Something to think about. Except I wanted my friend to be happy, so I'd have to live with whatever decision he made.

A few more puffy white clouds decorated the azure sky, but they presented no threat of rain. It was a day born for outdoor activities, and I imagined the park's ball fields and picnic areas, deserted during our morning run, were now full of townspeople celebrating the break from winter's misery. I filled my lungs with fresh, spring-like air.

I scurried down the sidewalk under the noonday sun, past the police station and town hall, which showed no signs of activity—typical for the closed town hall and a positive omen for the police. Hopefully, their day would remain peaceful. They might not have many more calm weekends if Simeon Kirby had his way. An influx of tourists would definitely keep our police force busy. Mainly on the weekends.

The Dandy Diner occupied the corner of Main and Pine next door to the Goodwill and across the street from the town hall. It functioned as a meeting place as much as an eating place, a favorite hangout for the Riddleton gossipmongers. They'd sit in the orange faux-leather booths for hours, sipping coffee and exchanging stories.

Angus served as gossipmonger-in-chief since he picked up snippets from everyone who came through and passed them on to anyone who would listen. Mostly for entertainment, though. No malice intended. Angus knew when to keep a secret and never revealed anything that might hurt someone, unless they happened to be a murder suspect.

When I entered, the diner was wall-to-wall people, and I recognized about half the faces participating in various stages of their dining experience. Good thing I'd left Savannah behind. No way to know which of the strangers would feed her treats and who might complain about her presence. Best not to take any chances.

Angus stood behind the counter, conducting his orchestra of waitstaff, cooks, and bussers as if they were members of the South Carolina Philharmonic. He shared a smile with each person he made eye contact with,

23

and his combover bounced across his shiny scalp every time he moved. He loved this place. I couldn't imagine him ever giving it up, even for the world's best retirement opportunity. Particularly when he knew he'd be turning it over to someone who didn't care about the customers, didn't care about the town, and didn't care about anything but profits.

Eric had somehow managed to snag our favorite booth in the corner. How he always did that, no matter how busy the place was, amazed and confounded me. When I asked him about it, he just shrugged and said he knew the owner. But that should only make a difference if Angus was forcibly relocating people when Eric walked in. No way we were that important, but knowing Angus, I wouldn't be shocked if it turned out to be true.

I slid onto the seat across from Eric. He looked up from his menu and grinned, bunching his cheek freckles together and creating laugh lines around his eyes. The guy was growing up. His skinny frame had filled out some in the last few months, and his orange hair had darkened into more of a deep red. He no longer reminded me of little Opie Taylor, although I could still see the resemblance at times like this.

"How's it going?" I asked, reaching for a menu of my own.

He lifted an eyebrow. "What're you going to do with that?"

"I'm going to decide what I want for lunch, just like you. What else would I do with it?"

"We both know what you're going to order. Why bother with the pretense?"

"What's that supposed to mean?" I set the laminated

page on the table and crossed my arms. "I have no idea what I want until I look at the choices. Just because the same things appeal to me every day doesn't mean I don't give everything else a fair shot."

"Methinks the lady doth protest too much."

I scrunched my lips together. "You'd better knock it off before we do the 'out, out damn spot' scene instead."

He flipped to the sandwich side of his menu. "Nothing like a little Shakespeare in the morning, huh?"

"It's afternoon."

"Which is why you're going to order a bacon cheeseburger, fries, and either a chocolate milkshake or a Mountain Dew, depending on how your day's been so far."

I pinched my brows into a fake glower. I hated when he was right. "One of these days, I might surprise you."

"Possibly, but not today, I suspect."

Before I could reply, our waitress, Penelope, approached with her order pad in one hand, the other self-consciously patting her dyed-red long hair. Must've been the inch of blond showing at her roots making her feel uncomfortable. First time I'd ever seen her behind on her hair upkeep. "You folks ready to order?" She immediately began scribbling.

"We haven't said anything yet. What are you writing?" I asked.

"I'm writing down your order while he finishes deciding. We're busy, so I'm saving time." She fussed with her hair again. "Is this a shake day or a Dew day?"

I *so* wanted to order something different to teach them a lesson, but I liked what I always got. Why should I punish myself because they were smart alecks? "It's a Dew day. Nothing bad's happened yet."

"Well, I hope it stays that way." She turned expectantly to Eric.

"I'll have the same, except with a Pepsi."

"Got it. I'll be right back with your drinks." Penelope tore our slip off her order pad and carried it to the front counter.

"Now that the challenging task of ordering lunch is complete, what have you been up to today?" I reached across the table for Eric's hand and traced his lifeline with my finger.

He shivered as I tickled his palm. "Not much. Relaxing on my day off." His emerald eyes glinted in the overhead fluorescent lights. "And making plans for Valentine's Day."

A boulder settled in my chest. I really didn't want him to do anything special. Too much pressure. "Oh? What kind of plans?"

"If I tell you, it won't be a surprise."

Uh-oh. What would I do if Angus was right? I loved him, but I was happy with the way things were between us. "It doesn't have to be a surprise. I enjoy spending time with you, even if I know what we're doing beforehand."

"Some things are better when they're unexpected. Valentine's Day plans are one of those things." He took a deep breath and let it out slowly. "Please don't spoil this for me, Jen. I want to do something nice for you. To show you how I feel."

Something nice? That didn't sound like a proposal. I relaxed a bit, and the boulder crumbled. "I won't. I promise."

"Thank you."

Penelope returned with the drinks, and we busied

26

ourselves by stripping the paper off our straws. I poked mine into my soda and wiped condensation off the glass with a napkin.

Eric sipped his cola. "I do have a Valentine's Day surprise I can share with you, but you have to swear you won't tell anyone else."

Oh, boy, a secret! I crossed my heart, zipped my lips, and threw away the key. "There. I swear. Now spill!"

"I'm serious, Jen. You can't tell anyone. Especially Brittany."

Brittany Dunlop had been my best friend since kindergarten. How could I keep a secret from her? As a rule, I spilled my guts the instant she walked into the room. "Why can't I tell Brittany? I tell her everything."

"I know, but you can't this time. Promise me, or I can't tell you."

"Fine. I promise, but this better be good."

His grin gave me the answer. "Olinski is planning to propose on Valentine's Day! He showed me the ring this morning. Brittany's going to love it, but you can't breathe a word to her about this. Olinski'll have my head fitted for a lampshade."

My eyelids stretched so wide they felt like they were being forced open. I covered my mouth with my hands, then squealed. "Oh my gosh! That's wonderful! How's he going to do it? Balloon ride? Skywriter?" Then I remembered *my* experience with him. "Never mind. His proposal to me was, 'Hey, let's get married,' while I was still wearing my high school cap and gown. No getting down on one knee, no mushy soliloquy. Not even a ring."

Stan Olinski was my former high school boyfriend and Riddleton's current chief of police. He'd been dating

Brittany for a little over a year, and they seemed well matched. Much better matched than he and I had ever been.

Still, a tiny twinge of jealousy galloped through my chest. I dismissed the silly feeling. I didn't want him back. Why shouldn't my best friend be happy with him?

"He's not the same guy he was back then. He didn't tell me his plans, but I'm pretty sure he'll do more than that this time."

"I hope so. He'd be lucky to have Brittany as his wife. She deserves better from him."

He took my hand. "So did you."

"Apparently not."

Eric wisely stayed silent. He'd reopened an old wound, and I suspected he knew it. Even though I refused to marry Olinski, his nonchalant assumption that I'd jump at the chance had always gnawed at me. He knew my plans didn't include cooking, cleaning, and popping out babies but was still shocked when I turned him down to go to college instead. And stayed angry with me for years afterward.

We'd agreed to get along for Brittany's sake, and for the most part, we did. Unless I found myself stuck in the middle of one of his murder investigations. Then, our relationship depended on whether he believed I'd interfered with it or not. And it didn't take much for him to decide I had. Of course, he was usually right, but I only did it because I had no choice. I had to save either myself or someone I cared about. That justified my behavior, in my opinion, but most of the time, he disagreed. The fact I usually turned out to be right in the end only made things worse.

A lull at the cash register brought Marcus to our

table to break the silence. Marcus Jones was the diner's assistant manager and a former felon, but he'd since turned his life around to provide a stable environment for his two young daughters. My pride in his accomplishments led me to rush to his defense when he'd been arrested for a crime I knew he didn't commit a while back. Fortunately, my efforts—classified by Olinski as interference—succeeded.

Marcus flashed his perfect white teeth. "Hey, ya'll. How's it going?"

"Not too bad." Eric moved over to make room for him. "Have a seat."

Marcus scooted into the booth next to him and glanced at each of us. "How come you so serious today?"

Eric shot me a warning glance.

My lips twitched, itching to blurt out my secret, but I'd promised. "No reason. We were just discussing the meaning of life and the mysteries of the universe."

"Sure you were. What's going on?"

Eric stepped in. "Nothing. Honest. What've you been up to?"

Under the table, my leg bounced, my knee colliding with the underside of the Formica. If I'd known how difficult it would be to keep my promise, I never would've made it. But then I wouldn't know my best friend was about to get engaged. I sighed and trapped my lips between my teeth as if that would help. It didn't.

"Not too much," Marcus replied. "Business as usual."

My conversation with Ingrid this morning popped into my head. "Not quite. I heard you received an interesting phone call the other day."

"You been talking to Ingrid."

"A little, while we were running. She didn't say much,

only that a guy you met in Sutton called you, and you seemed upset and wouldn't talk to her about it."

Eric laid a hand on my arm. "Jen, maybe he doesn't want to talk to you about it, either."

Marcus frowned at his hands for a moment, then sighed. "It's not a secret. The guy has a problem, and I don't know how to help."

"Tell us what's going on. Maybe we can do something." Eric folded his hands together on the table. "Even if we can't, talking to someone might make you feel better."

Marcus chewed on his lower lip and picked at his thumbnail.

"At least tell us who the guy is," I said. "Then, we can look into it on our own, and you won't have betrayed his confidence. It'll never come back to you. I promise."

"It's not that. I just don't want to dump you in the middle of another investigation that might get you in trouble. You've done so much for me. I can't do that to you again."

"Why don't you let us decide what we should do." Eric sipped his drink. "Tell us the story. I won't let Jen get into any more trouble."

He glanced at me, and I nodded. "Go ahead."

"Okay. The dude's name is Jaylon Barnes, and he was convicted of killing his brother five years ago, but the body was never found, and the evidence was all hinky. They didn't have nothing on him, and he swears he didn't do it."

I fought back a snicker. They all said that, and rarely was it true. But I had to hear Marcus out. This might be one of those cases, although I had no idea what I could do about it, even if the guy *was* telling the truth.

30

"Go on," Eric prompted.

"Here's the problem. The reason Jaylon was at Sutton County to begin with is he's real sick. Something about his kidneys don't work. He has to get treatment two or three times a week, or he'll die, so they transferred him from the prison to the jail to be closer to the hospital."

I reached across and squeezed his arm. "I'm so sorry, Marcus. Is he a candidate for a transplant? Have they put him on the list?"

"He's on the list, but way down 'cause he's a convicted murderer. It ain't supposed to be that way, but you know how it works in real life."

Eric locked eyes with me. We did. The man had no chance.

"What about a volunteer donor? Is there anyone in his family who's a match?"

"He only has his parents, and neither one of them is compatible." He tapped his fingers on the table. "There is one lady they found on the national donor list, but she won't do it since he's in jail for murder. The only way to save his life is to prove he's innocent and get his conviction overturned."

Eric blew air out through pursed lips. "And that's where we come in. He wants us to find proof he didn't kill his brother so he can get the transplant he needs to save his life."

Marcus nodded, a hopeful expression in his liquid brown eyes.

"Where did all this happen, Marcus? Which department had jurisdiction?" Eric asked, pulling out the cop notebook he always carried, on duty or not.

"Riddleton. I don't know who investigated, but

31

Jaylon made it sound like he didn't try very hard to find another suspect."

I tilted my head back to stare at the white-painted ceiling. He was asking the impossible. How could we find evidence the police missed five years ago? Where would we even start? "How sure are you he's innocent?"

"Almost 100 percent. Go see him. Let him tell you his story, and decide for yourself. If you think he's guilty, then forget I ever said anything. It'll be like we never had this conversation. But, if you don't, if you think he might be innocent, you have to help him. Please."

How could I say no to that? However, how could I, in good conscience, say yes? Marcus was begging for a miracle, and I couldn't be sure I had another one in me.

CHAPTER FOUR

After a restless night, I untangled myself from the sheets and rolled out of bed—despite Savannah's objections—around seven thirty Sunday morning. Marcus's story played on a loop in my head throughout the night. Torn between the choices, I had a different decision in my mind every time I awakened in the dark. By the time I gave up, it was a fifty-fifty split. Half check into Jaylon's situation, half leave it alone. That's where things stood as I started the coffeemaker and leashed Savannah for her walk.

We made the circuit in record time, Savannah spending much less time than usual on sniff stops. I couldn't tell what had her in such a rush today. Perhaps the neighborhood strays had left her fewer messages than usual, or she might be hungry and ready for breakfast. Whatever the reason, she zipped around the block like a greyhound chasing a mechanical rabbit, towing me along in her wake.

The air temperature wasn't quite as warm as this time yesterday, but it was comfortable enough, and the sun hovered above the Piggly Wiggly across the street in a partly cloudy sky.

The dying sputters of the magic machine that produced my morning elixir provided background noise as I filled Savannah's dishes with food and water. Her crunches accompanied the filling of my mug and the booting up of my laptop. She licked her bowl clean while I brought up my latest chapter, her satisfied burp serving as the concerto finale.

Even thinking about writing turned out to be a waste of time, in any case. I couldn't shake off the expression on Marcus's face as he told me his friend would die if someone didn't help him get his conviction overturned. The picture remained lodged in my brain like a splinter on the day before tweezers were invented. No matter how hard or often I squeezed, pushed, and prodded, I couldn't get it out.

I finished my coffee and poured another to carry as I paced the track around my apartment. Jaylon needed help. That left me with two questions: was he innocent as Marcus believed, and did I dare investigate a case the police considered closed? Did I dare risk the wrath of Olinski and company? It would be a dicey move at best.

At worst? Well, I didn't want to think about that.

On the one hand, why should they care if I looked into it? It was a closed case; they were satisfied the perpetrator was in jail, and, as far as they were concerned, justice had been served. If they were right, they had no reason to fear my findings. On the other hand, my poking into the case might make them defensive, leading me to wonder if they hadn't railroaded Jaylon as he claimed. A hint of a headache encroached on my temples. I rubbed them with my free hand.

Law enforcement officers hated being questioned, and

they hated being proved wrong even more. If I headed in a direction they disapproved of, someone in the department would likely try to discourage me at every opportunity. And given how often I'd been falsely accused since my return to town, it wouldn't be in my best interest to make enemies of the Riddleton police. However, I suspected it was already too late, where some of them were concerned.

I wanted to carry the coffeepot across the hall and discuss all this with Brittany but feared I couldn't keep Olinski's secret. I was so excited for her; I'd probably blurt it out when she opened the door. Then Olinski would hate me again, and Eric too, for betraying his trust. I clenched my free hand and gulped my coffee. Now, I was irritated with Eric for telling me.

A glance at the clock told me it was late enough to call my mother instead. It was my turn this week, and she got grumpy when I forgot. And I didn't like my mother when she was grumpy. I pulled up my contacts and pressed the photo of us at my college graduation. When I hit the green phone icon under MOM, she answered on the second ring.

"You're early this morning."

A complaint or comment? No way to tell yet. "I didn't wake you, did I?"

"No, we've been up for a while. How are you?"

"Pretty good. How about you?"

"Can't complain. We saw the doctor the other day, and Gary's still in remission, so we're cautiously happy."

My stepfather was diagnosed with colon cancer last year, and surgery along with chemo succeeded. So far. "That's great! I'm glad to hear it." Gary and I had our problems when I was growing up, but his illness had

35

brought us a little closer together. I no longer actively despised him as I once had, which I considered progress. "Mom, I need some advice."

"Advice from me? Since when?"

Oh boy, here we go. "Don't start. Please. I'm in a quandary and don't know what to do. Can you please just listen and tell me what you think?"

"Humph. All right."

I told her Jaylon's story and my reservations about getting involved, leaving out my fear of police retaliation. She believed the police never did anything wrong, and nothing I could say would convince her otherwise. "What do you think?"

"Should I tell you what I really think or say what you want to hear? I don't want to fight with you today."

Since I had no idea what I wanted to hear, that was an easy question to answer. "Tell me what you really think. I don't know what to do."

She sighed into my ear. "I think you're making this situation all about you. It doesn't matter what anyone else thinks. Do *you* think this man has been wronged?"

"I don't know. Marcus seems to believe the guy didn't do it."

"But you're obviously unwilling to take his word for it, so don't you think you should talk to the man yourself? Make up your own mind about his guilt or innocence, and then decide whether you should pursue it. Remember, if he's innocent, he could die waiting for justice."

When did getting justice for everyone become my responsibility? I'm only a writer. "But why do I have to be the one to do it?" An unpleasant whine had slipped into my tone.

36

"Because you can, dear. Because you can."

She was right, of course. I had to do it because nobody else would, and I couldn't live with knowing that a man died in prison because I wouldn't help him. There were no guarantees, of course. I understood that. I might look into it and not find anything worthwhile, or I might find something that could help him, and he still dies. Regardless of the outcome, I had to try.

I thanked her and disconnected the call. I knew what I had to do next. I had to visit Jaylon Barnes. There was no other way to tell if this investigation was a risk worth taking.

The Sutton County Detention Center was a brick building with a pyramid-shaped slate roof that took up an entire block in downtown Sutton. I eased my silver 2015 Dodge Dart into the parking lot and circled until I found an empty space in the last row of six. I hadn't expected this large a crowd. Sunday must be a prime visiting day.

I meandered toward the double doors, thinking of ways to establish a rapport with Jaylon. It shouldn't be too difficult, though. He was desperate for my help. Unlike most of the people I struggled to acquire information from, he ought to readily volunteer anything I needed to know. He had to convince me he didn't murder his brother. But first, I had to prove he could trust me.

Wiping sweaty palms on my jeans, I opened the door and entered the interior, heated beyond what the weather required. A Sutton County sheriff's deputy with sweat pooling on his brow stood beside an X-ray scanner to my right, and I emptied my pockets into a bowl. He waved me through the metal detector, where, on the other side, another deputy returned my keys, phone, and ID.

Directly ahead was an information desk staffed by yet another deputy. I explained why I had come, and she directed me to a door at the end of the sparsely furnished modern-motif lobby. I stepped through the steel door with a six-inch square window too small for even the tiniest prisoners to escape through. Plus, it was reinforced by wires, creating little diamond shapes within the glass. What was the point? Nobody's arms could be long enough to reach the door handle from that window.

Beyond the entrance was a room containing two more deputies—one male and one female. The man signed me in and collected the contents of my pockets to be stored in a paper bag with my name on it and mumbled that my belongings would be returned when I left at the end of my visit. Then, the woman patted me down to ensure I had nothing else on my person that Jaylon could use to attempt an escape. Good thing I left my file at home.

Only then was I allowed through the doorway into the room set up with tables and chairs like a dining hall or restaurant with no food service. My observations about the crowded parking lot were confirmed as I weaved my way through the tables occupied by orange-clad detainees and their visitors to the sole empty one at the front. At least Jaylon would have no trouble finding me despite not knowing what I looked like or that I would even be here today. I was the only person in the room seated alone.

I only had a few minutes to study the hall for character

ideas before a door opposite the one I'd come in opened. A young man wearing wire-rimmed glasses entered and looked around. His orange jumpsuit had short sleeves that hung down to the elbow and pants cuffs rolled at least twice to keep them from dragging on the ground when he walked. Close-cropped hair did little to hide his prominent ears, which stuck out on each side like car doors left open. At first glance, the kid couldn't be over eighteen, if that. But, of course, he had to be much older.

His escort pointed him in my direction, and he shuffled toward me. As he neared the table, the fatigue etched into his thin face became visible, and his eyes were puffy from lack of sleep. I had no idea what severe kidney disease was supposed to look like on a person, but this guy was definitely ill with something.

When he came close enough, I stood and stuck out my hand. "Hi, Jaylon. I'm Jen Dawson, a friend of Marcus Jones, and I wanted to talk to you about your case."

He lightly brushed my fingertips and eased into the seat across from mine as if it might break if he sat too hard. I suspected he was the one who might break. How could anyone believe a guy this fragile could kill someone? Marcus didn't mention how the brother died, but unless he used a gun, Jaylon had to be innocent. Although I'd been fooled before, so perhaps I should wait until I heard the whole story to decide.

"Are you a lawyer?" he asked in a low voice I strained to hear.

"No. Marcus told me a little about you, and I thought you could use some help. He said you needed a kidney transplant, and your only possible donor wouldn't give

39

you one of hers because you'd been convicted of murder. Is that right?"

He nodded and rubbed at a patch of dry skin on his forearm. "I didn't kill my brother, Ewon. I loved him."

"Why don't you tell me the whole story from the beginning?"

For the first time since he'd come in, he met my gaze full on. "What's in it for you? What do you care?"

"Well, I care for a couple of reasons. Number one, I know what it's like to be falsely accused. I had people on my side, and that made a big difference."

"So, now you're one of those do-gooders who think they can save everyone?"

My mouth slipped into a half-smile. "Not hardly. I can barely save myself most of the time. That's where those other people come in. Reason I want to help number two is Marcus cares about what happens to you. And I care about Marcus."

"He's a good guy. He didn't deserve to be in here."

"No, he didn't. And I helped him get out. Now, will you let me try to help you? What do you have to lose?"

He lifted one shoulder in a shrug. "Nothing I guess, besides getting my hopes up for nothing."

"I'm not making any promises. Obviously, I can't guarantee the outcome, no matter what, if anything, I find, but I'd like to try. So, will you tell me your story?"

He coughed into his hand, then cleared his throat. "Sorry. I'm not allowed to drink much, and my throat gets dry."

"Take your time."

He cleared his throat again, a dry, raspy sound. "My parents were married for about five years when the doctor told them they couldn't have any kids. My mom

40

told me they were devastated. They really wanted a family, you know? Anyway, a year or so later, they heard a three-year-old boy was available for adoption because his parents had died in a car crash, and he had no other family. My dad was an engineer, and my mom taught kindergarten. They had money and a big house with plenty of room for a baby, so they had no trouble adopting Ewon and bringing him home."

"That was nice of them to save that little boy."

"It was a dream come true, and everything was great for a while. Then, two years later, my mom got pregnant with me. Their miracle baby. Ewon was five by then and very happy being an only child. He had no interest in a little brother. He wanted my parents all to himself. After I was born, he started acting out."

"In what way?"

Jaylon stared at a spot over my head. "The usual stuff kids that age do, I guess. Throwing temper tantrums, refusing to do his schoolwork, being disrespectful to his teachers. My mom never went into detail, but by the time she told me all this, I could fill in the blanks for myself. I do remember hearing her and my dad talking about being afraid to leave me alone with him once. I didn't understand why, though."

Scary stuff. "How did you and Ewon get along?"

He shared a wistful smile. "I idolized him, but he wanted nothing to do with me. As I got older, we fought over everything. He made his resentment clear every chance he got, but I didn't understand what was happening until I was around ten or so. Basically, he hated me for being born. For stealing his parents away from him. I didn't know how to handle it, so I retreated into myself. I spent a lot of time alone in my room reading."

41

I could relate to that, having spent my teen years the same way. I waited for him to collect himself enough to continue.

"When Ewon was in high school, he started hanging around with some bad kids. They got into a lot of trouble, and my parents spent a bunch of time dealing with his issues. I retreated even further, determined not to make the same mistakes he did. Determined not to make a mess of my life the way he had.

"He left home after graduation, and then the real problems began. Drugs, petty theft, vandalism. Stuff he did as a kid, but he was an adult now. At least in the eyes of the law. He stole a car and went to jail for a few months, which seemed to help him. He learned how to fix cars and found a job when he got out. He moved in with his girlfriend. It really seemed like he finally had his life together."

Jaylon stopped and inhaled, seeming to have trouble catching his breath.

I gave him a minute. "Are you all right? Do you want to stop for today?"

"I'm okay." He coughed again, then nodded. "I want to keep going. I need to finish this, so you'll help me get out of here."

"You understand I can't guarantee that, right?"

"I do. I only hope you'll be willing to try. I know you have no control over the outcome."

At least the kid was realistic. I could work with that. "Okay, so what happened next?"

"When I graduated from high school, Ewon wanted me to come work with him. He wanted us to open a shop together. But I wanted to go to college and law school. He didn't like that much. We argued all the

42

time, but it didn't get really bad until he asked my dad for the money to open the shop by himself. My father turned him down. Told him he had to pay for my schooling and didn't have anything left over."

Tears washed his eyes, and he blinked them away. After a hard swallow, he continued. "Ewon was livid. He blamed me for destroying his future. That last day, we fought, and he got physical. He tried to hit me. I ducked, and he punched the wall instead. His hand started bleeding, which was the blood the police found in the house and on my shoe, which they used as evidence against me. Some of the blood also rubbed off my shoe onto the back of my truck when I was loading the rug my mom asked me to take to the landfill."

They really did convict him on circumstantial evidence. Of course, that didn't mean he wasn't guilty, only that the prosecutor didn't present any real proof. "Marcus told me Ewon's body was never found."

"Right. He left the house that day, drove away, and nobody's seen him since. The cops decided I'd killed him during the fight, rolled him up in the living room rug, and dumped him somewhere he wouldn't be found. But he was alive when he left. That rug was old, and my mother wanted a new one, so she asked me to get rid of it. But the police searched the landfill, and they couldn't find it. My mom testified she'd told me to take it away, but my attorney spoke to some people on the jury, and they didn't believe her because she didn't buy the new one until the next day. And because she was my mother."

His eyes filled with tears again, but this time the flood was too big to contain. He shrank into himself, seeming even younger than he already did. He wiped his face

43

and met my gaze. "I had nothing to do with my brother's disappearance, but my public defender didn't believe me. He didn't put up much of a fight, and now I'm going to die in prison."

"Not necessarily. Don't give up hope yet." I reached over and squeezed his hand. "Why didn't your parents hire an attorney for you?"

Jaylon showed a half-smile directed more at himself than me. "I told them not to. They'd just paid my tuition and would've had to take out a second mortgage on the house. I was sure I'd be acquitted since I didn't do it, and they had no evidence against me. Guess I was wrong."

The poor kid had sacrificed himself for the benefit of his family. Nothing I could say would make him feel better about the decision, so I changed the subject. "How was Ewon acting before he disappeared? Other than being angry with you. Anything unusual?"

"He was secretive, like something was going on. I think his friends got him into something, but he wouldn't say what. It was almost like getting the money from my father was his only hope to get out of it. When Dad refused—"

"Ewon had to go through with the plan to get the cash he needed to open the shop."

"Right."

"Any idea what that plan was?"

He shook his head. "It was something big, though."

I couldn't think of any more questions, but Jaylon had already given me much to think about. "Thanks for talking to me, Jaylon. I know how difficult it must be for you to have to relive it over and over again."

"Are you going to help me?"

44

How should I respond? It sounded like he might be innocent, but I needed to check into some details of his story before making a final decision. I didn't want to lie to him and say I'd help, but I didn't want to destroy his hopes, either. I walked the tightrope instead.

"I'll see what I can do, but I'm not making any promises, okay?"

His lips tightened. "I understand."

I hurried away before his resigned expression encouraged me to make a promise I might not be able to keep.

CHAPTER FIVE

The ride back to the bookstore Sunday afternoon seemed to take much less time than the drive to Sutton. I zoomed along the familiar roads with little traffic on autopilot. Jaylon's story swirled around in my head, along with potential ways to verify the details. I couldn't help but wonder, though, if the police and his attorney were unable to verify the facts as Jaylon related them, how on Earth would I? However, I suspected a lack of motivation might've hindered their efforts. A problem I didn't have.

The police only wanted a closed case and conviction, which they got without looking for any other suspects. The public defender assigned to Jaylon's case, most likely overburdened with more clients than any one attorney could properly serve, didn't believe his story. So why bother to see if it's true or not? Why bother to look for exonerating evidence or witnesses who weren't family? The short answer: he didn't.

The idea of accusing someone of doing a lousy job based solely on the word of the person convicted made me uncomfortable. I needed to speak with Jaylon's attorney myself. Perhaps he'd allow me a look at his

46

case files. There might be something in them he missed. I'd forgotten to ask Jaylon who represented him in court, but since trials were a matter of public record, it shouldn't be too hard to find out.

The police file on the case would be another source of information. If I could convince someone to let me look at it. Since I'd be hunting for their mistakes, I doubted they'd let me see it voluntarily.

Petitioning to see the case file through the Freedom of Information Act was also an option, but that would take time, and the cops would probably delay as long as possible just because they could. Perhaps Eric might consider reviewing it and telling me what he finds.

I pressed the icon next to Eric's name and put the phone on speaker. I usually hesitated to use speaker phone for a call, but I was driving. Safety first. Although, some people would probably die laughing if I ever said that out loud. I wasn't known for shying away from taking action due to safety concerns.

He answered on the second ring. "Hey, I was just thinking about you."

My cheeks warmed. "Anything good?"

"Always good! What've you been up to?"

I told him about my visit with Jaylon and gave him the abridged version of the story. "What do you think? Is he guilty?"

"I don't know. The jury thought so."

I sighed. "Yeah, but that doesn't mean he did it. After all, nobody ever found the body. We can't even be sure Ewon is really dead."

"True, but then where's he been all this time? Why would he just disappear like that? He had a girlfriend, a job, and a dream of opening his own auto repair shop. It doesn't make sense he'd take off and leave it all behind."

"Jaylon said Ewon was acting squirrelly during the days before his disappearance. Maybe something else was going on."

"Okay, but what?"

"Jaylon didn't know. He thought Ewon's friends might've pressured him into doing something illegal, and Ewon was trying to find a way out. That's why he picked that particular moment to ask his father for the money."

Eric breathed into the phone. "I don't know, Jen. You might be searching for something that isn't there. It seems all you have to go on is Jaylon's word that he's innocent. And his own lawyer didn't believe him. Why should he expect you to?"

I slowed as I approached the Riddleton town limits. "Public defenders get jaded after a while. You know how things work. Most of their clients are guilty and claim to be innocent. He probably assumed Jaylon was only another one of those."

"Let's say you're right. What about the Innocence Project or a similar group? The Carolina law school probably has one like it. Maybe you should try them. They know much more about investigating cases like this than you do. If you're sure he's innocent."

The big question. Was I sure? No, not yet. Jaylon's story was believable and credible, but, at this point, it was only a story. I needed something solid to go on. "Honestly, I'm not sure what I think right now. Is there any way you can pull the old case file and look it over for discrepancies? Something we might be able to use to convince them to help Jaylon? After all, the guy will die if he doesn't receive that transplant."

"All right, but you have to promise me, if I find anything, you'll take it to someone else. I don't like the concept of you investigating this yourself. We have no idea who else is involved, and they might be dangerous."

I couldn't make that promise, and frankly, he should've known better than to ask. "Why don't we wait and see what you find? Then we can decide what to do with it."

"Because I know you, Jen. If I find so much as a typo in a report, you'll go charging in. Risk your own life. Or at least your safety. And for what? For some guy you've only met once and aren't even sure about yourself?" A hint of frustration crept into his voice.

"You're right. I'm not sure. Yet. But if I decide to help, it'll be because I believe him, and we've found something to back up his story. Besides, Marcus trusts him, and I trust Marcus. That's the bottom line."

"Well, I'm not crazy about helping you put yourself in danger for some stranger."

What happened to the guy who had my back no matter what? "I'll be careful. I promise. Please check out the case file. Or at least give it to me so I can. If you find nothing, fine. But if there *is* something, maybe we can help this guy. Would you be able to live with yourself if Jaylon turned out to be innocent and died in prison because we chose not to help on the grounds it might be dangerous? I'm not sure I could."

He exhaled audibly. "Fine. You win. I'll see what I can find out tomorrow."

"Thank you. Call me later?"

"Yup." He hung up.

I rolled into an empty spot around the corner from Ravenous Readers. My hand shook, but I wasn't sure why. I'd had much worse discussions with Eric without a physical reaction. Perhaps it was only the stress of the day catching up to me. On some level, I felt Jaylon Barnes's life was in my hands, but I had no idea how to move forward or even if I should. Didn't I have enough of my own problems to worry about?

When I rounded the corner, a sea of pink assaulted my eyes. Lacey had begun decorating the front windows for Valentine's Day. An all-pink—except for his diaper—Cupid took up the whole of one window. On the shelf below, romance novels of all shapes and sizes rested on display stands. The main thing they had in common, besides their genre, was that their covers all had some shade of pink somewhere. Fortunately, she hadn't started on the other window yet, or I might be running for the bathroom, gagging.

Lacey and Charlie were both helping customers when I walked in, so I headed back to my office. I needed some time to think. Although it was a good possibility I'd done too much thinking already today. Maybe I should give my brain a break instead. I slipped into the chair behind my desk, rested my forehead on folded arms, and closed my eyes.

I had just begun to doze when a rustle in the doorway drew my head back up. Cowboy Charlie stood there watching me, dressed in jeans, leather chaps, ten-gallon hat, gun belt, boots, and spurs. Was it time for the showdown already? Couldn't be. It was after noon.

I lifted my eyebrows.

He gave me a crooked grin, missing only a piece of

straw clamped between his teeth. "Hi, Boss. I wanted to make sure you're all right. You seem a little down."

I really should tell him to stop calling me that since I'm not the boss anymore, but it made him happy, and Lacey didn't seem to mind, so I'd leave it be for now. I'd have to remember to ask her about it later, though. "I'm fine. Just tired, I guess."

"Why don't you mosey on home, then?" He hooked his thumbs in his gun belt, empty holster bouncing off his thigh. "I reckon we can handle things here."

No matter what else might be going on in my life, Charlie could always make me smile. I'd come to love him like family. Not my family, of course. I got along much better with him than I did them. Although I had to admit, my relationship with my mother and stepfather had improved significantly in the past year.

I stepped out from behind my desk and flung an arm around his shoulders. "Come along, cowpoke, the fence in the north pasture needs fixin', and we got cattle to herd."

He tipped his hat. "Yes'm. Reckon I'll have that fence fixed up right purty afore the cows come home."

Out front, in the real world, Lacey was ringing up a woman with straight brown hair resting in a line across the middle of her back. I could never stand to have my hair so long. It drove me crazy when mine fell below my collar. Not sure why; it just did.

When the woman collected her books and scurried out the door, Lacey pointed toward Cupid's window. "How do you like it so far?"

Oh, boy. I'd hoped she wouldn't ask me about her artwork. I channeled Daniel Davenport, the social-butterfly twin. "I can see how hard you've worked on

51

it. I think you've achieved your goal." Daniel would be so proud.

Lacey narrowed her eyes. "Yes, but do you *like* it?"

I couldn't bring myself to lie to her, but I didn't want to hurt her feelings either. I dodged the question one more time. "It's very . . . pink."

She rolled her eyes. "Never mind. I knew you'd hate it."

And yet you did it anyway. "I don't hate it. Pink isn't at the top of my preferred color palette, that's all."

"No kidding. But navy blue or black just didn't seem to suit the theme."

"I like other colors!"

"True, but none of them fit Valentine's Day. We're trying to attract new readers, not start a coven. We'll save that one for Halloween."

"Fair enough. I can wait. But I call dibs on Elvira, Mistress of the Dark."

"We'll discuss it when the time comes," she said, perfectly imitating my mother when I asked for a pony for my ninth birthday. Like the pony I never got, I suspected there'd be no Elvira next Halloween.

I stuck out my lower lip. "Fine."

Lacey collected her supplies and began outlining people reading books on the other window. At least she couldn't make them all pink unless she painted them all Caucasian and naked. While that might attract more attention to the store, I imagined the town council would frown on it. It'd be fun to shake the old fuddy-duddies up a bit, in any case.

At the coffee bar, Charlie restocked supplies with one hand and pushed buttons on his laptop with the other. I wandered over to fill my mug.

"Whatcha working on?" I asked, stirring cream and sugar into my coffee.

"Checking the email for online sales. Nothing today so far."

"That's all right. It'll catch on eventually. What we sell online is extra, anyway."

He pulled his ten-gallon hat low on his forehead. "I know. I'm still hoping it'll help us cover expenses, though. Maybe even turn a profit someday."

"At least we're okay for now."

"Thanks to Lacey and her husband buying in. What happens the next time we run out of money? What'll we do then?"

I blew the steam off my coffee and took a sip. "We've made many changes in the last few weeks, and our sales have increased. If we keep moving in the right direction, we won't have money problems again."

His expression brightened. "And there's always the new business we'll get when the resort opens by the lake. People are bound to come into town sometimes. If nothing else, they'll need something to read while sunning by the shore."

I wished I could share his enthusiasm for the project, but the picture of Myrtle Beach in July had entrenched itself in my head. I didn't want to live that way, even if it meant owning a wildly successful bookstore. Half of a wildly successful bookstore. I would have to get used to having partners. It'd only been a couple of weeks since Lacey, Ben, and I signed the papers. I'd give myself a couple more to adjust to the new dynamic.

Either way, I'd worry about all that later. At the moment, I had another mystery to solve. "Hey, Charlie, do you remember the Jaylon Barnes case?"

He furrowed his brow. "No, I don't think so. What was it about?"

"About five years ago, Barnes was convicted of killing his brother, but the body was never found. Ring a bell?"

His mouth formed a circle. "Oh yeah, I remember. The evidence was all circumstantial, but they convicted him anyway. I thought it was kind of strange, but obviously, the jury had more information than I did. I can't imagine they'd vote guilty if they weren't sure."

"Stranger things have happened."

"True. What makes you bring it up now?"

I told him Jaylon's story and the issues he currently faced. "He wants me to find enough evidence to overturn his conviction so the woman will give him her kidney."

"That's a lot to ask. What are you going to do?"

"No idea yet. I want to believe him, but I don't know if I should."

"You want me to do some poking around for you? Maybe I'll come across something that'll help you figure out the best thing to do."

"Sure, if you don't mind. I don't want to pull you away from anything you're already working on."

He peered at me from under the brim of his hat. "That's never stopped you before."

"All right, smarty pants." He was right, though. I'd often commandeered his unique skills to help me find information I could get nowhere else without considering what he might've already been doing. "I'm sorry. I'll try to be more respectful from now on."

His face reddened. "I was only kidding you. I'm happy to help." He started typing. "When did you say the trial was again?"

"Five years ago."

Images flashed across his screen. He turned to me. "Five years ago? Isn't that around the time the medical examiner said the skeleton you found when you were lost in the tunnel last December died?"

"Yeah, why?"

"What if the skeleton is Ewon Barnes?"

Holy crap! Why didn't I think of that? That would explain everything. Except who killed him and left him underground to rot.

Would that person turn out to be Jaylon?

CHAPTER SIX

Andy Kim rocked me gently awake Monday morning, but nothing about the song seemed gentle to me. I slapped the radio off and rolled over to go back to sleep. Savannah's nose poked me in the eye. I pulled my head away, blinking, and she sneezed on me. Yuk. Wiping my face on the comforter, I sat up. Sleeping in was clearly not on the menu today. Of course, if I wanted to sleep late, I should've remembered to turn off the alarm.

My German shepherd grumbled and stretched out her legs, effectively pushing me off the side of the bed. I landed on the floor with a thump, glared at her, then stood. So much for me being the alpha dog. It was obvious to anyone paying attention who ruled this pack. She noticed me standing and rolled over for a belly rub, her tongue lolling out the side of her mouth. If I didn't know better, I'd think she did it on purpose. When I didn't start scratching her tummy right away, she thumped her tail and squirmed on her back to get my attention. I ran my hands up and down her underside.

No, she's not spoiled at all.

After a minute, I stopped. "C'mon, little girl, let's go potty."

She leaped off the bed, carrying the comforter on her back, and charged into the living room. I threw sweats on over my sleeping shorts and T-shirt and made a pit stop of my own. Then I fished my Nikes from under the coffee table, checked the coffeemaker, and leashed her up for her morning rounds.

It was a nippy morning, and I hadn't worn a jacket, so I did my best to keep her moving; once again, she cooperated for some reason. I suspected she didn't appreciate being cold any more than I did, so we made it around the block in record time, arriving home before the coffee had finished perking. While the coffeemaker hissed its last, I fed and watered my girl, then settled on the couch, cradling cup number one in my chilly fingers. A satiated Savannah curled up beside me and laid her head in my lap while my mind wandered. A perfect way to start the day.

Charlie suggested Ewon Barnes might be the skeleton I'd found in the old Underground Railroad tunnel under St. Mary's Catholic Church. Rumor had it a frat boy had been lost down there in 1927, and I'd assumed that's whom I'd discovered until the medical examiner's report showed the remains were only five years old. There was no way to establish whether the man had died down there or the body moved after the fact, only that he was shot in the back of the head, execution style.

Did Jaylon Barnes know of the tunnels' existence? Not many people in Riddleton did. They hadn't been used for anything since the rumrunners evaded capture in them during the 1920s. Many of the entrances were sealed off with concrete floors or building foundations. At least the ones here in town. I couldn't be sure about the entries in the woods, and I suspected Lake Dester also made some inaccessible.

I pulled up the photos on my phone from when I'd found the bones while trying to wend my way out of the tunnel system. They'd turned out well, considering they were snapped in total darkness. Unfortunately, there wasn't much to see. A skeleton, like you might find hanging in a biology lab, covered by jeans and a T-shirt. One shot showed sneakers on his feet, but I couldn't make out what brand. I held the phone under the table lamp for a better look at some of the shadowy places. One of the drawbacks of snapping pictures in the dark.

Scrolling through the pictures taken from all angles, I noticed a dark spot on what remained of the left wrist, draped across what used to be a lap. I enlarged that section. It appeared to be a watch, but not an ordinary one. It had no face, only buttons and what seemed to be a tiny antenna. Strange. I'd never seen a timepiece like that before. How did he tell the time with it?

I slid from under Savannah's two-ton head and retrieved my laptop from my desk. Returning to the couch, I brought up my search engine and typed *watch with no face*. Lots of pictures of watches with covers and websites where you can buy them. Nope. Not what I'm looking for.

Okay, try again. *Watch with antenna and buttons* got me a list of sites to watch TV. I don't want to watch television; I want to know what this guy was wearing on his wrist. I sighed out my frustration.

Think, Jen.

58

Why would someone need an antenna on their wrist? What devices used antennas? Televisions, radios, phones. All used for communication. It could be a phone or an exercise tracker of some sort, but I'd never seen one with an external antenna.

What else did we use to communicate with each other? My brain flashed back to the string with a can on each end our kindergarten teacher had let us talk to each other with. Not quite what I needed. Then there were the walkie-talkies Brittany's parents gave her for Christmas one year. We played with those until they fell apart.

Hey, wait a minute. Did they make a walkie-talkie you could wear? I typed in walkie-talkie watch. Bingo! An army-style kids' toy appeared on the screen. I clicked on it and scrolled down to the specifications. It had about a three-hundred-foot range and a place to tell the time. Perhaps the one in the photo was an older model, or the picture was too dark for me to see clearly. Either way, it was exactly what the skeleton had on his wrist. Now, I only had to figure out what he used it for.

I wanted to call Eric and tell him what I'd found, but I didn't want to bother him at work or risk his partner and training officer, Detective Havermayer, answering his phone. Besides, he might be busy sorting through Jaylon's file. I definitely wouldn't want to interrupt that. If he finds something I can work with, we might solve both cases—Ewon's disappearance and the identity of the mysterious skeleton. Hopefully, Havermayer would leave him alone long enough to do the job properly. She might, as long as she didn't know he was doing it for me.

Francine Havermayer loathed me the first time we met a year and a half ago. No idea why. Since then, she's tried everything she could to put me in jail, where she obviously believed I belonged. If a candy bar disappeared from the Piggly Wiggly, she came looking for me. It made no sense. I'd never been in any trouble except that of my own making. And none of it was illegal. Foolish, maybe, but not illegal.

The only reason for her behavior I could ever come up with was that we're so different. While she dressed for work every day as if going to a magazine photo shoot, I preferred jeans and T-shirts or sweatshirts, depending on the time of year. She wore flats or sensible pumps. I lived in my Nikes. I'd never been to her home, but I suspected it was spotless, with nothing out of place. My apartment always looked like the aftermath of a kegger.

Basically, we had different outlooks on life. She saw the world as black and white. People were good or evil, with nothing in between. I was more of a gray kind of person, able to see both sides of a situation. At least, I tried to. As a writer, I understood that nothing was ever as it seemed. There was always a story. She had no patience for what she called my overactive imagination. Sometimes, I pitied her. Perhaps she sensed that, and that's what bothered her most of all.

Regardless, it was time to put my imagination to work. I had a chapter to finish and a few hours before meeting Eric for lunch. I picked up where I'd left off and immersed myself in the fictional world of the Davenport twins.

Angus was balanced in the diner's Main Street window when I arrived, outlining his Valentine's Day design.

Apparently, he'd decided to go for it. Too soon to tell what *it* was, though. Whatever it turned out to be would be unique and well presented, I was sure. Angus was a talented artist, which surprised me because he was a bank loan officer in New Hampshire before moving to Riddleton and opening the diner. Nothing against New Hampshire or banks, but when I encountered creative flair, the last person I thought of was a banker.

I'd made it before Eric for once, so I got to snap up our corner booth. Somehow, no matter how many folks were in the restaurant, our booth was always available when we wanted it. The fact that it was empty eliminated my earlier theory that Angus moved people when we came in. My new idea was that he must have a reserved sign on it, only visible to people other than Eric or me. That had to be it.

I slipped onto the orange seat and took a menu from the condiment holder, sitting against the wall below an ad for *The Thin Man* circa 1934. Above my head was a Fifties-era poster depicting the Marlboro Man riding through the desert on his horse. The ambience Angus had created here was the part I loved best, having spent the better part of my childhood watching black-and-white movies with my stepfather. One of the few interests we had in common.

Penelope swung by after taking an order from a group of guys who worked at the hardware store. "Dew or shake today?"

"Dew, please." It occurred to me as she walked away that after all the years she'd been delivering my cheeseburgers and drinks, I knew almost nothing about her. Not even her last name or how long she'd been in Riddleton. And worse than that, I'd never asked. A despicable lack of curiosity for a mystery writer. Or a human being, for that matter. No wonder I had so much trouble making friends. I did a lousy job of being one.

Eric interrupted my downward spiral with a smile and a kiss. "Hi. What're you thinking so hard about?"

Penelope dropped off my drink and scurried away.

"Nothing important. How's your day been?"

He sat across from me. "Interesting. I've been reading Jaylon Barnes's file."

That got my attention. "Oh? What did you find?"

"It was a pretty straightforward circumstantial case. He and his brother argued on the day Ewon disappeared. The argument got physical, but nothing major, just pushing and shoving. Then, according to Jaylon, Ewon got mad and swung at him. He ducked, and Ewon punched the wall, splitting open his knuckles. Blood dripped everywhere, including, again, according to Jaylon, on Jaylon's shoes and the wall. Unfortunately, there were no witnesses to corroborate the story, and the detectives didn't believe him."

All exactly what Jaylon had told me. So far. "Did the Barnes brothers still live with their parents?"

"Jaylon did. Ewon had a place with his girlfriend in Blackburn. Either way, the parents were both at work at the time of the argument."

"What did the girlfriend say about it?"

"She said she never saw Ewon again after he left to talk to his brother about working in the shop with him."

"Did the detectives believe her?"

Eric shrugged. "As far as I can tell. They had no reason not to. From how that file reads, they were convinced the brother did it from the beginning."

62

I leaned against the back of the booth. "What's her name? I think I'd like to talk to her."

"Eliza Naismith, but good luck finding her. She disappeared right after the trial. Nobody in Blackburn's seen her since, from what I've heard."

Interesting.

Penelope appeared holding her order pad in one hand and a Pepsi in the other. She set the drink and straw down in front of Eric. "Ya'll ready to order?"

"I'll have the usual," I replied with a smile. No point in pretending I might order anything different. Everybody knew better.

Eric said, "I'll have the same."

"Got it. We'll get that right out to you." She turned away.

I stopped her. "Wait. What's your last name?"

She tapped her pen on her lower lip, studying me. "Ulrich. With a C-H pronounced like a K. Why?"

"I realized I've known you for years and still don't know anything about you. I'm sorry about that."

Her cheeks reddened, matching the hair she twisted around her finger. "No problem. I doubt more than ten people around here know anything about me."

"Well, now it's eleven."

She gave me a quick, closed-mouth smile and hurried toward the counter to turn in our orders to the cook.

"I think you embarrassed her," Eric said, touching my hand.

"I didn't mean to. I just thought I should get to know her better. She's been around a long time, and I see her almost every day. How long has she worked here? I know she'd been here a while already when I moved back to town."

He scrunched his eyebrows. "I'm not sure. Five or ten years, maybe? You'll have to ask Angus."

I would, but not right now. "What else did you find in Jaylon's file?"

"Nothing you don't already know. A neighbor saw him loading a large rug into his truck the afternoon his brother disappeared. He said he took it to the landfill, per his mother's request, but it never turned up in the search. The assumption was he buried it in the woods somewhere it would never be found."

"Jaylon told me his mother asked him to take it away because she was buying a new one. The old rug was worn and tattered."

"He told the detectives the same thing, and the mother backed him up, but nobody believed her. They figured she was just covering for him. Particularly since she didn't buy the new one until the day *after* the last time anyone saw Ewon."

"Covering for one son accused of murdering the other? Why would she do that?"

He tore the corner off his napkin and rolled it between his fingers. "The detective who wrote the report thought it might be because Ewon was adopted, and Jaylon was her firstborn. Her real son."

"Jaylon said she called him her 'miracle baby.'"

"Could be motive to lie."

I propped my elbows on the table. "I find that hard to believe."

"Maybe she figured she'd already lost one son; why risk losing the other?"

He had a point. "That's possible, I guess. Did you find anything else that seemed off? Something I can work with?"

Penelope brought our food, and we salted and ketchupped while Eric considered his response. I knew he didn't want me to get involved, and I could tell he struggled with what or how much to say. Clearly, he'd noticed something that would pique my interest. I waited.

After downing a bite of his burger, he said, "I did have a few questions while I read, but I'm not sure they necessarily mean anything."

"Like what?"

"Well, for starters, what happened to Ewon's car? He owned a black 2010 Toyota Corolla. Assuming he drove himself to the house, and Jaylon was alone cleaning up after the murder, where was the car Ewon drove to meet his brother? It never turned up anywhere, and Jaylon couldn't have taken it too far away because he'd have had to walk back. There's no public transportation in Riddleton other than the bus from Blackburn to Sutton, which only runs twice a day. Once in each direction. He didn't have time to clean up the house, roll up the body, drive the car to Blackburn, catch the bus, take the rug to the landfill, and make it back home before his mother came home from work."

"What if Ewon got a ride from someone? Then his car wouldn't have been there for Jaylon to have to get rid of."

"Even so, he still had a Toyota Corolla that disappeared at the same time he did. What happened to it? And who did he get a ride from? Nobody has owned up to driving him there."

"All questions nobody asked, I assume?"

Eric dunked a fry in his ketchup pool. "You assume correctly."

"What other issues did you have?"

"According to the ME's report, there was blood at the crime scene, but not very much. You'd expect to see at least a little more blood if Jaylon had beaten his brother to death, as the prosecutor claimed. But there was nothing besides the few drops on his shoe and a little on the wall near the dent they assumed was made by Jaylon smashing his brother's head into it. And Jaylon's mother told the detectives he was wearing the same clothes when they picked him up he had on in the morning before she left for work. There was no blood on his clothing."

"But if Jaylon strangled him or broke his neck while smashing his head, there wouldn't be much blood."

"True, but Ewon would've tried to fight back if he was conscious, and there's no reason to believe he wasn't. At least in the beginning. They found no scratches or bruises on Jaylon. If nothing else, blood would've transferred from his bleeding knuckles to Jaylon's shirt when Ewon grabbed it to push him away."

Something Jaylon's public defender could've used to create reasonable doubt and didn't. "What else?"

"The only other thing that bothered me was the rug. The detectives believed Jaylon buried the rug, along with his brother, in the woods. But if that's true, we run into time trouble again. They searched everywhere he could've gotten to in his time frame and found nothing. But, if we go with Jaylon's story about the landfill, he had plenty of time to be home before his mother arrived."

"Only the rug wasn't there."

"They interviewed a worker at the landfill who said people stole things from there all the time. A good-sized

Oriental rug would be an excellent find, even if it were a little beat up, so it being missing didn't strike me as all that inconceivable. However, if someone stole a rug with a dead body in it, wouldn't they have reported it to the police?"

"Probably, unless they were afraid of being arrested for theft."

Eric shook his head. "Garbage is considered abandoned, so no crime in taking it."

"Okay, but most people don't know that."

"True. Even so, they still would've left it somewhere it would be found, but not tied back to them. I mean, who would want to risk being caught hauling a dead body around? The rug was never seen again anywhere around here."

I shifted a French fry to the other side of my mouth. Eric had given me a lot to think about that the original detectives on the case hadn't bothered themselves with.

It seemed Jaylon might've been telling the truth all along.

CHAPTER SEVEN

When I returned from lunch, the bookstore had four people milling around, including a man, two women, and a child around seven years old. Lacey had continued her work on the window across from Popping Pink Cupid but had stopped to help the customers, and Disco Charlie was serving a muffin to one of our female guests, his purple paisley satin shirt sleeve fluttering in the manufactured breeze.

Our business had experienced a significant increase in the past few weeks, mainly driven by the new Used-Book section we'd added. However, we still sold just as many new books as before. For once, I was happy to have been wrong about used-book sales cutting into our new book sales. Moreover, we had more patrons coming in who also indulged in specialty coffee and pastries, which moved our bottom line a little closer to what we'd need to survive.

As soon as the woman carried her muffin and coffee to a table, I made my way to the coffee bar.

Charlie looked up and greeted me with a smile. "Hi, Boss. How's your day been so far?"

"Not too bad," I replied, glancing up at the ceiling.

"Would you like me to install a disco ball up there for you?"

He struck John Travolta's famous pose from *Saturday Night Fever*—right leg forward, right hand raised with the forefinger pointed, and left arm angled at his side—and sang a slightly off-key falsetto rendition of "You Should Be Dancing." All eyes in the store turned toward us.

The Bee Gees had nothing to worry about, though. My ears grew hot, and I winced at the sudden attention. "All right, all right. I get it. And for everyone's sake, don't quit your day job!"

He rearranged the muffins on the tray to fill the empty spaces. "I'd never quit. You couldn't manage without me."

I reached under the counter for my mug. "I'm not entirely sure about that, but I know I wouldn't want to."

"Even better." He clumped his glittering purple platform shoes around to my side of the counter and inspected the pastry case glass for fingerprints. "What can I help you with, Jen?"

"Why do you ask?" I filled my mug with coffee from the urn.

"You have that I-have-a-mystery-to-solve look about you today. And I know you were preoccupied with that sick guy in jail yesterday. I only figured you'd made up your mind about helping him, and there might be something I can do to lend a hand."

Interesting. Charlie had a well-hidden, intuitive side. Or perhaps I'd never looked beyond his clothing and unusual behavior. *My bad.* "You're right. I've decided to help Jaylon Barnes if I can. I believe he's telling the

69

truth." I sipped my coffee, the fragrance almost as stimulating as the caffeine within. "And since you volunteered, can you locate his parents for me? I'd like to speak with them if possible."

"Sure. What're their names?"

Crap! I'd forgotten to ask Eric. "I don't know, but they're undoubtedly in his records or a news article someplace. On his birth certificate, for sure, if you can find it."

He puffed out his chest, satin shirt pulling at the buttons. "Oh, I can find it, all right. Don't you worry. I'll even tell you where you can find them by the time I'm through."

I smiled behind the cup at my lips. "I'm counting on it." Turning to watch the browsing customers, I remembered something else I needed from him. "Also, Ewon Barnes had a girlfriend, Eliza Naismith, who nobody's seen since Jaylon's trial. Can you find her for me too?"

His grin spread from ear to ear. "Gotcha covered, Boss."

The last customer left, and Lacey climbed onto the window shelf to finish outlining the readers on the glass. Her borders were pink, matching the Cupid across the way. But, I hoped she'd only chosen the color because pink was light enough to cover with just about any other. Otherwise, Ravenous Readers would look like a Pepto Bismol factory blew up in it for the next ten days.

"It's shaping up well," I said. "As always. Did you ever consider becoming an artist?"

Lacey paused for a moment, then replied, "Not really. I had my sights set on winning Olympic gold in the four hundred meter. Drawing was just a hobby I used to wind down at the end of the day."

"That was before your injury, right?" Lacey didn't talk about that time in her life much.

"Yes, I tore my ACL in college, which didn't heal as well as we'd hoped after the surgery. I could still run, but not fast enough to make the team."

"I'm sorry."

"Thanks, but it turned out all right. I got married, had my kids, and now I have another one on the way. I only traded in one dream for another. I'm happy with my life the way it is."

Amazing how positive she was about everything. Many people would be consumed by anger and resentment. Myself included. "Did you never wonder what might've been?"

A faraway look crept into her eyes. "Sometimes, right before I fall asleep late at night, I have the old daydream again. You know, the one where I break the tape at the finish line, and the crowd's cheering? Next, I'm standing at the top of the podium, hand over my heart while they play 'The Star-Spangled Banner.' Then, my son wakes up calling for me after a bad dream, and I remember how much better what I have is. How much more important my family is."

"Speaking of having one on the way, how've you been feeling? Any more dizzy spells?" Lacey was three months pregnant and had some issues a few weeks ago that resembled the problems she'd had when carrying her daughter. Problems that'd been near life-threatening.

She knocked on the wooden shelf. "So far, so good."

"Happy to hear it. Maybe you *were* only dehydrated, as you thought."

71

"Maybe. Now I'm drinking enough to float both of us to England."

I laughed. "Guess we'd better stock up on toilet paper."

"I already did."

Somehow, even though I meant it as a joke, I wasn't surprised she'd already thought of it. Lacey was efficient in ways I never could be, no matter how hard I tried. I spent most of my time firmly entrenched in my own head, oblivious to much of what went on around me. Lacey lived in reality, often able to anticipate and solve problems before they happened. I was lucky to have her as a partner. Something I'd surely recognize as soon as my ego adjusted to the power shift.

I swallowed the last of my coffee and hit the urn for a refill. Charlie looked up from his computer and asked, "Are we ready for a new batch yet?"

Since I was too short at five-foot-six to see into the two-foot urn when it sat on the three-foot-high counter, I tilted it and sloshed the contents around to gauge approximately how much remained. "No, I think we're okay for now. It's about a third full."

As I stirred cream into my cup, the front door bells signaled a new arrival. Lacey was busy painting the world pink, so I headed in that direction, freezing in my tracks when I saw Simeon Kirby come through the doorway, his collar-length brown hair slightly mussed from the breeze outside.

What does he want?

He glanced around, and when his gaze landed on me, headed straight to where I stood. "Good afternoon, Ms. Dawson. Do you have time for a little chat? I have a proposition I think you'll be interested in."

72

My imagination wasn't adept enough to come up with anything he could propose that I might want to hear. Still, alienating someone on his way to becoming an influential figure in town wouldn't be a good idea. Guess I'd learned a few things from Daniel after all.

I plastered on a smile. The one I usually reserved for "*When's your next book coming out, Jen?*" conversations. "What can I do for you, Mr. Kirby?"

He smoothed back his hair and ran a hand over his close-clipped more-salt-than-pepper beard. "Is there somewhere we can speak that's more private?"

I couldn't think of a legitimate reason to say no. Telling him the idea of being alone with him gave me the creeps, while being the truth, wouldn't work since he'd given me no reason to feel that way. And yet, I did. "We can talk in my office if you'd like."

He tugged on his light-gray suit jacket and adjusted his dark-gray tie before silently following me to the back. I offered him a chair, then perched in mine, clasping my hands on the desk, waiting for him to speak.

Clearing his throat, he pulled on his shirt collar, seeming uncomfortable for the first time since, well, ever. All the time he'd been in Riddleton, he presented himself as calm, collected, and reserved. A professional businessman with an almost icy demeanor. What about speaking with me could possibly make him uncomfortable? Perhaps one of the grapes in the grapevine had told him how I felt about his plans.

Watching him fidget made me wonder if perhaps what I thought mattered to people around here, and that concerned him. Nah. I wasn't even a tadpole in Riddleton's pond. So, what was his problem?

73

He finally settled himself and met my gaze with his muddy brown eyes. "Ms. Dawson, I'd like to buy Ravenous Readers. I promise my offer will be agreeable to you."

"It's not for sale," I replied, knowing I should consult Lacey first but choosing to believe she felt as I did. That my friend Aletha's dream wasn't disposable at any price. When Aletha Cunningham left Ravenous Readers to me in her will, I vowed to run the business as she would've wanted. Which included protecting it against predators like Simeon Kirby.

"You haven't even heard my offer yet."

I sat back in my chair. "It doesn't matter. This store is not for sale."

"I'm willing to give you twice what the place is worth. You'll never get an offer like that from anyone else."

Huh. That didn't make any sense. "Why are you so anxious to buy a bookstore that only breaks even during a blue moon? What's in it for you?"

He stroked his beard again. "Does that really matter?"

"It does to me."

"Let's just say it fits my plans to do so."

Tension lifted my shoulders toward my ears. "From what I've heard so far, I'm not particularly fond of your plans. Why should I want to help you?"

He leaned forward. "Because it's in your best interests. I'm willing to pay you enough money to open any kind of business you want, anywhere you want. What don't you like about that? It's a win-win situation."

"Only if I want to go somewhere else, which I don't."

Kirby sighed. "All right. Open up something else here. There are plenty of options that'll fit with my overall vision for Riddleton."

"Who died and left you in charge? I'm happy with the business I have. I intend to keep it, and there's nothing you can do about it."

He stood and stepped toward me, forcing me to look up at him to maintain eye contact. "I can make life difficult for you if you don't sell."

Now, he sounded like the mob boss I'd once thought he was. I rose to reduce the gap. "I don't give in to threats, Mr. Kirby. Now, I think you should leave."

"And I think, perhaps, you should discuss my offer with your partners." He planted his hands on my desk, scowling, face inches from mine. "After all, it's not entirely your decision to make anymore, is it?"

Anger heated my cheeks, and I faced him down. "Goodbye, Mr. Kirby."

He turned and stormed out without another word.

I scurried behind him to ensure he didn't make a fuss in front of customers or blindside Lacey. No scene, but he slammed the front door so hard the windows rattled. Lacey, Charlie, and two women at the coffee bar all stood, mouths open, looking at each other. Charlie offered the customers free cookie samples to distract them. Quick thinking.

Lacey climbed down out of the window. "What was that all about?"

I gestured toward a wingback chair. "Have a seat."

She cocked an eyebrow, puzzled. "What's going on, Jen? What did Kirby want?"

Blowing out a lungful, I took the other seat across from the couch. "You might as well sit; you're going to end up down there anyway."

The seat cushion puffed as she lowered her weight

into it. "All right, I'm sitting. Tell me what happened, or I'll reach over and throttle you!"

While I doubted she'd actually follow through on her threat, there was no reason to hold back. Other than my fear of what her reaction might be. And that self-serving motive wasn't good enough. "Kirby wants to buy the bookstore."

"What? Why?"

"He wouldn't say, but it kind of fits with our suspicion that he wants to own the whole town. Or at least control it."

Lacey considered me, chestnut brows pinched, mouth set in a line. I could picture the hamsters running on their wheels in her head. Was she considering selling? I hoped not. With our partnership being fifty-fifty, it could lead to a nasty fight.

"What do you think he wants to do with it?" she asked after a minute.

"The town or the store?"

"The store, silly. We'll worry about the town later."

I trapped my bottom lip between my teeth. "I don't know, maybe we should worry about the town first. By the time we get around to it, it might be too late."

She crossed her legs at the knees, then thought better of it. "I think you might be overreacting a bit. How much did he offer us?"

"He didn't give me an exact number, but he claimed it would be twice what the store is worth. When Charlie and I checked out that flash drive we assumed Kirby dropped in the store a few weeks ago, there were what appeared to be valuations of all the businesses in town. He pegged Ravenous Readers at fifty thousand. So, twice that would be—"

76

"A hundred thousand. Forget it. It's a good figure, but Ben and I would lose half our investment right away."

I shook my head. "I wouldn't let that happen. You'd get it all. Except, I already told him the store wasn't for sale at any price."

Her jaw fell. "You did what? Without discussing it with me first?"

My belly churned, making enough butter for the whole town. "I'm sorry. It never occurred to me that you'd even consider selling. I thought you wanted this place to succeed as much as I do. You do, don't you?"

"Of course I do. But I'd also like the opportunity to voice my opinion on decisions like that. We're supposed to be partners!"

I pulled my legs beneath me on the chair, and my cheeks burned. I'd definitely messed up this time. Lacey had every right to be upset. Now, I had to find a way to make it up to her. "I'm still adjusting to the changes around here. And you know me, I hardly ever think before I speak. It's one of my most endearing qualities, remember?"

My attempt at a grin fell flat as Lacey crossed her arms, scowling.

"I'm truly sorry. Kirby knows about our partnership, and I'm sure he's expecting a call saying you've outvoted me. He was flabbergasted when I turned him down. He won't be the least bit surprised at the reversal."

"Reversal? No way! I don't want to sell the store any more than you do. I just want to be consulted on the decision, that's all. I think I'm entitled to that courtesy, don't you?"

The butter in my belly softened as relief took its

place. "Yes, I absolutely agree. I promise I'll do better next time."

She scowled and said, "You'd better," then smiled.

"Yes, ma'am. Are you sure you don't want to discuss the offer with Ben before making a final decision?"

"Ben has nothing to do with this. He's not only a silent partner, he's deaf and blind too. This store is our baby. Yours and mine." She shot me a side-eye. "Unless you keep making me mad. Then I'll bump you off and hide your body where nobody will ever find it, and it'll be all mine. Got it?"

We burst into giggles.

All was forgiven. This time. But my luck was sure to run out one of these days.

CHAPTER EIGHT

I spent the afternoon helping customers while Lacey completed her work on the windows. The Cupid side remained a Palais de Pink, but the readers' side turned out well, with five men and women of varying ethnicities engrossed in romance novels of varying colors. The arrangement seemed fair. One half of the décor to Lacey's taste, the other half to mine. Fifty-fifty. Just like the store itself.

If only I could remember that when it mattered.

Around five thirty, I started packing up my things to go. I had a dinner date with Eric. Nothing special, just the usual dinner and a movie. A nice, peaceful evening at home. Exactly what I needed. Some people—Brittany and Angus, to name two—accused us of being unwilling to commit to anything more, but Eric and I were comfortable with each other and our relationship. And comfortable with being comfortable. We wanted nothing more right now.

Eric had been promoted to detective only a few months ago. Still in training, he needed to focus on becoming the best detective he could be. I'd recently accepted an offer from my publisher for two more books in my series and had to concentrate on writing them both before the end of the year. Fireworks and shooting stars required more time and energy than either of us had to spare. We didn't need those things to know we loved each other.

I slid my laptop into my messenger bag and headed for the front of the store. Before I could get past the stockroom, my phone buzzed with a call. Brittany's college graduation picture covered the screen. *Uh-oh.* How could I talk to her without revealing Olinski's proposal plans? I'd never even tried to keep a secret from her before. For the first time ever, I considered letting the call go to voicemail. I couldn't do that to my best friend, though.

Sergeant Schultz's famous line in *Hogan's Heroes* ran through my head like a mantra:

I know nothing! I know nothing!

I continued repeating it to myself while I swiped the screen.

"Hey, Britt. What's up?"

"Olinski had to go to Sutton this afternoon, and he's going to swing by the barbecue place on the way home. Since we always end up with too much food, we thought you and Eric might like to join us. Around six thirty?"

No, no, no, no, no! There would be food and wine and chit-chat. I'd never be able to keep my mouth shut. Especially after the alcohol hit me. *What am I going to do?* Unfortunately, I had no legitimate reason to say no. The four of us often got together for meals. What could I possibly give her as an excuse? I'm an idiot who can't keep her mouth shut?

"Jen? Are you there?"

I know nothing! "Yeah, I'm here. Sorry. That sounds great. We'll see you then."

I hung up and called Eric to tell him about our change of plans. He shuffled papers in the background, then said, "I have a couple of reports to finish up, so I'll meet you there. And, remember, don't say a word about Olinski's Valentine's Day plans. Promise me you won't."

"I promise."

Oh, boy . . .

At precisely six twenty-nine, I escorted Savannah across the hall to Brittany's apartment. I didn't dare risk nobody else being there when I arrived. Brittany and I would get to talking, something about weddings or relationships would come up, and I'd spill the beans. Nope. Not gonna take that chance.

My timing was spot on. Brittany and Olinski were unpacking the food, and Eric showed up a minute later. Perfect. No secrets would be revealed tonight.

Savannah charged into the kitchen to supervise the food service while I opened the door for Eric. His black suit jacket was slung over one shoulder, and he'd loosened his tie. Fatigue etched lines on his boyish face.

"Hey, babe," I said, then kissed him. "You look tired. Tough day?"

"Just paperwork. And I'd rather run a marathon backward in high heels than do paperwork. Less exhausting."

"I'm sorry." I gestured toward the couch. "Sit down, and I'll get you something to drink."

"Thanks, but I've been sitting all day. I'll take a beer, though."

Eric followed me to the kitchen, where Olinski

81

already had a cold bottle waiting for him. He chugged about half, belched, then said, "I feel better already."

I peeked over the half-wall divider and found Savannah parked at Brittany's feet, politely waiting for something to fall into her territory. "Is she in your way, Britt?"

Brittany smiled at my German shepherd and emptied a barbecue container onto a serving dish. "No, she's fine. I'm used to it."

She pulled a strand of her flyaway blond hair away from her eye and pushed her oversized tiger-striped glasses back into position. She'd changed out of her work clothes into jeans and a Support Your Local Library T-shirt.

As Riddleton's town librarian, Brittany was responsible for generating supplemental revenue to keep the library stocked with the books the townspeople wanted to read. Like mine, except she still hadn't ordered a copy yet. I might just have to break down and buy one for the shelves myself.

Olinski dumped the baked beans into a bowl and threw the container in the trash. "All right, everyone. Come and get it!"

Bottle and two glasses in hand, Brittany asked, "Jen, you want some wine?"

No, I definitely shouldn't drink. Once buzzed, I couldn't control what came out of my mouth. Absolutely no wine! "Sure, sounds great. Thanks."

Apparently, I couldn't control my mouth even without wine.

We heaped our plates with barbecue, beans, and coleslaw. Brittany handed me a full glass. I knew I shouldn't drink but gulped half of it down anyway. The

82

alcohol hit my empty stomach like a wrecking ball slamming into a skyscraper. And the results would likely be the same. This was going to be an exciting evening.

Olinski and Eric exchanged uncomfortable glances. Eric leaned toward me and whispered, "Take it easy. You know how you get when you drink."

I kept my head down as the wine heated my face. "Don't worry. I'll be fine." I zipped my mouth shut and threw away the key again for emphasis.

Brittany cocked her head in my direction. "What's that all about?"

"Nothing!" Olinski, Eric, and I all said at once.

She froze with a serving spoon full of barbecue hanging in midair. "Seriously, what's going on? What're you all hiding?"

Olinski wrapped his arm around her shoulders and squeezed. "Obviously, they have something they don't want to tell us yet." He grinned at me. "Maybe Jen's pregnant."

I narrowed my eyes and pursed my lips in an "I'm gonna get you for that" look.

Brittany's eyes widened, and her mouth fell open. "Are you?"

"What? No!"

"Oh. Too bad. I was looking forward to being an aunt."

Savannah poked her, looking for a handout. I pointed at the dog. "You already are. See?"

"Not quite what I meant, but I'll take it." She slipped Savannah a hunk of barbecue and patted her head while she swallowed without chewing. "Aunt Brittany loves you."

Olinski and Brittany camped on the couch, and Eric

and I sank into the love seat opposite. Olinski downed a forkful of barbecue, then said, "Eric, tell me about this closed case you've been looking into lately?"

Eric flushed, creating a colorful backdrop for his freckles.

Olinski trained his gaze on Eric's. "Did you think I wouldn't find out?"

"No, sir, I was sure you would. It wasn't meant to be a secret."

"Good. I wouldn't like it if you tried hiding things from me."

"Of course not," Eric replied, shaking his head. "I'd never do that. I have no reason to."

"Glad to hear it." He forked up a load of coleslaw. "What's the sudden interest in Jaylon Barnes? He killed his brother, and now he's doing life. Case closed."

"That's the thing. He might've been wrongfully convicted." Eric looked at me. "Jen can explain it better than I can, but I had some questions about how the investigation was handled."

Olinski turned to me, chewing, a fleck of slaw stuck in the corner of his mouth. I picked up the story from the beginning when Marcus first told me about it, then sent it back to Eric. "Eric went through the case file and found some issues the detectives never investigated. Things that could support Jaylon's version of events."

Eric told him about the timeline problems and the missing rug and car. Olinski stabbed a chunk of barbecue and chomped while considering what we'd said.

Mouth empty once more, he asked, "You really think this guy might be innocent?"

I laid my fork on my plate. "I don't know, but I think

84

there are enough questions to make it worth taking another look at."

Olinski looked squarely at me. "You know how I feel about you interfering in police investigations."

"I do, but—"

He put up his hand to stop me. "However, I like the idea of leaving a possibly innocent man in prison even less. Especially one who might die because he can't receive proper medical care." He stirred the beans on his plate, pushing them farther away from the coleslaw. "This is a closed case. I can't reopen it without hard evidence to justify it."

I held my breath. Was he going to let me run with it? "I'm willing to do the legwork. Find the necessary evidence. All I need is access. I'll take care of the rest."

"Access to what?"

"The case file, witnesses, and the detectives who originally investigated the case."

I swigged wine while waiting for his response. Not the wisest of ideas since my head already floated a bit. And I'd caught myself twice sneaking a peek at Brittany out of the corner of my eye, on the verge of grinning. I folded my lips between my teeth.

I know nothing!

Olinski took a deep breath and ended his internal debate. "All right, Jen. I can't stop you, but you need to be careful. When you talk to the detectives in particular. They're not going to like you second-guessing their work. The good news is, they're both retired, and neither one still lives in Riddleton. The bad news is they still know people who do. People who can make things difficult for you." He turned to Eric. "Let her see the file and help when you can without getting yourself in trouble with Havermayer. She's not gonna like this either, but at least she didn't have anything to do with the original case. Maybe she won't take it personally."

Yeah, right. Havermayer takes everything personally if I'm involved. "Thank you," I said, nodding at Olinski.

He lowered his caterpillar eyebrows beneath the black rims of his glasses. "Don't thank me yet. This isn't going to be as easy as you think. And I'm not doing it for you. I'm doing it for Jaylon Barnes. Convicting an innocent man leaves a stain on the whole justice system. Makes a mockery of it. Find me something solid enough to get him out, or at least grounds for a new trial, okay? And if you discover he's guilty, I expect to hear about that, too."

"If the proof is there, either way, I'll find it." I squeezed Eric's hand. "*We'll* find it."

Brittany raised her wineglass in a toast. "To the truth!"

We all clinked our glasses and bottles together. "To the truth!"

She set her glass on the coffee table. "Great! Now that's settled, who wants to watch a movie?"

All hands went up. We definitely needed something to lighten the mood. Hopefully, it wouldn't be a rom-com or something that would get me thinking about Olinski's proposal. While the three of them bickered over what to watch, the wine pushed my thoughts into "woe is me" territory. Not a happy place for me to be.

Brittany was about to get engaged. Lacey would have a new baby in a few months. And here I was, treading water. Eric and I loved each other. What kept us from moving forward? Sure, we had our careers to focus on, but did one necessarily have to preclude the other? Or was that just a choice we made? An excuse to keep us from committing to our relationship?

Olinski and Brittany stared into each other's eyes, the love there for all to see. And they didn't care who was watching. Olinski had never looked at me that way. And to be honest, I never looked at him or anyone else that way, either. Did I have it in me to feel that much for someone? Or did fear always make me hold something back?

What was I afraid of? I wanted to believe it was all the troubled relationships I'd had in the past, but the truth is, I'd never fully committed to anyone or anything. Not even my writing. Perhaps that was the real source of my reoccurring writer's block. If I didn't really try, I couldn't fail. If I never entirely devoted myself to a relationship, I'd have nothing to lose when it ended. Huh. Good thing I'd probably remember none of this in the morning.

I emptied my glass and reached for the bottle. As the alcohol took hold in my brain, Olinski's secret buzzed around like a swarm of fireflies trapped in a jar, begging to get out. I tried to focus on the movie, but it was no use. The screen was swimming a race my eyes couldn't follow. I needed more food and something non-alcoholic to drink if I was going to survive this dinner without making a fool of myself or an enemy of Olinski.

I set my plate down on the coffee table and slowly stood, freezing when my head whirled like a merry-go-round run amok. After a moment, I regained my equilibrium and moved toward the kitchen. Brittany had to have something other than beer or wine in her refrigerator.

Eric looked up. "Are you okay, Jen?"

"I'm fine. Just getting something else to drink. I think I've had enough wine for tonight."

Brittany said, "There's some Coke and juice in there."

"Thanks. Anyone else need anything?"

Nobody did, so I cautiously moved around Savannah, who was prewashing Brittany's plate. From the empty space on the coffee table, it was clear she'd already taken care of Olinski's. I maneuvered around the dog's tail and stepped on Olinski's sparkling dish, which my girl had abandoned on the other side of the couch. My foot slid back, and I lurched forward, flailing my arms to regain my balance. But I couldn't get back something I never had in the first place.

My front foot landed on its side, and I dove face first for an up close and personal look at Brittany's carpet. Savannah rushed over, stuck her nose in my eye, and then licked my face to make it all better. I pushed her away and sat up. She took my push as a sign I wanted to play, grabbed a napkin off the coffee table, dropped into a play bow, and then zoomed around Brittany's apartment.

Eric rushed over, sidestepping the galloping German shepherd, to where I sat. He squatted to my eye level. "Are you all right? Did you hurt yourself?"

I could hear Brittany and Olinski trying not to laugh in the background. They failed, and my face felt like a barbecue ready for the steaks. No pain anywhere, but I suspected that would change when I sobered up. "I'm okay. I didn't hurt anything but my ego."

He helped me to my feet, and I brushed myself off, almost falling over again when I bent to reach my knees. Only Eric's grip on my arm kept me upright.

"Come on, hon," he said, leading me toward the door. "Let's get you home and put you to bed. You'll feel better in the morning."

I grinned at him playfully. "Will you be joining me?"

His face turned red. "I don't think so. You're in no condition to give consent."

"That's implied, darlin'. You should know that by now," I said with a wink and a drunken leer.

He draped his arm around my shoulders, and I gave him a side hug. I waved to Brittany and Olinski, who laughed hysterically, and Eric guided me out the door and across the hall.

CHAPTER NINE

Tuesday morning, I woke up with a blacksmith pounding horseshoes in my head. Savannah slept in her usual place, attached to my side, and I vaguely remembered Eric rising early and leaving for work. Unfortunately, that was all I recalled about him being there, but I wouldn't tell him that. Hopefully, he wouldn't bring up the subject.

I kept my eyes closed, head still, trying to piece together what had happened last night after we started watching the movie. No idea which one we'd settled on or what we talked about when the Jaylon Barnes discussion ended. I was almost positive, though, I'd revealed no secrets. Relatively sure I'd remember the ensuing blowout had there been one. Other than that, I had nothing. Just a black hole where the evening should've been.

Slowly and carefully, I eased apart my sticky eyelids, praying I hadn't left the blinds open. The sun streaming through would be like laser beams aimed at my eyeballs to keep the smithy's fire fueled. The last thing I needed right now. This morning, water, coffee, and pain reliever were the only items on the menu. Not necessarily in that order.

90

A darkened room greeted me. Either I'd closed the blinds last night, or Eric had before he left. Either way, the pounding maintained its steady rhythm. No blast of light exploded in my brain. I debated remaining in place until the pain receded, but my bladder had other ideas. And I imagined Savannah's did, too. Oh boy, I had to walk the dog. Maybe the lady in Georgia who gave her to me would take her back for the day.

Not a chance.

I slid my legs out from under the comforter and lifted my head off the pillow. No change in pain level, so I held my breath and sat up on the edge of the bed. The pressure lessened, and I actually felt a little better. Not much, but enough, so I risked standing up and tottering to the bathroom, using the wall for support.

My German shepherd showed her first signs of life when she jumped down and followed me. Good. I couldn't stand the prospect of going to the bathroom alone for the first time in a year and a half. It'd been so long I'd grown accustomed to having company everywhere I went whether I wanted it or not. One of the perks of dog ownership.

Teeth brushed and hair combed, sort of, I carried a couple of pain caplets to the kitchen and downed them with a bottle of water. By the time I finished dressing, the pills had taken the edge off, and I was ready to brave Savannah's walk. She waited patiently by the door with her leash in her mouth. A not-so-subtle hint.

An overcast, windy day awaited us at the bottom of the steps. I shivered in my sweatshirt, debating whether to run upstairs for a jacket. My head vetoed the idea of me running anyplace, and I concurred. I'd have to tough it out.

Guiding the dog through a business-only trip around the block, remnants of my conversation with Olinski ran through my mind. He'd renewed my faith when he encouraged me to check into Jaylon's conviction and gave Eric permission to help. I understood why it all had to be unofficial, however. If he reopened the investigation after they'd received a guilty verdict, it would cast shadows on the efficiency and integrity of his police department. Not to mention ruffle enough feathers to keep a whole flock of geese warm in Alaska. Better I take the heat than the chief of police.

I felt confident, though, that Olinski would act on whatever I found. He seemed genuinely concerned about the possibility Jaylon hadn't committed the murder he'd been convicted of. Or at least that all the questions in the case hadn't been adequately answered. He'd tasked me with addressing them now without getting myself in trouble. Of course, that part would be much easier if I had a badge and a gun to back me up. *Not gonna happen.*

However, I had Eric's help this time, which was the next best thing. Not that he hadn't wanted to help me in the past, he'd just never had permission before. When we made it back to the apartment, I fed and watered Savannah, threw a cup of coffee in the microwave, and called him, hoping I'd forgotten nothing important from last night.

He answered on the third ring. "Hey, babe! How're you feeling?" The chuckle in his voice told me he had a reasonably good idea of how I felt.

"I'm all right. A bit of a headache, but nothing I can't handle."

"Glad to hear it. You were pretty smashed last night."

Embarrassment burned my ears. "Too much wine on an empty stomach. I didn't do anything stupid, did I?"

"You mean like tell Brittany Olinski plans to propose on Valentine's Day?"

Oh, no! Please tell me I didn't. "Yeah, like that."

"Nope. I was very proud of you." He cleared his throat. "But you did take a pretty good tumble trying to get to the kitchen. I'll bet Brittany and Olinski are still laughing."

I blew out a sigh. "Well, I'm glad I could entertain you all." I examined my arms for bruises and felt the parts of my legs I could reach without bending down. All clear. "I should charge extra for that."

"We'll double your pay. Will that cover it?" He shuffled papers in the background. "Listen, I'd better get back to work. Havermayer'll have a fit if I don't get these reports done."

The microwave dinged. I retrieved my coffee and added cream and sugar. "She has a fit no matter what you do, but I'll let you go. Do you mind if I swing by and pick up the case file on my way to the store?"

"Case file? Oh, you mean Jaylon Barnes. Sure, I have it right here."

"Thanks. And thank Olinski for me. I don't remember if I did last night."

"I will."

"Eric, do you think that skeleton might be Ewon Barnes?"

"The skeleton in the tunnel?" He hesitated. "I don't know. The timing's right, but it could be anybody who disappeared back then. I should check the missing persons reports when I have time, just in case."

"Wouldn't the cold-case squad have already done that?"

"They should have, but who knows?"

"True. Thank you."

"You're welcome. See you soon. Love you."

"Love you too." I grinned as I disconnected the call. He told me he loved me. He'd said it before, but somehow, the casual way he expressed himself this time made it seem more real, like it was something I could take for granted. Not in the bad sense, but so I could count on it. He'd be there for me no matter what. A wave of warmth gathered in my chest.

I changed into jeans and a clean sweatshirt and relaxed onto the couch beside Savannah. When I stroked between her eyes, she closed them and drifted into her post-breakfast nap. The mug warmed my hands, and the fresh-brewed, albeit reheated, coffee aroma tickled my nose. The day's first cup was always my favorite, and I savored the drink and the peaceful time I spent enjoying it. Usually, the calm before the storm, as my mother liked to say.

When the bottom of my cup revealed itself, I put on my Nikes and woke the dog. "C'mon, kid, we have to go to work."

She blinked her sleepy eyes at me but didn't budge. No problem. I knew she'd be wide awake as soon as I moved. No way she'd agree to be left behind. Too bad I couldn't send her in my place. I'd love to relax with another cup of coffee. I imagined Jaylon Barnes felt the same way; however, if he didn't have that option, then neither did I. At least until I was convinced he deserved to be in prison. And that hadn't happened yet.

Eric was busy with Havermayer when I stopped by the police station, so I grabbed the file off his desk and left, hoping nobody would stop me on the way out. No sense in starting unnecessary trouble. Lacey had closed the book on Story Time when we arrived at the bookstore, and stood by the register, sipping ginger ale and munching on crackers. Her morning sickness must be acting up. I couldn't imagine dealing with that kind of nausea every day. Or being pregnant, for that matter. The picture of me walking around with a skin-covered beach ball between my ribcage and my hips wouldn't come into my mind. Nope, not for me.

I followed my prancing dog to the counter. "You okay?" I asked Lacey.

She took another swig. "I'm fine. Nothing to worry about." Lacey could be dying and would give me the same answer. And I thought *I* was tough. She had me beat by miles.

"Have we been busy?"

Lacey reached under the counter for the bag of dog treats. Savannah spun around before finally settling into a sit. "Not too bad. We had eight for Story Time. Charlie's been a big help." She glanced in his direction and smiled. "Or should I say, the Lone Ranger?"

"What?" I turned to look at him. He wore powder-blue pants with a matching pullover shirt, a red kerchief around his neck, a black mask over his eyes, a Stetson on his head, and, of course, his gun belt and cowboy boots. I laughed and shook my head. "Let me guess, he finally figured out a new outfit."

"Yup."

"Is Silver tied up in the alley out back?"

"I've been afraid to look, but I think Tonto's in the stockroom, rearranging books."

I did a double take, then realized she was only joking.

A good thing. We couldn't afford anyone else on the payroll. Although, I wouldn't mind the help catching bad guys. "You want to take a break for a while? I can cover things here."

"Nah, I'm good. I want to finish up the second window. The readers need clothing."

"Probably a good idea. We don't want to leave them naked long enough for Charlie to think up a matching outfit."

"No kidding. Although, I'm worried about Cupid encouraging him to come in wearing nothing but a diaper."

Great. Now, I'd have that image stuck in my head all day.

I wandered back to the coffee bar to fill my mug with the day's second cup. Waving to Charlie, I said, "Nice duds."

He twirled like a model at the end of a runway. "You like it? I had to special order the suit. It cost a bundle, but it's worth it, don't you think?"

Oh, brother. "Absolutely. It's very authentic."

"Thanks." He pointed to the police file I held by my side. "Is that something for me to work on?"

"Probably, but I won't know until I go through it. Did you have any luck finding Jaylon Barnes's parents?"

"I did, but still nothing on the girlfriend. It's like she disappeared with Ewon."

I didn't want to say it out loud, but Eliza Naismith might've taken off with Ewon, leaving Jaylon to stand trial for a murder that never happened. Except she was there for the trial. Did she join Ewon later, after his brother was convicted? I might never know.

"Okay, so tell me about the parents."

Charlie slid a sheet of paper from under his laptop. "Richard and Regina Barnes split up after Jaylon's trial. She still lives in town, and he moved to Sutton to be closer to his work." He handed me his notes. "Their addresses are here. I'll keep working on the girlfriend."

I took the paper and slid it into the folder. "Thanks, Charlie. Hopefully, there'll be something in the case file we can work with. I really need to get this guy out of jail if I can."

"Let me know what I can do to help."

"Will do." I carried the file back to my office and parked behind my desk. Savannah trotted in and grabbed her stuffed bone to poke me with. "Not right now, little girl. I have work to do."

She sat beside me, dropped the toy in my lap, and waited for me to throw it. Poor neglected thing. Nobody ever paid her any attention. I grabbed the slobbery bone and shook it in front of her. She jumped up and danced around the desk. "Go see if Uncle Charlie wants to play," I said, throwing the toy through the doorway into the hall by the stockroom. She took off after it. That should keep her busy for a minute.

I opened the file and studied it piece by piece. The investigating detectives were Larry Smith, who'd retired to Florida last summer, and Jeremy Conway. Hopefully, Eric knew where he'd retired to, and it was someplace close. I'd rather interview the detectives in person, but I wasn't about to drive all the way to Florida to do it.

The crime scene photos offered almost nothing in the way of evidence a crime had even taken place, let alone that Jaylon had murdered his brother. There was a shot of a dent in the Sheetrock wall with a few drops of blood around it, just as Eric had described. Another had a little blood on the floor. Again, not enough to show Ewon had been beaten to death as the prosecutor insisted. The last picture was of the brand-new living room rug.

The next page gave me the name of Jaylon's public defender: Quinn Simmons. I added contacting him to my to-do list. Perhaps he could shed some light on why he was convinced Jaylon had committed the murder. I suspected I already knew, but also had to consider the possibility it was more than his vast caseload and cynicism.

Witness statements were short and to the point. Nobody had seen anything except the neighbor who noticed Jaylon loading the rug into his truck, but Jaylon and Ewon had been arguing before Ewon disappeared. That was it. As far as I could tell, the detectives hadn't tried to elicit any more information or looked for any evidence to back up a different theory. Jaylon and Ewon fought. Ewon was missing and presumed dead. Therefore, Jaylon was responsible.

How did the prosecutor convince a jury of Jaylon's guilt with no evidence?

It didn't make any sense. Eric suggested I contact someone who specializes in these cases. Maybe he was right. I got on the computer and searched blindly for someone in South Carolina who could help. I stumbled on the Palmetto Innocence Project and dialed the number on their website, then jotted it down on the back of an envelope.

The phone rang four times before being picked up by a woman. "Palmetto Innocence Project. This is Debbie. Can I help you?"

I crossed my fingers that she could. "Hi, my name is

Jen Dawson, and I have a friend who's been convicted of a crime he didn't commit."

"I'm sorry to hear that. Can you tell me about it?"

I told her everything I knew, including what I'd found in the case file. Or hadn't found.

"That's awful. Do you have any evidence he didn't commit the crime? Any witnesses or an alibi that wasn't followed up on?"

"Well, no. But it seems pretty clear the prosecutor didn't have any evidence he *did* commit the crime. Or that a crime was even committed. His brother's body was never found. For all we know, he could still be alive."

Debbie remained silent for a minute, then said, "Have you any proof of that? Has he been seen anywhere? Used his credit cards? Any activity in his bank accounts?"

My grip on the phone tightened. "No, not that I know of. I have the police file, and his financial dealings aren't mentioned. Right now, I'm wondering if they ever checked."

"I'm sorry. I wish we could help, but without new evidence, we have nothing to work with. Bring me some proof your friend is innocent, and we'll do everything possible to get him a new trial. Until then, there's nothing we can do."

Tears of frustration burned my eyes. "I'll see what I can find. Thank you for your time."

I ended the call and sat with my head in my hands, mentally begging the blacksmith to take a coffee break. I was Jaylon's only hope. It was all up to me, but could I do it? Could I save his life?

I wished I knew.

CHAPTER TEN

When I surfaced from my dive into despair and self-doubt, I went back to work. Quinn Simmons topped my list of people I needed to talk to. My buddy Google told me he'd left the public defender's office and gone into private practice chasing ambulances. Apparently, the never-ending stream of guilty-until-proved-innocent clients had burned him out on criminal defense. Couldn't say I blamed him.

I dialed the number on the screen, expecting a secretary to answer the call who'd insist I make an appointment. Instead, I heard a deep, booming voice that must've served him well in the courtroom, if his goal was scaring the right verdict out of the jury.

"Quinn Simmons."

After a long breath to recover from my surprise, I told him who I was and what I wanted. "Is this a good time to talk?"

"I'm a little busy right now, but I can give you a few minutes. I'm not sure I have anything to say that'll help you, though."

"I appreciate you speaking with me. Jaylon felt that you believed he was guilty and behaved accordingly. Did he have that right?"

"No, he most certainly did not!"

His vehement denial vibrated across the airwaves. As he continued, I pulled the phone away from my ear to protect my eardrum.

"Every client is entitled to a vigorous defense, and that's exactly what Mr. Barnes received. I never asked him if he'd done it and never formed an opinion about his guilt or innocence. It didn't matter. I defended him to the best of my ability."

That didn't say much for his abilities.

"I'm sure you did, but I had some questions about details that didn't make it in front of the jury. For instance, what happened to Ewon Barnes's car? His vehicle disappeared the same day he did and hasn't been seen since."

"Since Barnes insisted his brother drove away, and there were no witnesses to corroborate his claim, I thought it unwise to bring it up because the prosecution would only insinuate Jaylon had disposed of it."

"But they didn't have any evidence to support that assumption."

"Ms. Dawson, juries don't always rely on the evidence. It would've been enough for the prosecutor to plant the idea in their heads. I saw no advantage to bringing up the subject."

His response boomed into my ear, and I pulled the phone away again. A few more minutes of this conversation, and I'd come away with an even bigger headache. No point in continuing this discussion, so I changed the subject. "I only have one more question, Mr. Simmons. Ewon's body was never found. If Jaylon rolled it up in the rug and disposed of it as the prosecution described, why do you think it was never

101

discovered? Since he worked alone, Jaylon couldn't possibly have transported the rug to a place so remote nobody would stumble across it in what would've had to be a shallow grave. All before his mother came home from work. And the body still hasn't been located five years later. How do you explain that?"

"I don't have to explain that. The only evidence I had to work with was Barnes's claim he'd taken the rug to the landfill, where the police didn't find it. I had nothing to present to the jury that would've affected their votes one way or the other."

"But, what if the police didn't find it in the landfill because someone stole it? An Oriental rug that size would be a premium find, and the police didn't search the area until several days after Jaylon dumped it. Not until Ewon was reported missing."

"I agree that's quite possible. But, in the courtroom, it doesn't matter what I think, only what I can prove. And I couldn't prove that's what happened."

I sighed in frustration. "But, isn't part of your job as a defense attorney to plant seeds of doubt in the jurors' minds? Prosecutors have to prove their case. All you needed was reasonable doubt. The car and the rug were both obvious ways to do that."

"Hindsight is twenty-twenty, Ms. Dawson. I wish you luck in your endeavor, but I strongly suggest you don't do anything to smear my reputation, which will force me to take action against you. I did the best I could with what I had to work with. Now, if you don't mind, I have a trial to prepare for."

"Certainly. Thank you for your time. Good luck with your trial."

I hung up and rested my phone on the desk. If Mr.

102

Simmons handled his upcoming case the way he'd dealt with Jaylon's, his client needed all the luck in the world.

Penelope was delivering food to our table when I arrived at the diner for my one-thirty lunch date with Eric. I waited for her to finish before sliding into my seat and giving him a puzzled glance. "What's this?"

He laughed. "I don't have much time for lunch, so I went ahead and ordered for us."

I grabbed a napkin from the dispenser and spread it across my lap before adding ketchup and salt to my fries and an extra dollop of ketchup to my burger. "Why? What's going on? Do you have a new case?"

"No, nothing new, but I'm making some headway with the missing persons files. Two potential matches so far. I want to finish before Havermayer figures out what I'm doing."

"You have Olinski's permission. Why all the secrecy?" I bit into my bacon cheeseburger, and ketchup dripped out the side onto my finger. I stuck it in my mouth.

He downed a bite of his burger. "Havermayer had just been promoted to detective when this case came up. She had nothing to do with it, but she worked with the guys who did on other cases. I don't want her giving me a hard time about reopening it."

"She can't do anything to you."

"No, but she can find a bunch of other things for me to do, so I don't have time. I'm sure there's a backlog of filing to be done somewhere. Like in the dumpster."

I rolled a fry in ketchup and popped it in my mouth, giggling. "And if there isn't, she'll create a backlog just for you."

"Or something worse. Especially if she figures out

103

you're involved. And if she notices what I'm working on, she'll assume you're involved."

"I'm sorry about that. I hate that she gives you so much trouble because you're my boyfriend. It's not fair. And what's worse is I don't even know why she has a problem with me."

"I still haven't figured that out." Eric shoved a fry in his mouth. "There doesn't seem to be any reason for it. Not that I can see, anyway."

"Tell me about it." I shook my head and bit into my burger again. No ketchup making a run for it this time.

Eric changed the subject. "I ran a DMV check on Ewon Barnes's car this morning."

I swallowed my bite. "Oh yeah? What did the Department of Motor Vehicles have to say for itself?"

"Not much. All I found was his expired registration from five years ago."

"Did you try surrounding states?"

"Nothing in Georgia, Florida, or North Carolina. I even checked sales records. Nothing there either. The car's just gone. Vanished, like its owner."

I drew a face in my ketchup with a French fry. "I wonder if the killer dumped it in the lake to get rid of it. If it's out in the deep part, we'd never find it." The depth of Lake Dester was almost two hundred feet at its deepest point. If Ewon's car was down there, even a year without rain wouldn't expose it.

"Even if we did find it, that might end up pointing back to Jaylon."

"Except he'd have had to sink the car in the middle of the afternoon, or his mother would've seen it when she got home. Too many people around that time of day, even during the week. It had to be somebody who could hide it elsewhere until after dark. After midnight, probably, to avoid people partying on the shore in the evening."

"True. And he'd have to push it out far enough to be too deep for swimmers to find." He stopped chewing and stared at me. "Do you think the mother might be involved? That would eliminate all the timeline problems because Jaylon wouldn't have to finish everything before she came home."

"The detectives checked her alibi. She was at work until five that day."

"That doesn't mean she didn't help with cleanup and disposal."

"Disposal of her son's dead body? I don't know about that, but I guess anything's possible. I'd like to think Smith and Conway would've considered that possibility, though."

I had to face it. The car was probably a dead end. "What about Ewon Barnes himself? Any activity on his driver's license, like a speeding ticket?"

"I checked that, too. There's nothing there. His license expired last year, and he didn't renew it. No activity in his financial records, either. Our only options are he changed his name and went completely off the grid, or he really is dead."

Definitely not what I wanted to hear. "You know, even if he's dead, it doesn't mean Jaylon killed him."

Eric balled his napkin and dropped it onto his half-empty plate. "I know, but proving someone else murdered him will be next to impossible after all this time. It would be a lot easier if we could find some evidence that he's still alive."

"Except there doesn't seem to be any."

"Yet."

"It would be nice if we came across something, however. I called the Palmetto Innocence Project this morning. There's nothing they can do unless we find new evidence that Jaylon is innocent or Ewon is alive. If we do, they might be able to get him out."

"That stinks. I'd hoped they could help us find that evidence. I imagine they have too many cases to do that kind of legwork, though." He reached over and took my hand. "Don't lose hope yet. We're just getting started. There are many more avenues we haven't explored."

I'd have to take his word for it since I couldn't think of a single one. But he was right. We were just getting started. There had to be something somewhere that would back up Jaylon's story. I only needed to find it.

After a glance at his watch, Eric said, "I hate to do this to you, but I need to get back. I want to finish going through those missing persons reports. Maybe we'll get lucky and be able to eliminate Ewon as the skeleton."

"Good idea. Who knows? You might be able to solve at least one case today."

He stood, then bent over to kiss me. "See you later?"

"You bet."

I pushed French fries into the shape of a house, trying to work out what to do next. Maybe Charlie had found Jeremy Conway, and I could talk to him this afternoon. If nothing else, he could explain why he was so sure Jaylon had killed his brother. Perhaps he'd even have enough to convince me.

Fat chance.

Angus slid into the booth across from me, inching the table in my direction. I'd been so engrossed in my thoughts I hadn't even noticed his approach. Good thing he wasn't here to kill me. I'd surely be dead.

"What're you thinking so hard about?" he asked, pushing Eric's plate to the side.

"Trying to figure out how I'm going to prove Jaylon Barnes didn't murder his brother."

He squinted at me, then raised his eyebrows in recognition. "Oh, is that the guy Marcus has been talking about?"

I nodded and messed up my ketchup face with the end of a fry. "He asked me to help him get his conviction overturned. The only way to do that is to find proof he didn't do it. And the police did a lousy job of investigating, so I'm basically starting from scratch."

"What's the problem? It's not the first time you've had to do that."

"Maybe, but all the other times, I at least knew the people involved. Usually, because I was one of them. I don't know anything about this guy or his family."

Angus waved to Penelope and lifted his fingers toward his mouth as if drinking from a cup, holding it by the handle. "Why don't you tell me what you know so far? I might be able to help."

Why not? I had nothing to lose. I filled him in on what Jaylon had told me and everything Eric and I had learned since Sunday. Penelope brought him a cup of coffee, and he studied me thoughtfully as he sipped the aromatic brew. I waited for him to share what was on his mind.

Half a cup later, he asked, "How old did you say that skeleton was?"

"About five years. Why?"

He set his coffee on the table and folded his hands

together. "Well, somebody told me a story a few years ago, and I'm wondering if it might be connected."

Yippee! Years-old gossip. Just what I needed to confuse things even more. Still, every once in a while, Angus had useful information. Might as well give it a listen. "Really? Tell me about it."

Massaging the back of his neck under his white shirt collar, he said, "I guess it would be around five years ago now, three guys robbed the Blackburn City Jewelry store and got away with two hundred and fifty thousand dollars' worth of merchandise. They were never caught, and the jewelry was never found or offered for sale publicly or privately. According to the story, the stash is hidden somewhere around here, in Riddleton."

Why was he telling me this? "You think the skeleton might be one of the jewelry store robbers? Left behind to guard the stash?"

"I don't know. Could be. Maybe one of the robbers killed the others to have the proceeds all to himself."

"Okay, but what does this have to do with Ewon Barnes?"

Angus sipped his coffee. "Maybe he was one of the jewelry store robbers who got killed. Didn't you say Jaylon thought his brother was being pressured by his friends to do something he didn't want to do? What if his friends wanted to rob a jewelry store?"

Jaylon also said his brother needed money to open the auto repair shop, and if he couldn't get it from his father, he'd have to find it another way. Or, was Jaylon possibly part of the crew and murdered his cohorts to keep it all for himself? That would explain why none of the jewelry was ever seen again. Jaylon was arrested a few days later.

"Angus, you might be on to something."

Unfortunately, his helpful gossip made my problem a lot more complicated. Now I was back to wondering if Jaylon had murdered his brother after all. I rubbed my temples. Angus had not only given me useful information, he'd also brought back my headache. "I'll have to give that story some thought."

"Happy to help!" He drained his cup. "Hey, did you hear that a psychic showed up at the police station today offering to help with the skeleton investigation? She said she had a vision."

How did he know all this stuff? And why didn't Eric mention it when he was here? "A psychic? Really? No way. Who told you that?"

"I have my sources."

Sources? Cops with big mouths trying to seem more important than they are, most likely. "All right, tell me about her. What did she see in her vision?"

"I don't know. They didn't say."

"Didn't say or didn't know?"

He shrugged.

Helpful. "No problem, I'll ask Eric about it later."

The front door swung open, and Angus turned in that direction. "You might not have to." He jutted his chin toward a heavy-set blond woman wearing an orange muumuu covered with pineapples entering the restaurant. "That's her."

Her bobbed hair framed a full, round face adorned with thick-lensed brown glasses. Apparently, her sight was all internal. She looked around the diner, spotted me in the corner, and headed directly for my table.

Angus touched my arm. "I guess you can ask her yourself."

109

"I guess so. I wonder what she wants."

She sallied up to us, muumuu swinging around her lower legs, her gaze fixed on me. "You are Jennifer Dawson. Yes?"

Her thick Russian accent offset a deep-pitched voice that sounded about as real as the cartoon character Natasha Fatale. Boris Badenov must've been waiting in the car. "Yes. Can I help you?"

She pushed into the booth beside Angus, leaving him no choice but to move over. The oversized peace sign she wore around her neck scraped the tabletop. "I am Madame Crystal Moon. I have message for you."

"A message? From who?"

Crystal lifted her palms to shoulder level, showing off the rings that adorned every finger. A jewel-encrusted dolphin bracelet dangled off her left wrist. "The spirits give me message. I know not who. But is important you listen."

Was she for real? It was all I could do to keep from laughing. There had to be a carnival in town I hadn't heard about. *Who put her up to this?* "Look, miss, I appreciate the joke. It's hilarious. Just tell whoever sent you that you got me, okay?"

She slapped a hand on the tabletop hard enough to turn all eyes in the room toward us. "Is not joke! Is very important message. You must listen. You must listen, or you die!"

I looked at Angus. He lifted his eyebrows. "I don't know, Jen. Maybe you should pay attention to her." His lips twitched. "We certainly don't want you to die."

Unbelievable. I shot him an eye roll. "You're joking, right?"

He curled his lips behind his teeth to suppress a smile.

110

"No, not at all. This lady is obviously quite serious. I don't want anything bad to happen to you."

"All right, Angus, I'll hear her out. Just for you." I turned to Crystal. "Tell me the message, please."

Crystal leaned her ample bosom over the table and pointed an index finger so close she almost touched the end of my nose. Her gaze locked on to mine, and icy fingers walked down my spine. I shivered, then shook it off. This woman couldn't possibly be any danger to me.

After a minute-long staring contest, I said, "Miss Moon? The message, please?"

"Madame Crystal!"

"Okay, Madame Crystal. Will you please give me the message?"

"Beware the golden bones!"

I laughed. "Are you kidding me? What does that mean?"

She sat back and crossed her arms. "The spirits no tell me what message means. Just deliver to you." She leaned over the table again. "You must listen! Beware the golden bones!"

Oh, brother.

CHAPTER ELEVEN

Beware the golden bones? What in the world did that mean? Crystal Moon hoisted her garish muumuu out of the booth, pushing the table another inch in my direction, and left the diner without another word. Angus sat across from me, his jaw hanging and brows furrowed, mirroring my confusion.

I propped my elbows on the table and cupped my chin in my hand. "Well, what do you think?"

"Don't ask me. I have no idea what it means, let alone how it might kill you."

"She's nuts. That has to be it. Her parents never should've given her that crystal ball to play with when she was a baby."

"No kidding." Angus turned as a large group entered the restaurant. "I'd better get back to work. If you figure it out, let me know. In the meantime, I'll start asking around about her."

"We can compare notes later." I followed him to the counter and flagged down Penelope for my check.

She waved me off. "Eric took care of it on his way out."

I handed her a tip and ducked out the door, still

112

baffled by Crystal's words. She'd been so serious about the so-called message from beyond. Too serious to say something so ridiculous. But she didn't seem to think it was. Did she truly believe I'd die if I didn't heed her words? As ridiculous as the whole thing seemed to me, I thought she did. A cloud of dread brought the hair on the back of my neck to attention.

Though it was only three in the afternoon, the air outside had chilled. The sun was going down and taking the temperature with it. I shoved my hands into my jeans pockets and my teeth chattered, but I couldn't be sure if the weather or the spooky pronouncement from Crystal accounted for the reaction. Probably a little of both. Her words rattled around in my head on the way to the bookstore.

Beware the golden bones.

What gold? And what bones? Was she talking about the skeleton? There was nothing golden about those bones that's for sure. Only the desiccated remains of what had once been a living human being. No money in that unless I auctioned them off to some mad scientist on eBay. Besides, they were the property of the Sutton County Medical Examiner's office at the moment. No auctions in my immediate future.

I shook off the pall and strolled into Ravenous Readers. Savannah flew up the aisle to prance circles around me since I'd abandoned her in foster care. I squatted to her level, corralling her for a hug, and she squirmed to escape. Not this time, though. I needed her furry warmth to soothe me, but I wasn't sure why. What about Crystal, and her message, had bothered me so much?

The message was silly. It meant nothing to me, yet

somewhere deep in my psyche, I quaked like a three-year-old with a monster in her closet. I needed to put it out of my mind. Distract myself. I released my imprisoned dog and headed for the coffee bar. Maybe Lone Ranger Charlie had found something I could follow up on.

I reached under the counter for my mug as Charlie replaced a nozzle on the espresso machine. "Everything okay?" I asked, watching him work. Replacing expensive equipment was the last thing we could afford right now. We had enough trouble restocking the inventory we sold, let alone anything else.

He held up the part. "What, this? It's fine. Just needed a little cleaning. We're slow, so I figured I'd knock it out now instead of waiting until after we close. You never know what might happen between now and then."

"Sounds good." I should know that by now. Sometimes, it seemed I was a useless appendage around here. *So, what're you gonna do about it, Jen?* Good question. "Any luck finding those detectives we talked about?"

"Actually, yes." He finished his chore, wiped his hands on a clean towel, and reached for his notepad. "Here you go."

I tore the top sheet off and squinted at his hieroglyphics. Clearly, penmanship was never his best subject. As best I could make out, Larry Smith had retired to Boca Raton in Florida, and Jeremy Conway lived near Lake Dester.

While I'd love a trip to Florida at this time of year, planning a visit to Detective Conway made more sense. I may well do that this afternoon if he was available. "Thanks, Charlie. I'll start on this right away. For your next project, can you see what you can find on Madame Crystal Moon? She's supposedly a psychic who showed up in town today. She says she had a vision about the skeleton, but I don't have any details."

"A psychic? In Riddleton? What's she doing here?"

"Beats me. That's what I'm hoping you'll find out."

"Sure thing. I'll get right on it."

I waved at Lacey in the stockroom, who was gathering books for the shelves, then went to my office. After punching Jeremy Conway's number into my phone, I leaned back in the chair and put my feet up on the corner of the desk. The phone rang four times before a man with a raspy voice answered.

"Hello?"

I sat up and dropped my feet to the floor. "Hi, is this Jeremy Conway?"

"Yeah, who's this?" he replied, his gruff tone suspicious.

After explaining who I was and why I'd called, I said, "I'd love to speak with you in person. This afternoon, if possible."

"I don't know what I can tell you that isn't already in the case file. Why are you looking at this case, anyway? It was open and shut. There was never any question in my mind that Barnes killed his brother."

That was the problem. If he never questioned it, he never looked at anyone else. How could I answer without telling him I thought he did shoddy work? I called on Diplomat Daniel. "I understand that, and I'm not saying you were wrong. I guess I'd like a little insight into why you felt that way. There's probably nothing to Jaylon's story, but I'd feel better knowing your side."

When he didn't reply, I continued, "It'll only take a little of your time and go a long way toward alleviating my concerns."

I almost saw him shrug when he said, "Sure, why not? If you want to waste your time, have at it. Can you be here by four? I have dinner plans."

My phone screen showed 3:22. If the Robot Woman in my GPS didn't let me down, I'd make it. Barely. "I can be there. See you then. Thank you."

He hung up without a response then texted me the address, which Charlie'd already given me. I plugged it into my phone's navigation app. On my way out, I stopped by the front counter to ask Lacey to mind Savannah for a while longer. Given Conway's apathy, bordering on hostility, on the phone, I suspected I'd be back long before the shop closed at six.

RW guided me west over the mile-and-a-half-long dam, and I fought the low-hanging sun shining directly in my eyes. This trip had better amount to something given the difficulty I had getting there. No guarantees, though. I suspected Conway would be uncooperative at best. At worst, he'd be openly antagonistic to my questioning his conclusions. Still, the detective might give something away without realizing it. And that would make it all worthwhile.

About halfway across, I glanced in my rearview mirror. The naked bones of Simeon Kirby's resort-in-the-making marred the lakeside landscape. When the skeleton was clothed with walls, stucco, and a shingled roof, and guests began pouring in from all over the Southeast and beyond, Riddleton would never be a small cozy town again. My heart shriveled. I pressed my lips together and focused on not driving over the side into the lake.

116

The glare made my hands barely visible on the steering wheel by the time RW instructed me to turn into the dirt drive leading to a house set back in the woods. Overhanging branches shedding pine needles like Savannah's fur in August shaded me from the sun, and I blinked to help my eyes adjust. For the first time since I'd left Riddleton, I relaxed my grip on the wheel.

The A-frame cottage was about the size of my four-hundred-square-foot apartment, with an unfinished plank walk, which seemed to have been there since the dam was completed in 1930, leading to the front door. It had board siding painted blue and a shingled roof that needed replacing. It reminded me of the Jolly Green Giant's daughter's dollhouse. Probably all Conway could afford after retiring on a small-town detective's salary. Still, it was more than I could afford now or possibly ever at the rate I was going.

I noticed no vehicle parked near the house but took a chance he might be home, anyway. After all, we had an appointment. Had he changed his mind? Perhaps he'd had second thoughts about hearing what I had to say. Or worse, maybe he'd had second thoughts about how well he'd investigated Ewon's disappearance and decided to avoid the discussion altogether.

The walkway boards creaked under my weight as I tiptoed across, avoiding the weak and rotting planks. Breaking an ankle wasn't high on my to-do list today. The front door opened before my knuckles came near it, and a sixtyish, white-haired man wearing jeans and a dirty gray T-shirt stared at me. He ran his fingers over the three-day growth on his chin, and the sour alcohol stench blasting me came from him, not the beer can he gripped in his other hand.

117

I stepped forward, grateful I wasn't his dinner date for the evening. "Detective Conway? I'm Jen Dawson. Thank you for seeing me." I stuck out my hand.

He ignored it and stepped aside to let me in. I masked my surprise when I saw the newly remodeled interior. Fresh paint, new furniture, and a spotless glass coffee table filled the main room, and the kitchen sported twenty-first-century appliances newer than mine.

Turning to him, I smiled to open him up. "This is lovely. Did you do the work yourself?"

He gestured for me to sit on the plush chocolate-brown couch across from a gas fireplace, which warmed the room to a comfortable temperature. "Some. I did the painting but had to contract out for the electrical and gas lines." His shoulders relaxed a bit. Mission accomplished.

"You wanna beer?" he asked, showing me his can as he flopped into a cracked leather recliner. The only old thing in the room. It must've been his favorite chair for the last forty years.

"No, thank you. I don't want to take up too much of your time. I know you have plans."

A smile tugged at his lips when he emptied half his can in one swallow. "All right, let's get to it, then. What do you wanna know?"

"As I mentioned on the phone, I'm curious why you were so sure Jaylon Barnes murdered his brother. The evidence didn't seem that overwhelming to me."

He lifted a bushy black-and-gray eyebrow. "Is that your professional opinion?"

Blood rose into my face, which heated even though I understood he was only trying to put me in my place. "No, I've never been in law enforcement, but I'm no stranger to these kinds of cases, either."

118

"I've heard about you, you know. You're that nosy mystery writer who thinks she knows more than the police." He settled his right ankle on his left knee.

Nosy mystery writer? I counted to five to maintain my composure. He wanted me riled up so he'd have an excuse to be angry, too. "It's true, I'm a mystery writer, but my experience comes from being a suspect myself. Accused like Jaylon Barnes by detectives with flimsy circumstantial evidence and not much else."

Conway thumped his foot to the floor and leaned toward me. "The evidence against Barnes wasn't flimsy, as you put it. We had him cold. He slammed his brother's head into the wall, rolled him up in a rug, and hauled him away. We found blood on the wall, the guy's shoes, and his truck. He had no alibi and plenty of motive. What more did we need? Case closed."

"What about Ewon's car?"

He froze with his beer can halfway to his mouth. "What?"

Gotcha! "Ewon Barnes's black 2010 Toyota Corolla was never seen again after he disappeared. What happened to it?"

"What difference does that make?"

My mouth opened and closed like a fish scooping up pellets before they reached the bottom of the tank. Did he seriously not understand the relevance, or was he only excusing his sloppy police work? "Well, since it's pretty clear Jaylon Barnes didn't have time to kill his brother, dispose of the body in the rug, and get rid of a car before his mother came home from work, I think it makes a big difference. It points to someone else as the killer."

"Or somebody helped him." He polished off his beer

119

and crushed the can with one hand, dropping it on the table beside his chair. It bounced off onto the floor. "Nothing you can say will make me doubt our conclusions. Jaylon Barnes is a murderer, and he's exactly where he belongs. You need to leave this thing alone." He stood and stepped forward in a feeble attempt to intimidate me. "Whatever you think you know, you're wrong."

I held his gaze. "I'm not saying I know anything. All I have right now is questions. Help me find answers to them. Please! A man's life is at stake."

Conway pointed toward the door, controlling his anger with gritted teeth. "Get out of my house, and don't come back."

"One more question, please, if you don't mind."

He ran a hand through his greasy shoulder-length hair. "What?"

"Did you ever suspect that either of the Barnes brothers was involved in the jewelry store robbery in Blackburn that happened around the same time Ewon disappeared?"

"I don't know anything about crimes in Blackburn. Why would I?"

"Don't the departments communicate with each other?"

His eyes flashed. "When necessary, sure. They must not've thought there was any connection because I never heard a word about it."

"Well, now that you know, do you think they might've had something to do with it?"

"No. Now go! I don't have time for this nonsense."

Hostility rolled off him in waves, catching my breath in my throat. I rose and put up my hands. "Okay, no problem." As I started toward the door, I made one more attempt to make him see reason. "Look, I'm not trying to discredit you or your work. I'm trying to help a dying man receive the care he needs to stay alive. Surely you can understand that?"

"All I see is a nosy little puke trying to make me look bad." He pushed me over the threshold. "Get lost. If you step foot on my property again, I'll shoot you. You understand?"

Did I believe his threat might be credible? Yup. He'd shoot me and likely get away with it. I nodded and backed away, trembling. I felt his eyes watching me until I slid into the driver's seat and closed the door. Only then did he retreat into the house. I rested my forehead against the steering wheel, regaining my composure so I could safely drive home.

That went well.

CHAPTER TWELVE

Wednesday morning, I awoke to Bryan Adams blasting from my clock radio, doing everything he does for *me*, and bacon sizzling in the kitchen. Savannah was suspiciously absent, so I threw on my sweats and headed for the kitchen to see if the cooking fairy had finally appeared. Maybe I could get a lesson or two before they left again.

When I peeked around the corner, the baritone of fresh-brewed coffee joined the mezzo-soprano of bacon in a mouth-watering duet. A few steps into the living room brought Eric into view, wearing his suit minus the jacket, protected by the Santa-covered apron Brittany had given me as a joke last Christmas. He flipped the eggs in the frying pan, then handed me a cup of coffee, already fixed.

"Good morning, sunshine," he said, grinning.

"Morning. This is a nice surprise. What are you doing here?" I sipped my coffee, letting the mellow flavor swirl around my tongue, waking up my tastebuds. "And how did you get in?"

He waggled his blond eyebrows. "Wouldn't you like to know?"

"Actually, I would." I set my cup down and skirted begging-dog Savannah to embrace him from behind, burying my nose in his back while he slid the eggs onto a plate. The mix of laundry detergent, shower soap, and Eric warmed me inside like the springtime sun after a long, cold winter.

The toaster popped, and I snagged the two slices of browned bread and slathered them with butter. After a diagonal cut, I laid them beside the eggs. "My guess is you borrowed Brittany's key. I'll have to talk to her about that."

"And what will you say?" He collected two slices of bacon from the paper towel used to drain the grease and laid them on my plate. "There you go. Enjoy!"

"I need to take Savannah for a walk first."

"I already took her. Fed her, too. Relax and enjoy your breakfast."

My mother was right. Eric really was a keeper. I'd never felt so safe and so loved with anyone else. "Thank you. This looks great!" I bit into a slice of meat, and it was perfect. Not too crisp, not too soggy. "Mmmm. Delicious. Kudos to the cook."

Eric blushed and cracked two more eggs into the pan. He never did know how to handle a compliment. He must not've received many growing up because flattery seemed to embarrass him. I couldn't say for sure since he never talked about his family or childhood and wouldn't say why. I figured it was either because his growing-up years were very good, and he didn't want me to feel bad by comparison, or they were terrible, and he didn't want to relive them. Either way, he'd tell me when he was ready.

I sat at the table, enjoying my coffee, until he joined

me. "Anyway, I would remind Brittany it was inappropriate to provide the key to my apartment to any strange man who asked for it."

"Hey! I'm not just any strange man, you know." He buttered his toast and carried his plate to the table.

"You're the strangest man *I* know."

"How so?"

"You hang around with me voluntarily, don't you? That makes you pretty strange in my book. In anyone's book. Just ask your partner."

He grimaced. "I'd rather not, if you don't mind."

"I don't blame you." I dunked a piece of toast into an egg yolk. "What's the occasion this morning? You don't usually make me breakfast. Not that I'm complaining."

His grin sent a shiver into my nether regions. "I missed you. I worked late last night and didn't get to see you. I thought this would be a nice way to catch up before we both have to go back to work."

I reached over and squeezed his arm. "And you were right. Thank you." I pushed an egg around my plate. "Maybe you should keep that key. I'll get Brittany another one."

His brows shot up. "You mean it? I thought you wanted to take things slow."

The words had popped out on the spur of the moment, and now I had to think about them. Did I regret what I said? No, I didn't. I wanted Eric to have a key to my apartment. I trusted him more than I'd ever trusted anyone. "A girl's allowed to change her mind, isn't she? On second thought, give it back." I'd finally figured out what to give him for Valentine's Day.

He dropped the key into my hand, struggling to mask his disappointment.

I took his hand in both of mine, gazing into his eyes. "I love you."

"I love you, too. Now, eat your breakfast before it gets cold." Eric forked eggs into his mouth. "How did it go yesterday? You make any progress on the case?"

"I spoke with Jeremy Conway, and he was downright hostile about me looking into it. I knew he wouldn't like it, but I didn't expect him to be so nasty about it." I bit into my toast, concerned about how much to tell him.

Eric was protective, and I didn't want him to do anything stupid, like challenge Conway to pistols at twenty paces. I opted not to tell him about the threats. I had no reason to return to the cottage, so Conway had no reason to shoot me. With luck, and reasonable caution, I wouldn't regret that decision later.

"That doesn't surprise me. I didn't know him very well, but word around the station was he has a big ego. I can't imagine he appreciated you challenging his findings."

I snickered. "Believe me, he didn't. He got angry when he couldn't convince me Jaylon was guilty just because he said so."

"Sounds like him. What's on your agenda for today?"

"Charlie located Jaylon's parents for me, so I'll speak to them if possible. How's the missing persons hunt going?"

"Good. I finished the local files last night and located three potential matches altogether. One was found dead a couple of years ago, so that leaves two: Ewon Barnes and a guy named Lyle Pipkin, who disappeared at the same time Barnes did. Too much of a coincidence for my taste. I think the disappearances are related somehow."

I munched a strip of bacon, wiping my greasy fingers on my napkin. "You could be right. I'm not big on coincidences, either. It's worth looking into, anyway. Do you collect DNA when someone files a missing persons report?"

"Sometimes, when it's available. In Ewon's case, they didn't bother since they had Jaylon dead to rights. Or so they thought. Lyle was reported missing by his parents, but he was living with his girlfriend at the time, and she refused to cooperate with the investigation. The parents didn't have his comb or toothbrush to get DNA from, but they agreed to let us have their DNA for a possible familial match if we find someone to match them to. The Blackburn cops thought the girlfriend might've had something to do with Lyle's disappearance, but they couldn't find any evidence to back it up."

"Strange she wouldn't want to help find her missing boyfriend. But people do weird stuff all the time, so who knows? Maybe she just hated cops." After dabbing the grease off my lips with a fresh napkin, I said, "You know, Angus told me an interesting story yesterday that might be related, too."

"Oh?"

"It was something about a jewelry store robbery that happened around the same time." I repeated the story as close to word for word as I could remember. "And the jewelry was never found. You think the skeleton might be one of the thieves?"

"Could be, but that would mean Ewon or Lyle possibly robbed the jewelry store. Of course, we have to consider the prospect the skeleton isn't related to this, only someone who disappeared and was never reported missing."

"You mean like a homeless person?"

"Or someone with no family or friends to make a report. We might eliminate both Ewon and Lyle and be right back where we started."

The eggs soured in my stomach. "I hope not."

Eric wiped his mouth and placed his plate on the floor for Savannah to prewash. "I heard you met Crystal Moon yesterday. What did you think?"

I laughed. "She's interesting. I'll give her that. Cuckoo for Cocoa Puffs."

"That's one way to put it. She came by the station yesterday to tell us she had a vision about the skeleton you found committing a robbery. A golden aura surrounded it."

My eyebrows shot toward my hairline. "She said she had a message for me. 'Beware the golden bones.' That must've been what she meant. Sounds like she's warning me off my investigation and trying to insinuate herself into yours."

"It's a little strange. She came to us so we *would* investigate. And then she tries to discourage you. Why us and not you? It doesn't make any sense."

"No, it doesn't." I glanced at the clock. It was almost eight. "Shouldn't you be getting to work? You know how Havermayer feels about you being late."

He scrunched up his cheek freckles. "I know. She needs to lighten up a little."

"Yeah, like that'll ever happen."

Eric donned his suit jacket and straightened his solid blue tie.

"Thank you for breakfast. It was very sweet of you."

He gave me his Opie grin. "It was, wasn't it?"

"All right, don't get full of yourself." I punched him lightly on the shoulder.

"Ow!" He pulled me into his arms and kissed me, his lips soft at first, then demanding on mine. He broke off before I wanted to let go of the warmth cascading through my body. "How's that for sweet?"

I arranged my expression into my best "come hither" look and ran a hand over his chest. "Why don't you stick around for a few more minutes, and I'll show you?"

He groaned. "I wish I could, but, well, you know . . ."

"I do." I kissed him on the nose and walked him to the door. "Try to have a good day. And stay out of trouble."

"I'll do my best."

I closed the door behind him and rested my head against it, letting the heat dissipate into the painted wood. As much as I would love to forget everything and spend the day with Eric, we both had work to do. Jaylon Barnes remained in jail, and every day he spent there was one day closer to the end for him.

I wished there was a way for me to talk to the potential donor, but the registry kept that information confidential. The only hope was to get Jaylon's conviction overturned. And that was a slim hope at best. Still, I had to try.

After gathering the breakfast remains from the table, I collected the dishes off the floor. Savannah had done an excellent job of prewashing, as always. She was the perfect child. She never had to be reminded to do her chores. And she accepted her allowance in edibles and belly rubs rather than insisting on cash. Couldn't ask for more than that.

I dumped the plates in the sink to wash when I got home and retrieved the note Charlie had given me with Richard and Regina Barnes's addresses on it from the pocket of my jeans. They'd likely be at work at this hour of the day, but I had to do something. Jaylon had mentioned his father was an engineer and his mother a kindergarten teacher. But that was back when they adopted Ewon. They could be doing anything now. Or nothing.

Since Regina still lived in Riddleton, it made sense to start there first. If she wasn't home, I could go on to the bookstore from there since Richard was most likely at work on a weekday. Maybe I'd get lucky, and she'd be available for a conversation. Either way, I wouldn't waste half the morning driving to Sutton for nothing, doing it that way.

I dressed in khakis and a white linen blouse under a red sweater vest. She likely wouldn't talk to me if I showed up in my usual jeans and sweatshirt. Might as well try to make a more professional impression for a change. I enjoyed wearing real clothes every once in a while. I just didn't want to make a habit of it. People might get the wrong idea.

Savannah watched me from her perch on the couch, hope pulling her head up every time I wandered near her leash. I disliked leaving her behind, but I had to do some things without her. Someday, when our country evolved, I'd be able to take her with me everywhere. I suspected that wouldn't be anytime soon, though. For today, she'd have to make do with a hug goodbye, a chew stick to keep her occupied for a few minutes, and my assurance I'd be home soon.

When I pulled up to the old two-story farmhouse on farmland since subdivided into double-wide mobile-home plots, a gray late-model Nissan Sentra was parked under a carport alongside. Either Regina had more than one vehicle, or I'd lucked out, and she was home.

The newly repainted porch with pillars supporting the roof extended all the way across, with a swing on either side of the door and a table with four chairs on one end. I imagined the Barnes family once sitting around that table, enjoying lemonade on a hot summer afternoon. And now the parents were divorced, one son was presumed dead, and the other in prison for killing him. A wave of sadness washed into my gut. An entire family destroyed in a day.

I tapped on the door and waited for a response. When none came, I tried again, hoping Regina hadn't heard my first attempt. Otherwise, she wasn't home, and I'd made the trip for nothing. This time, however, footsteps sounded from deep in the house.

A tall, silver-haired woman wearing a casual floral-print housedress covered by a ruffled yellow apron opened the door. A confused expression flitted across her face. "May I help you?"

I smiled broadly to show I was friend, not foe. "Are you Regina Barnes?"

"Yes." She wiped her hands on the apron. "What can I do for you?"

Now came the tricky part. Convincing her to speak with me. "My name is Jen Dawson, and I was hoping you could spare a few minutes to talk to me about your son, Jaylon."

"Jen Dawson. Your name sounds familiar. Have we met?"

"No, ma'am. I'm—"

Her eyes widened. "You're the mystery writer. I remember now. I loved your book! When's the next one coming out?"

I camouflaged the grimace that automatically accompanied the question with a closed-lip smile. "It was supposed to be out in April, but my publisher pushed the release up to November, for some reason. Not soon enough for me." Nine more months before the questions would stop. Worse than having a baby, in my mind, though I doubted Lacey would agree.

She stepped away from the doorway. "Please come in. Would you like some tea? I just made it fresh."

I followed her through the tastefully furnished living room. "Yes, please. If it's not too much trouble."

"It's no trouble at all."

Regina held the swinging door to the kitchen open for me and retrieved a pitcher of sweet tea from the refrigerator. "Do you mind if we talk in here? I have cookies in the oven and don't want them to burn."

The sweet aroma seeping from the oven had my mouth watering, and I hoped she'd offer me a taste when they were done. Especially if they happened to have chocolate chips in them. "In here is fine with me, Mrs. Barnes."

She set a full glass on the table and gestured for me to sit. "Please call me Regina."

I pulled out a ladder-back chair and settled into it. "Thank you, Regina."

"Now, what did you want to know about Jaylon?" she asked, sitting opposite me.

"Anything you can tell me that might help me help him." I recounted the story as Marcus and Jaylon had told it. "I believe he's innocent and want to do what I can to get his conviction overturned so he can get the kidney he needs."

A tear slipped from the corner of her eye. She swiped it away. "I'm not sure what I can tell you that I haven't already told everyone else."

I gave her a minute to compose herself, then softly said, "Why don't you start from the beginning? You never know what might be the clue that solves the case, so to speak."

Regina stared into her drink, searching for the words to describe the situation that had obliterated her family. After a moment, she began with Ewon's adoption and continued through the same tale Jaylon had told me. When she finished, anger clouded her eyes. "My son is innocent. He would never harm anyone, let alone his own brother."

"What do *you* think happened to Ewon?"

Her lips tightened. "I don't know. I want to believe he's alive somewhere. Maybe he had an accident and got amnesia or something."

A mother's wishful thinking. Unfortunately, that didn't happen nearly as often in real life as on TV. "Perhaps. Can you think of any reason Ewon might just take off? Was anyone threatening him?"

"Not that I know of. Although, he did hang with a pretty rough crowd for a while. Maybe they didn't like that he'd turned his life around."

"Jaylon seemed to think his friends had something

132

planned and pressured Ewon into joining them. There was a jewelry store robbery in Blackburn around the time Ewon disappeared. Do you think he could've been involved, and maybe that got him killed? Or he ran to avoid being arrested?"

After a long moment of contemplation, she replied, "It's possible. He was acting oddly in the days before he disappeared. And when my husband refused to give him the money to open his repair shop, he became angry. He mostly blamed Jaylon, though it wasn't his fault. But then, he'd blamed Jaylon for everything he didn't like all his life. I taught school for twenty years and never saw so much resentment in a child as Ewon had for Jaylon."

"How did Jaylon feel about Ewon?"

A small smile creased her lips. "He idolized his big brother. Followed him everywhere until Ewon became physical with him. Then Jaylon just retreated into himself. Spent a lot of time in his room."

"Physical, how?"

"Nothing major. Pushing and shoving to get Jaylon away from him. That sort of thing."

"Is it possible Ewon disappeared to get away from Jaylon? To start a life without the constant reminder his father favored his brother over him?"

Anger roiled in Regina's eyes again, and she tightened her hands into fists. "No. If he did intentionally disappear, it was to ruin Jaylon's life. He wanted what Jaylon had but wasn't willing to do the work to get it." She pounded a fist on the table. "Ewon ruined our family long before he left. He tore us apart. Constantly forced my husband and me to choose between him and Jaylon."

I leaned back in my seat, unconsciously putting distance between myself and the anger I saw brimming deep inside the woman sitting across from me. What had just happened?

Is it possible Regina killed Ewon?

CHAPTER THIRTEEN

I learned little I didn't already know from my conversation with Regina Barnes but came away unsettled nonetheless. Although she clearly loved both her sons, she harbored a deep resentment for Ewon she might not realize existed and couldn't always hide. Could she have tried to eliminate the problem to save her family, not considering the possibility Jaylon might end up a victim, too? If so, why wouldn't she confess to save her remaining son? I couldn't imagine any mother allowing her child to go to prison for a crime she committed. Not even mine at her worst.

The short drive to Ravenous Readers allowed me little time to think about the situation, which was probably a good thing. The likelihood that Regina murdered her son or encouraged him to leave town without calling him back when Jaylon went on trial for his murder was slim.

Unless she did ask Ewon to come home, and he refused in order to punish his younger brother for slights both real and imagined. Either way, if she knew where he was, she would've told the police. Maybe. There might be circumstances in play I didn't know yet.

Eric called as I parked, and I filled him in on my conversation with Regina before exiting my Dodge. When I finished, I said, "Now, part of me wonders if she didn't have something to do with Ewon's disappearance."

"I can't imagine it," Eric replied. "What kind of mother would let her adult son go to prison for something she did?" He hesitated. "Although, if he was a minor at the time of the crime, maybe because he'd get a much shorter sentence and likely be released when he turned twenty-one. I've heard of cases like that. But Jaylon got a life sentence, and she said nothing. I just don't see it."

I had to agree. "Regina didn't strike me as someone who would allow that to happen. But, you have to admit, people do a lot of crazy things to save themselves."

"True, but not in this case, I don't think. How about I look into her and see if I can learn anything to support your theory?"

Warmth crept into my chest, and I smiled. He really was a terrific guy. "Sounds good. Let me know what you find." I hesitated for a second, then said, "I love you."

"Love you, too. I'll talk to you soon."

I climbed out of the car and went into the bookstore. Lacey looked over from the bookcase she was dusting and waved. "What're you smiling about?"

"Nothing." The heat moved from my chest to my cheeks. "Aren't I allowed to smile?"

Lacey grinned. "Of course you are. You just never do. Not for no reason, anyway."

After an eye roll and a headshake, I said, "Guess I must have a reason, then."

"Good for you." She returned to her dusting, then stopped again. "You'll never guess who was in here this morning."

136

I froze halfway to the coffee bar. "Who?"

"Simeon Kirby."

"What did he want?"

"Same as last time. He wants to buy the store. I told him no, same as you."

I started moving again and grabbed my mug from under the counter. "Good. Now he's heard it from both of us. Maybe he'll leave it alone."

"I wouldn't count on it."

Me neither. When my mug was full, I added cream and sugar and sipped. "I wish I knew why he was so determined to buy us out. What does he want with the place? It makes no sense."

"Not to us, maybe, but he clearly has a plan for it he's not sharing."

"I guess. Whatever he's doing, he's really getting on my nerves!"

Charlie came out of the stockroom wearing his Ravenous Readers uniform with a fistful of napkins and a box of coffee stirrers. "Who's getting on your nerves? Me?"

"No. Why would you think that?"

He shrugged. "I know I can be annoying. My mother used to tell me that all the time."

"We love you just the way you are. Don't worry about that. Simeon Kirby is the problem. I wish he'd go back where he came from and leave Riddleton alone."

"I know, Jen. Change isn't your favorite thing, but his resort might be good for us. What do you have to lose by giving him a chance?"

Is he kidding? "My sanity, for one thing."

He stuffed the napkins into the dispenser. "Way too late for that, I'm afraid."

I narrowed my eyes at him. "Just for that, I'm putting you to work."

"What do you think I've been doing?"

"Nothing constructive, I'm sure." I winked so he'd know I was only teasing.

"Uh-huh. What do you need me to do?"

"Before we get to that, what's with the uniform? You meet another girl?" I asked, eyeing him up and down. A few weeks ago, Charlie had worn his khaki pants and red polo shirt every day in anticipation of a visit from an online girlfriend. She never showed.

"What? No." He gave me a sheepish grin. "I got busy and forgot to do laundry last night. This was all I had clean."

That was a switch. Typically, work attire was the first thing to hit the laundry basket. I guess that depended on your definition of work attire. "Well, did you win your game, at least?"

"No, but I moved up two levels and gained some great weapons."

"Not too shabby. Let's see how you do with this one. The Blackburn City Jewelry store was robbed around the same time Ewon Barnes disappeared. Can you check into it and see if he might've been involved? Look for a guy named Lyle Pipkin, too. He vanished when Ewon did. It seems an odd coincidence, don't you think?"

"Could be. I'll see what I can find."

"Thanks." I refilled my cup and headed back to the office. Might as well try to get some writing done while I waited for Richard Barnes to get home from work.

I managed about a thousand words by the time my phone screen showed 5:15. Not too bad. I'd had worse days. Some better, too. Right now, though, it was time to find out what Mr. Barnes could tell me about his sons. If Lady Luck shined on me today, he'd have some information I could use to help Jaylon.

But if he knew something exculpatory about Jaylon, why wouldn't he have told the police? I didn't want to consider that he might have, and the detectives ignored it, but after my conversation with Jeremy Conway, I had to wonder.

Charlie tapped on the door before I could gather my things to leave. "You got a minute? I think I've found something you might be interested in."

"Sure. Whatcha got?"

He landed in the chair in front of my battleship-gray desk. "Well, I think I read every newspaper article about the robbery. There were three guys—two tall and thin, who seemed young, and one heavy-set man who stood silently by the door. The shop owner, a woman, couldn't describe them better than that because they all wore parkas and balaclavas. Unusual way to dress around here, for sure."

I bridged my hands under my chin, elbows on the desk. "How could she tell how old they were if she couldn't see them?"

"She said she could tell by the way they moved. They flitted around, smashing cases and gathering watches, bracelets, and rings. One of them ran in the back to clean out the safe and grab the special orders they were working on."

"Okay, what else?"

Charlie leaned forward with his forearms on his knees. "Promise you won't get mad."

Intriguing. "Why would I get mad?"

"Just promise."

"All right, I promise. Now, what did you do?"

He cleared his throat. "I knew you were busy, and I wanted to show you I could do more than research on the computer, so I called the Blackburn police and tried to ask the detectives some questions about the robbery."

Uh-oh. No wonder he thought I might be angry. "What did they say?"

"Nothing. The guy started asking me all kinds of questions about why I wanted to know. I tried to explain, but he wasn't buying it. Then he asked some things that made it sound like he thought I had something to do with the robbery, so I hung up."

My mouth made a circle. "Charlie, that was risky. What if he traced the call? They could be on their way to arrest you right now."

"It's all right. I fixed it." He shared a Cheshire cat grin. "I called Eric, and he said he'd take care of it."

"And did he?"

"Yup. He just called me. He explained everything to the detective and got some information from him. Their prime suspects for the two young guys are Ewon Barnes and Lyle Pipkin."

Holy cow! There really *was* a connection between the robbery and the disappearances. "Why do they think those guys were involved?"

"They'd committed robberies together before, although nothing like this one, and both disappeared without a trace. They still don't know who the third guy might be."

I sat up. "That *is* interesting. And very helpful. Thank you." I pointed a finger at him. "But don't you dare do anything that foolish again without talking to me first. Got it?"

His face turned the color of his polo shirt. "Yes, ma'am, but you haven't heard the best part yet."

"Oh? What's that?"

"The jewelry store robbery happened the same day Ewon Barnes disappeared."

Whoa! "You're right. That is the best part. Thank you, Charlie." I glanced at my phone to check the time. Five thirty. "I have to go. I want to catch Jaylon's father when he comes home from work. See you tomorrow?"

He stood and said, "I'll be here."

After digging the address out of my pocket, I punched it into my navigation app and walked onto the sales floor. Robot Woman immediately instructed me to continue straight on Main Street. Repeatedly.

Lacey laughed and shook her head as RW kept interrupting me when I told her where I was going.

"Hey, Jen!" she said when I reached for the doorknob.

I stopped and turned. "What?"

"Don't forget to go straight on Main Street."

The thumbs up I flashed her was an acceptable substitute for the single finger I wanted to use before opening the door. "See you in the morning."

RW chipped in her two cents. "Continue straight on Main Street."

"Oh, shut up!" I stuffed the phone in my pocket and headed out to my car.

The road to Sutton was congested with rush-hour traffic as people swapped their workplaces for the comforts of home. I'd never had a regular job, so the closest I ever came to a commute was trekking from my college dorm room to class and back again. Not exactly a grueling process unless I was running late, which seemed my norm. Mainly when I started writing *Double Trouble* in my junior year. I didn't make it anywhere on time after that.

When I reached the Sutton city limits, RW started barking orders at me. Apparently, Richard Barnes lived in town, but not quite the town I was familiar with. I navigated a maze of narrow streets I hadn't known existed until I finally pulled up to a beige, ranch-style house with a shingled roof. The painted brown front door peeled in places as if the wood was shedding its skin. The dreaded Sutton Brown Snake.

A stocky, balding man wearing gray slacks and a white dress shirt with a loosened gray tie answered my knock. He carried a sandwich in one hand and swallowed a bite before saying, "Can I help you?"

"Hi, are you Richard Barnes?"

"Yeah, but everybody calls me Ricky." His gravelly voice sounded like a lounge singer who'd consumed a lifetime's worth of whiskey and cigarettes between sets at the Holiday Inn.

I explained who I was and what I wanted, and he stared blankly, squeezing dents into the soft white bread in his hand. Guess he wasn't going to let me in. I couldn't blame him for not wanting to talk about what was probably one of the worst periods of his life. But I needed to know more about his sons.

"Mr. Barnes, it's very important that I speak with you. I promise I'll only take a few minutes of your time. I want to help Jaylon if I can."

He stepped aside and waved me in. "Call me Ricky."

"Yes, sir."

The darkened living room enveloped me like I'd

wandered into a black-and-white movie where a bad guy lurked in every shadowed corner. Only one small lamp burned on an end table beside the brown leather couch, and I squinted to take in my surroundings. The walls were bare, and no personal mementos adorned any surface. Not a single photograph of his family, no doodads or knickknacks anywhere. Definitely a bachelor pad.

He gestured toward the couch. "Have a seat. I'll be right back." After a few steps, he asked, "You want a beer?"

"No, thank you."

"Suit yourself." He disappeared into what I assumed was the kitchen, stuffing the rest of his sandwich into his mouth. I hoped he chewed before swallowing. My Heimlich maneuver was a little rusty.

I sat on the end of the couch by the lamp and squirmed to make the stiff material fit my bottom. The end table had a small drawer in it. It could be he kept his photos in there. I was dying to put a face to Ewon's name. I hadn't been able to investigate any of Regina's belongings since she herded me into the kitchen and kept me there. The cookies were worth it, however. She should've been a baker instead of a kindergarten teacher.

A glance over my shoulder revealed no sign of Ricky, so I pulled the drawer open for a quick peek. It was empty. However, as I leaned over to open the drawer, my heel contacted something under the couch. After another glance at the kitchen door, I squatted and peered beneath, spotting a small container. Reaching for it, my hand came out with an old cigar box, like the kind my grandfather used to have. I flipped up the lid. Inside, I found a diamond ring and a walkie-talkie watch, the

143

same as the one in the picture of the skeleton. Guess his kids played with them, too.

The kitchen door squeaked open, and I threw the box back under the couch. When I looked up, Ricky was studying me.

His frown sent a cascade of adrenaline rushing through my veins, and he clenched his fists by his sides. He vibrated with controlled anger. My hands shook as an icicle dripped down my spine.

What have I gotten myself into?

CHAPTER FOURTEEN

I swallowed hard and took a deep breath to compose myself before facing Ricky's wrath.

"What're you doing?" he asked, his scowl deepening.

Think fast, Jen.

I pulled my most innocent facial expression out of my hat. "Nothing. I needed to tie my shoe. I should double-knot them like I did as a kid, but I always forget."

He stared at me and silently sipped his beer.

Sweat soaked my underarms. "What? You don't want me to trip and fall, do you? I might get hurt. Then you'd have to take me to the hospital. It would be a big ol' mess. You don't want that, do you?"

His inscrutable face softened, and he dropped into the armchair across from me. "What did you want to know about my boys?"

I couldn't tell if he believed my excuse based on his sphinxlike expression, but I continued. "If you don't mind, can you start at the beginning? What were they like growing up?"

After a long pull on his beer, he said, "Ewon was a troubled kid from the start. He was three when we adopted him, and we had no idea what he'd been through or inherited from his biological parents. He was getting better, though. Then we got pregnant with Jaylon."

Funny how Regina never mentioned Ewon was a problem child *before* Jaylon came along. "What happened then?"

"He was okay during the pregnancy, but once Jaylon was born, he started creating problems. He couldn't stand sharing our attention with anyone, let alone a new baby. Ewon resented Jaylon from the start, and the boys fought constantly, sometimes violently. It was like living in a combat zone at times."

Same story I'd heard from Regina and Jaylon so far. They'd either done a great job of synching up, or it was the truth. "That must've been tough on all of you."

He loosened his tie a little more and crossed his legs. "It was, but the real trouble began when Ewon started high school. He made some friends who led him in the wrong direction. Drinking, drugs, shoplifting. You name it; they tried it. The more time we spent dealing with Ewon's issues, the more Jaylon retreated into himself. He spent more time alone in his room than anywhere else but school. There were days when we didn't see him except for meals. Some days, not even then."

"Jaylon mentioned that Ewon went to jail. Do you mind if I ask what for?"

"The idiot stole our neighbor's Mustang and took it for a joyride. No big deal, except he was high and ran it into a power pole. The car was totaled, but at least nobody was hurt."

"That explains the jail time. How did he adjust to prison life?"

"Surprisingly well, and it seemed to help him. He took an auto repair course and came out determined to change. But his friends wouldn't let go. They kept trying to drag him back in like they were a gang or something."

"Were they?"

Ricky downed the rest of his beer and set the empty can on the end table. "No, not officially. They didn't have a name or anything, but they all got matching tattoos and operated with the same kind of mentality. Once you're in, there's no getting out. And I really do believe Ewon wanted out."

I asked Ricky if he thought Jaylon had murdered his brother. He said no, but if Jaylon believed Ewon was about to do something that would hurt the family, he might've tried to stop him, and something went wrong.

"Do you think that's what happened?"

He moistened his lips and thought for a minute before saying, "I don't know. Maybe."

He'd given me a new possibility to consider. The idea that Jaylon killed Ewon to stop him from doing whatever his friends wanted him to do, like robbing a jewelry store. But the jewelry store robbery occurred the day Ewon disappeared, and the Blackburn police believed he was involved, discrediting the theory. If the cops were correct, Ewon had to be alive that evening. A headache started to form behind my eyes, and I massaged my temples.

"Ricky, there was a jewelry store robbery in Blackburn the day Ewon argued with Jaylon. Do you think Ewon could've been involved?"

"No way. Why would he ask me for money if he was going to rob a jewelry store?"

147

The answer to that question seemed obvious. Ewon didn't want to participate in the robbery but needed funding for his repair shop. When his father turned him down, he felt like he had no choice. But I kept the thought to myself, suspecting Ricky understood that too. "True, but the Blackburn police believe he was involved. Do you have any idea why?"

"Nope. First I've heard of it." He looked away and rubbed the nape of his neck. "The only thing I can think of is they're lumping him in with his friends. His buddy Lyle always joked about someday robbing a bank or jewelry store or something. Maybe the cops knew that and figured he finally did."

I sat up on the edge of the couch, and the leather creaked. "Lyle? As in Lyle Pipkin?"

"Yes, why? Do you know him?"

I shook my head.

"He and Ewon have been friends since they started high school together. Lyle was the one always getting Ewon into trouble."

"Did you know that Lyle disappeared at the same time Ewon did?"

His turn to sit up. "No. I just figured he stopped coming around because Ewon was gone. He didn't come over much after Ewon moved to Blackburn anyway."

"You're probably right. Did Ewon and Lyle have any other friends?"

"There was a big kid named Josh who used to hang around them sometimes. That's all I remember about him, though. I only saw him once or twice, and he didn't say much."

Could Josh be the silent third man at the robbery?

148

I glanced at my feet, behind which the cigar box lay hidden. Should I risk asking him about what I'd seen? Perhaps he was only upset about me invading his privacy rather than what I might've discovered. Either way, I had to know. The worst he could do was throw me out. "Ricky, I wasn't entirely truthful earlier. I did peek into the cigar box you have stashed under the couch. I apologize. Sometimes, my curiosity gets the better of me."

"It's all right. I don't have anything to hide. It's just some personal stuff." His eyes took on a faraway look. "The walkie-talkie was Jaylon's. He and Ewon both had one when they were kids. Regina let me keep it in the divorce. And the ring's hers too. She insisted I take it back. Guess she didn't want anything to remind her of me."

She gave back her engagement ring? *First time for everything.* "I'm sorry. And please forgive me for invading your privacy like that."

He shrugged with an expression I couldn't interpret in his eyes, leaving me feeling disconcerted. I inhaled to steady myself. My next question might stir up a reaction, and I needed to be prepared. "Where were you the day Ewon disappeared?"

"At work. All day. The police checked."

I couldn't think of any more questions, although a dozen of them would probably come to me on the drive home. I did remember to ask Ricky about the divorce, something I'd forgotten during my conversation with Regina, and he said the stress of losing both sons was too much for their marriage to handle. That made sense. The grief had to be overwhelming; each would remind the other of what they'd been through just by being there. I couldn't imagine any relationship withstanding that.

As I left Ricky's place, I didn't feel like I'd learned much except for Ewon and Lyle being friends. Still, it was something I didn't know before. When I opened my car door, I noticed a black Ford Bronco parked across the street a couple of houses down that hadn't been there before. I gave myself a mental shrug while climbing into the driver's seat. Could be anybody.

It concerned me how quickly Ricky could transform. Between his temper and Regina's, growing up in the Barnes household had to be challenging for the boys. Ewon seemed to be the only son who inherited their volatility, even though he wasn't related by blood. How did Jaylon manage to escape? Maybe he didn't, and I gave him no reason to show his other side during our chat at the county jail.

Accepting there was no way I could remember the way through the maze I'd traveled to get here, I instructed Robot Woman to take me home. When I reached the road back to Riddleton, I glanced in the rearview mirror, and the Bronco hummed along a few cars behind me. While it seemed strange, it might be nothing. Plenty of other places to go before leaving town. No doubt they were picking up takeout for dinner or something. Nevertheless, I'd still keep an eye on them to be safe.

When the Ford continued to follow me even as I crossed the dam, I called Eric and told him. "I know there's most likely nothing to worry about, but I wanted you to know, just in case."

"I'm glad you called. Let me know if they're still there when you get past all the housing developments.

150

Don't do anything crazy, like driving around in circles. You'll tip them off if they *are* following you. Then they might do something dangerous, like run you off the road. Let me handle it. If there's even anything to handle."

"Okay." I hung up.

The Bronco stayed with me, and a ball of dread formed in my belly. I called Eric back, and he said he'd take care of it. I didn't ask how, but I saw him parked in front of the community center across the street from my apartment when I pulled into my parking space. The Ford kept going, and Eric waved at me and dropped in behind him. Hopefully, Eric wouldn't end up following him all the way to Blackburn.

I trotted up the stairs to receive my enthusiastic greeting from Savannah. Poor baby had been alone all day. I leashed her up for a walk, and when we hit the bottom of the stairs, she flooded the oak tree. Good thing it'd been around for a hundred years. Otherwise, she might've drowned it.

Back home again, I fed and watered her. She scarfed her dinner without chewing and washed it down with half a bowl of water. I stretched out on the couch and phoned Eric for an update. His cell rang in the hallway outside my door. Savannah ran to warn off the intruder while I went to let him in. Not the first time my dog and I were at odds with each other about a visitor. When I opened the door, he grinned and waggled his phone.

I shot him a pinched-lip glare. "Wouldn't it have been easier to knock?"

He pulled me in for a hug. "I just got here. Besides, it was more fun this way."

Savannah pushed between us, and Eric squatted to pet her. I went to the kitchen and retrieved a bottle of wine for me and a cold beer for him. When I returned to the living room, he was sitting on the couch, and the dog was stretched across his lap. *Where's Norman Rockwell when you need him?* The scene belonged on the cover of *The Saturday Evening Post.*

I pushed her rear end over to make room for me. Never dreamed I'd one day have to fight my dog for attention from my boyfriend. And she'd win. Could be worse, though. They could hate each other.

Eric urged her off his lap, and she ran to get her favorite tug toy. I sipped my wine, watching the children play, and a bubble of warmth surrounded my heart. I couldn't remember ever being this happy in a relationship before. Eric brought out my best and loved me despite having seen me at my worst more times than I could count. Sure, we had our difficult moments, but we always worked through them together. If the idea of marriage to anyone didn't send me into a panic, I'd consider marrying him.

A touch of anxiety squeezed into my bubble. How long before I messed things up? Sabotaging relationships was one of the things I did best. Sometimes, it seemed I didn't want to be happy. Perhaps, somewhere deep down inside, I didn't believe I deserved to be happy, although why I would feel that way, I couldn't fathom. Parental indoctrination, perhaps. My stepfather was never my biggest fan. Something to discuss with my shrink, Dr. Margolis, at our next monthly session.

Savannah finally tired of playing tug with Eric and stretched out on the carpet with her toy and chin between her forelegs. The love in her eyes as she watched us told me she was a happy little girl, though. The only thing that mattered.

Eric tipped his beer into his mouth for several swallows before saying, "Boy, that dog sure can wear me out."

"At least she gets tired now. Remember when she was a puppy?"

His eyes widened as he took another pull on the bottle. "No kidding. I don't miss those razor-sharp teeth, either. My arms always looked like I'd been bagging cats."

I snorted wine up my nose and coughed. "Hey, no jokes when I'm drinking."

"Who's joking? My uniform had short sleeves. Everyone stared at me. Olinski used to ask if I'd been out catting around every time he saw me. He knew it was the puppy, but he liked teasing me, anyway. Of course, he was still a detective then, so he could get away with it."

"You seem to have survived." I snuggled in next to him. "What was the deal with that Bronco? Was it following me?"

"Yeah. I talked to him when he cruised by the bookstore and stopped in front of Antonio's. It was Jeremy Conway."

"The detective who worked on Jaylon's case? What did he want with me?"

Eric squeezed me closer and rested his chin on my head. "He's upset about you looking into his case. Thinks you're trying to undermine him and spoil his reputation."

"What reputation? I'd never heard of him until you gave me the case file."

"You know how these detectives are. They're all legends in their own minds."

I poked him in the belly. "You're a detective."

"And I'll be a legend one day, too." He downed the last of his beer. "Anyway, he's keeping an eye on you. I told him to lay off. You weren't doing anything wrong. I'm not sure he'll listen, though. He's pretty steamed."

"Do I need to be worried?"

He stood. "I'd be cautious. I can't stop him from driving around, but if he approaches you or bothers you in any way, let me know. I can bust him for stalking."

"I'd rather it didn't come to that."

"Me too," he said over the clink of beer bottles in the refrigerator.

"Would you bring me the wine?" I emptied my glass. "And what do you want to do for dinner? Or did you eat already?"

"I wasn't sure when you'd be home, so I grabbed a burger after work. Sorry."

I refilled my glass. "No problem. You'll be hungry again in a little while." Eric could eat six times a day and never gain an ounce of fat. A fact I found more than irritating. I gained weight just looking at food. Of course, I rarely only looked. Especially if chocolate was involved.

He eased back in beside me. "Probably. I discovered something this afternoon you might find interesting."

"What's that?"

"Regina Barnes spent some time in an institution after Ewon disappeared. I had to do some digging since her medical records are confidential, but she has bipolar disorder that went undiagnosed until she was admitted."

Good grief! That must've been horrible for all of

them. Particularly for Regina, having to deal with runaway emotions and never knowing why. But, between an unmedicated bipolar mother and a father with a hair-trigger temper, those poor boys never stood a chance. No wonder things turned out the way they did. Now, I only had to figure out which one killed Ewon and let Jaylon take the blame for it. And I thought *I* had family problems growing up.

CHAPTER FIFTEEN

I was buried deep in my writing Thursday morning, on a roll for the first time in weeks, when my phone rang. I grumbled words I couldn't repeat in public under my breath, finished the sentence I was working on, then snatched the phone off the desk. It was Lacey. She never called me. It had to be something bad.

I swiped the screen, hoping she wasn't having a bad run of morning sickness or worse. "Hey, Lacey, what's going on? Are you all right?"

"I'm fine, Jen, but you'd better get down here."

My morning coffee sloshed in my otherwise empty belly. "Okay, why?"

"Somebody broke into the bookstore last night."

Oh, crap! "I'm on my way." I disconnected and ran into the bedroom to gather yesterday's clothes off the floor. No time to hunt for something clean.

Savannah followed, prancing with excitement, when she saw me getting dressed. "Not this time, kiddo. There'll be too much going on." She sat anxiously, bushy tail sweeping the carpet. Of course, she didn't understand a word I said, but I didn't have time to explain it to her.

After dressing, I gave her a chew stick, which she promptly dropped on the floor at my feet, making her feelings about being left behind crystal clear. Nothing passive-aggressive about *this* German shepherd, without a doubt. But I couldn't give in to her disappointed face, however much I might've wanted to. Instead, I kissed the top of her head, scratched under her chin, and said, "I'll be back soon. I promise," then bolted out the door.

On my way down the steps, I debated whether to walk or drive. Driving won. Walking would take too long, and since the police station was right next door to the bookstore and the cops would likely walk, my car wouldn't be in the way. Two minutes later, I parked around the corner from Ravenous Readers and ran in.

The police had the front door propped open so the crime scene techs could go in and out without touching anything, and Eric stood by the coffee bar, directing traffic. Lacey and Charlie were huddled together by the checkout counter. I tiptoed around the books covering the floor and approached them. I threw my arms around both their shoulders and asked what happened.

Lacey turned to me, and tears leaked from the corners of her eyes. "Somebody trashed the place for some reason last night. As far as I can tell, nothing's missing, and it doesn't look like the cash register was even touched. It was just straight-up vandalism."

Charlie piped up. "I left my backup laptop by the coffee bar, and it's still here, too. They did a lousy job of it if they were trying to rob us."

I glanced down at the display cases in front of me, and they'd been emptied. The floor behind was littered with booklights and journaling gift sets, and it appeared the bookmarks had been tossed up in the air to land wherever they would. "Have either of you been in the back yet?"

They both nodded. "More of the same," Charlie said. "For some reason, they left the coffee bar alone, though. I thought that was strange."

"Me too. They could have hurt us badly by destroying our equipment. It would've cost hundreds, if not thousands, of dollars to replace it all." I watched the techs work for a minute, hoping my stomach would settle. My heart rate reached allegro, which probably didn't help my belly much. I turned back to Lacey and Charlie. "Well, it could've been a whole lot worse. Nothing's missing, and nobody was hurt. It'll take us a while to clean up the mess, but we'll get it done."

"You bet we will, Boss. We'll get started as soon as the cops are done with the place," Charlie said, brushing dust off his long-sleeve white button-down shirt tucked into khaki pants and covered with a blue-and-white argyle sweater vest. He'd topped off his ensemble with shiny brown loafers on his feet, heavy black eyeglass frames with no lenses, and a pencil tucked behind his right ear.

"Sounds like a plan. What're you supposed to be today?"

He pulled out his pencil and waved it at me. "I'm a nerd. Can't you tell?"

"From the 1950s?"

Lacey snickered. "Oh, so you decided to be yourself."

"The heck with both of you," he said, but he didn't mean it, and we all knew it.

"I'm going to talk to Eric and see what he knows," I said.

I navigated the central aisle to the coffee bar, where

Eric instructed one of the newer techs. I waited until he finished, then stepped up to him. "Good morning. What do we have here?" I asked, sweeping one arm around the store.

He hugged me. "Hey, babe, I'm so sorry. Are you okay?"

"I am now," I replied, squeezing him tighter. "Why would somebody do this to us?"

"I don't know. I guess when we figure out who, we'll know why. Is there anyone you can think of who has a grudge against you I don't know about?"

I pulled away. "You think that's what happened?"

"Well, according to Lacey and Charlie, nothing was taken, so unless a couple of high school kids got drunk and broke in, it's the only logical explanation. And since the lock was picked, I'm ruling out teenage vandals. It's unlikely they'd have the tools or the know-how to get in that way."

"What about the Internet? They have tutorials on bomb making; why not lock picking?"

"Maybe, but I still think it's unlikely. Vandals wouldn't have bothered picking the lock. A rock through the door glass would get them in a lot easier."

"In that case, the only person I can think of is Simeon Kirby. He's been adamant about buying the store and gets very angry when we turn him down."

Eric shook his head. "I'll talk to him, but I can't imagine a successful businessman doing this. Surely, he's been turned down before."

"From the way he reacted, I'd say he's used to getting his way. He's pretty determined to not take 'no' for an answer. Besides, he wouldn't have done it himself. He has more than enough money to hire someone. And he did sort of threaten me with repercussions if I didn't give in."

"What kind of repercussions?"

"He didn't say. It was one of those mob boss kind of threats. All intimidation, no details."

"Okay, I'll check him out. Who else?"

I thought for a minute, then remembered the black Bronco. "What about Detective Conway? He's mad at me, too."

"I'd have an even harder time believing he's involved. He's a retired cop, for Pete's sake. Why would he risk losing his pension just because he doesn't like that you're looking into one of his cases? I'm sorry. I don't see it."

I searched my memory for another possibility but came up blank. I had my share of people who didn't like me for various reasons, but I couldn't think of one who would trash my store to make a point. "All right, that's everyone I can come up with. Who do you think might've done this?"

He took my hand. "I don't know. Maybe the techs will turn up something helpful. Either way, I'm going to find out who it is. Don't worry about that."

I kissed him softly. "I know you will."

Eric entwined his fingers with mine as I observed, perhaps sensing the despair building in my mind, threatening to overwhelm me. I squeezed his hand, gratefully drawing on his strength. And grateful that I didn't have to wear the "everything will be okay" mask for Eric that I'd donned for Lacey and Charlie. While deep down, I knew the store would be fine, eventually, I also knew it was okay to grieve for what we'd lost, not in property or money, but in our sense of security. Our safe space had been violated for no

160

discernible reason. It would take all of us a while to get over that.

The worker bees buzzed around, dusting smudges and collecting everything that might be considered evidence, but I had little hope they'd find anything useful. Ravenous Readers had hundreds of customers who'd touched or dropped something in the store. We cleaned house daily but couldn't possibly keep up with every little smear.

I realized that I hadn't seen the stockroom for myself or checked my office yet, so I reluctantly released Eric's hand and headed back there. The stockroom had books all over the floor. Mainly used ones we hadn't had room for on the shelves yet, but some new ones as well. The intruder had ignored the cleaning supplies, which could've destroyed all our backstock if poured out. Strange how the two areas that would've hurt us the most, had they been tampered with, were untouched.

What if the goal was to inconvenience us rather than cause financial hardship? To send a message we haven't figured out yet. Who would do that? Simeon Kirby was the first person to spring into my mind. Perhaps the message was: this is how life will be from now on, so you might as well sell while you can. And it made the omissions make sense, too. He wouldn't want to be forced to spend money replacing inventory and equipment we'd already paid for when he took over.

I still had to consider Detective Conway, however. He was angry enough to follow me; why not vandalize my business too? That seemed a bit of a stretch, though. Eric was right about that. There was a vast chasm between tailing me to see what I was doing and committing a crime to scare me off doing it. I doubted he'd make the leap. Still, I'd keep him in the back of my mind. *Anything's possible.*

So, who else did that leave? Ricky Barnes, maybe? If he killed Ewon, they certainly wouldn't want me to continue investigating. But would he have the wherewithal to pick a lock? It's not as easy as it seems on TV. Of course, he could've hired someone with the necessary skills. Perhaps Eric had it backward. If we could figure out the "why," it might lead us to the "who." Either way would be fine with me.

I gave up on speculating and went to the office. No surprise, the desktop had been cleared onto the floor, file cabinets emptied, their contents joining the mess. However, the computer remained undisturbed. Another costly piece of equipment ignored. It didn't even seem that anyone had tried to access it. Clearly, the culprit had no interest in proprietary information either. Not that we had anything worth breaking in for.

Before I could return to speculating about who vandalized the store and why, loud voices drew me back onto the sales floor. It sounded like an argument between a man and a woman at the front door, which a police officer currently guarded. Lacey and Charlie blocked my view, so I couldn't see who was doing the arguing.

As I moved in that direction, the woman yelled, "I must see her right now!" in a heavy Russian accent. The voice belonged to Natasha Fatale, AKA Madame Crystal Moon.

"What's going on here?" I asked when I arrived.

The cop replied, "This lady insists on speaking with you. I told her she couldn't come in, but she won't listen."

162

"Thank you, Officer." I pushed past him onto the sidewalk. "I'll take care of it."

I led the flustered psychic around the corner so we'd be out of the way of the techs still running back and forth between the store and the police station. Her blond hair tufted in places as if she'd run her fingers through it while the hairspray was still wet, and today, she wore a green muumuu covered with bananas. She either had Hawaiian ancestry or she had a real thing for baggy dresses covered with fruit. Her blue eyes bulged behind her brown-rimmed glasses, so I'd better find out what she wanted to talk to me about before we played marbles on the sidewalk.

"What can I do for you, Ms. Moon?"

She pulled her shoulders back and stuck her chin out. "I am Madame Crystal. You will address me as such."

Well, la-di-da. I sealed my lips to suppress a smirk. "Yes, ma'am. What can I do for you, Madame Crystal?"

"You did not listen. Now you are in danger."

"In danger from what?"

"I do not know. The spirits, they did not say. Only say you must stay away from golden bones. This is not joke!"

I had no idea how to respond. I'd never encountered anyone so comical and yet so serious at the same time. "If you tell me what the golden bones are, I promise I'll be happy to stay away from them."

"This is message for you. I do not know about bones. Only see vision."

"Okay. What exactly did you see?"

She closed her eyes and tilted her head back so far

163

I thought she'd fall over. "I see bones from man, covered in gold, and hear voice say your name."

I waited for her to return to this plane of existence, then asked, "Were the bones a skeleton? Like someone dead for a long time?"

"Yes. Skeleton. Covered in gold. Golden bones."

Could she mean the skeleton in the tunnel? I shook my head. This was ridiculous. Unless she was trying to frighten me away from investigating the skeleton for some reason. Did she have something to do with his death? Or know who did? "Madame Crystal, why are you trying to frighten me? Who are you working with?"

Her eyes widened and bulged even more. "I work with spirits. I deliver message. Nothing else." She stepped back. "I go now. You listen, you live. You do not, you die. That is all I will say." Madame Crystal pivoted on her heel and marched away.

I watched her go, my jaw hanging as if the hinges had broken.

Eric came around the corner and took my arm. "What was that all about?"

I closed my mouth and looked at him. "I wish I knew."

164

CHAPTER SIXTEEN

The clock had almost struck two by the time the last member of the Riddleton Police Department left the store. Except for Eric, of course. He'd finished taking our statements an hour ago but hung around for moral support. Part of me loved him for that, but the other part wished he'd get out there and find who did this. The war between my sides was never-ending.

I surveyed the damage. Merchandise covered the floor, all of which would need a damage inspection before we could even think about trying to sell it again. The doorways and knobs were covered with black streaks we'd have to scrub off before reopening, and the gargantuan task that lay ahead of us overwhelmed me.

Given the amount of black powder all over the store, nobody could accuse the fingerprint techs of doing shoddy work. Unfortunately, it was unlikely anything good would come of it. The best we could hope for would be finding identical foreign prints in multiple areas. The odds of that happening equaled those of being struck by lightning.

Eric put his arm around me but said nothing. Perhaps he sensed I needed time to process. Or maybe he'd just run out of things to say. I suspected it might be a little of both. Add fatigue, despair, and a little bit of salt, and the resulting stew would include my entire emotional spectrum.

I eased out of Eric's grip and turned to face my coworkers. "It looks like we've got our work cut out for us this afternoon. How about we head to the diner for a quick lunch break before cleaning up? My treat. That'll give us a little time to regroup."

Charlie and Lacey nodded, dejection plain on their faces. I'd expected pushback from Lacey, but she offered none. Her demoralized expression settled in my belly like a stone, crushing my appetite and making me question my decision. We needed a break, though, whether we ate anything or not.

We silently filed out the door, and Lacey locked it behind us, although why she bothered was beyond me. The damage was already done. What more could they do to us? Habit, most likely. Locking the proverbial barn door after the horse had already bolted.

Eric and I held hands as we trudged down the sidewalk past the police station and the town hall, heads down to avoid the glances of passersby. I couldn't face the compassion in their eyes. I had enough pity for myself to tread water against. Adding theirs might put me under for the third time.

Angus had finished his Valentine's Day window scenes, and thankfully, with no pink involved other than the skin color of some of the people depicted. On one side, he'd painted a man on one knee, proposing to his girl while a restaurant full of diners looked on, smiling. He really did have marriage on the brain for some reason these days. The other window depicted the same

166

man and woman kissing as the onlookers stood and applauded. I guided Eric into the diner so he wouldn't get any crazy ideas.

Our favorite booth was available, as always, and the four of us sat down. We'd barely glanced at our menus when Penelope approached the table. "I'm so sorry, y'all, about what happened to your store. If there's anything I can do to help, please ask me."

"Thank you, Penelope. That's very kind of you," Lacey replied. "All that's left to do is clean up."

"I get off at three. How about I come over and help? I can put stuff away if y'all tell me where it goes."

I studied her over the top of my menu. "That's very nice of you, but we can't ask you to do that. It's a real mess over there."

"You didn't. I volunteered, and I'll be there at three fifteen whether you like it or not." She grinned. "I'm assuming today's a shake day?"

"Extra, extra large. I might even need two. I'll let you know. And thank you for offering to help us out."

Penelope took the rest of the drink orders and scurried to the counter to fill them.

"That was nice of her," Eric said. "An extra pair of hands will help a lot. Especially since I have to go back to work."

Charlie reached over and tapped Eric's arm. "Yeah, you need to find whoever did this and put him away forever."

"I don't know about forever, but I'll definitely put him, or *her*, away. Don't worry."

Her? I'd never considered the culprit might be a woman. Whom did Eric have in mind? Surely, not Madame Crystal. I couldn't see her doing that kind of damage. She might break a nail. "Eric, who are you considering? I can't think of a single woman who would ransack the bookstore. What reason could she have?"

"I can't either. I'm only trying to be politically correct. We don't know it's a man just because we can only think of men with motives. Therefore, it could also be a woman."

Not quite what we had in mind when we asked for equality. "Thanks. That's very judicious of you. Now, make sure she doesn't get a sentence twice as long as a man would've in the same circumstances, and you'll have hit the mark."

"Thankfully, sentencing is out of my hands."

Before I could reply, Angus came up to us. "Hey, guys, how are you? Any news on who trashed your place?"

I shook my head. "Not yet. Eric's working on it."

"Unfortunately, I haven't heard anything either. The gossip train's stuck at the station."

It figured. The one time I needed to know what my neighbors were up to, Angus had nothing. "That's okay. I'm sure you'll let us know if you do."

"Of course. And I'm coming over after we clear out to help clean up."

"What about the diner?"

"Marcus can handle it. I want to help. It's the least I can do after you helped me when I was shorthanded."

"True. And that turned out so well, too." I chuckled. I'd tried to play server one day when Angus didn't have one and spilled drinks everywhere. He finally told me to sit down and gave me a master class on how it's done—handling it all himself.

168

"It's the thought that counts. I'm helping, and that's that."

I didn't bother to try to talk him out of it. He was a good friend, and we needed a few of those right now. Maybe more than a few.

Penelope returned to take our food orders, and we sat silently after she'd gone. None of us wanted to discuss what happened to the store, and chit-chat seemed sacrilegious. How could we talk about the weather or the great movie we'd seen when everything was a total mess? Our business, anyway.

We'd all put so much of ourselves into that bookstore, only to be reminded how quickly it could be destroyed. I sipped my chocolate milkshake, the blended ice cream, syrup, and milk calming my stomach. Or maybe only freezing it so I couldn't feel the pain anymore. Whatever. As long as it worked.

When our food arrived, I broke the silence. "I suppose we need to make a game plan for undoing the damage in the store."

Charlie lifted an eyebrow. "Seems pretty simple to me. Just put everything back where it belongs, right?"

I added ketchup to my fries and burger. "When you put it like that, I guess it is. I only thought we might do it in an organized fashion."

"What did you have in mind?" Lacey asked, slathering ranch dressing on her chef's salad.

Other than pretending to be in control of the uncontrollable? "I thought we should divide the store into sections, each taking one. Then we can allocate the volunteers where they're most needed, with one of us directing traffic in each section, so to speak."

Lacey forked up some lettuce and ham. "We only

169

have two volunteers, so putting them to work somewhere shouldn't be difficult."

"Actually, it's a bit more complicated than that," Ingrid said, approaching our table.

Eric stopped with a fry halfway to his mouth. "What do you mean?"

"Well, I'm volunteering to help, for one thing." She smiled. "And there's a crowd waiting outside the store for another."

Charlie swallowed the chicken strip he'd stuffed into his maw. "They probably don't realize we're closed today."

Lacey and I exchanged glances, then I said, "Maybe, but when have we ever had a crowd come in all at once?"

"I'm going to check it out." My elbow in Eric's ribcage encouraged him to move so I could get out of the booth.

He cleared the way, and I followed Ingrid outside. A dozen people in obvious work attire—jeans and T-shirts, and some carrying gloves—stood in front of Ravenous Readers. I recognized Nancy from the Snip & Clip and Amanda from the vet's office.

I stared at Ingrid with my mouth hanging open.

She shrugged. "The mayor emailed everyone on the town's mailing list, asking for volunteers. Didn't she tell you?"

"Uh . . . no. If she had, I wouldn't have been sitting in the diner feeling sorry for myself."

"Well, with all these people here to help, you need to keep your pecker up."

I gave her a side-eye. "I don't have a pecker."

Ingrid laughed. "It's just an expression, luv. You would say, 'Keep your chin up.' Is that better for you?"

"Much. At least it's anatomically correct." I laid a hand on her shoulder. "While I get them started, would you mind asking Eric to box up my lunch? And tell Angus I'll need snacks and drinks for all these people."

"Sure thing."

Ingrid returned to the diner, and I started down the street toward the group. Riddleton's mayor, Veronica Winslow, stood on the top step when I passed the town hall, smiling and waving, her auburn hair drifting in the slight breeze.

"Thanks for the help," I said. "You should've told me what you were doing, though."

Her green eyes twinkled. "Where's the fun in that?"

I rolled my eyes and kept walking.

When I reached the chattering crowd, I raised my hands to attract their attention. "Hi, everyone! Thank you all so much for coming. I'm sorry we kept you waiting."

I unlocked the door. They trooped in and huddled by the windows, surveying the mess.

"Boy, they really got you good, didn't they?" Nancy said.

All I could do was nod. I didn't want her to see me cry.

After assigning each person their own section, I said loud enough for everyone to hear, "The books need to be shelved alphabetically by author. If you're unsure if one goes in your section, set it aside, and we'll take care of it later. Also, if you find any that are damaged, please set them aside, too. Thank you again for your help."

Eric, Lacey, Charlie, and Ingrid came in a few minutes later.

Eric came over, kissed me, and handed over the remains of my lunch. "I wanted to check and see if you needed anything before I go back to work."

A good place to hide? "I'm fine, thanks. I can't believe all these people showed up to help us."

"There are a few benefits to small-town life. Aren't you glad you decided to stay?"

I smiled up at him. "As a matter of fact, I am. For more reasons than that one."

"I'll call you if we learn anything. Otherwise, see you for dinner?"

"You bet. With all this help, we should be done by then."

He waved to Charlie and Lacey and ducked out the door. They beckoned me over.

I joined them. "Okay, so how do you want to handle this?"

Lacey replied, "I thought Charlie and I should tackle the stockroom. Are you okay with supervising out here?"

"Sure. That's a good idea. I know how particular you are about arranging your backstock," I teased.

"I like being able to find things when I need them. You got a problem with that?" The sparkle in her eyes gave away that she was joshing me.

"Maybe, what's it to ya?" I asked, giving her the same in return.

She smiled and winked, then dragged Charlie to the back by the arm. Poor guy always got caught in the middle. I suspected, however, he wouldn't have it any other way.

The bells over the door jingled, and I turned to find Penelope squeezing a large cardboard box through the doorway, followed by Angus carrying a cooler. He pointed Penelope toward a table in the back out of the way. I hurried to get there first to push two tables together for them.

"Thank you both for this," I said as they dropped their loads. "Angus, I'll come by and settle up when I get through here."

He pulled a few ice-cold water bottles out and lined them across one table. "Nonsense. This is on me. You have enough to worry about right now."

"No, sir. I appreciate the offer, but it's too much. I'll pay for it."

"Wait a minute," he said, touching my arm. "You said I could help, right?"

"Well, yes, but—"

"This is me helping. Now shoo! Get back to work, or no snacks for you!"

Penelope snickered, giving up on pretending she wasn't listening as she unloaded chips and cookies from her box.

I turned her way, grinning. "Go ahead, keep laughing. I'll get Nancy to dye your hair blue instead of red next time. Or better yet, both!"

"Maybe she can add a white stripe down the middle. Might as well be ready for the Fourth of July," she said with a smile.

"Absolutely! Then you can be the grand marshal in the parade."

"Ooh! I'll get to ride in the back of the principal's convertible."

"Hey, Jen?" a voice from behind me called.

When I turned my head, Nancy stood beside me with a concerned expression.

"What's up?"

She proffered a slip of paper she held in her hand.

"This fell out of one of the writing books when I put it on the shelf. You should take a look at it."

I accepted and unfolded it. Printed in large block letters were the words:

LEAVE IT ALONE OR NEXT TIME THERE WON'T BE ANYTHING LEFT TO CLEAN UP!

CHAPTER SEVENTEEN

The paper vibrated in my shaking hand. It took a moment for me to realize it wasn't fear coursing through me but fury. *How dare they?* Haven't people figured out by now that threats like this only made me more determined? I would never let a bully intimidate me. Not in high school, and definitely not now.

I wanted to crumple the note and throw it away, but it was evidence. Although I doubted the person who wrote it had left anything helpful behind. This guy was no amateur. There wouldn't be a single trace of anything we could use to identify him. *Or her.*

Holding the slip pinched between two fingers, I retrieved my phone from my back pocket and called Eric. A minute later, he burst through the door with Havermayer close behind. Surprisingly, she hadn't participated in this morning's evidence collection, letting Eric take charge. Perhaps she'd finally let him take on a little responsibility. More likely, though, she thought the situation was beneath her.

Eric rushed up to me and asked if I was okay.

"I'm fine. Mad as hell, but fine."

He laughed and said, "That's my girl. Let me see it."

I handed him the note.

Havermayer squeezed in beside him. "Where did you find this?"

"Actually, Nancy found it in a book."

She dropped her dark eyebrows and flashed shamrock eyes at Nancy. "Which one?"

Nancy hesitated, then ran a hand through her multi-colored spiked hair and stepped forward, holding up a copy of *On Writing Well*. "It fell out of this one."

Havermayer snickered. "I guess someone's trying to tell you something, Jen."

I curled my lip at her. "Ha-ha. From what I saw, they're telling me to stop doing whatever it is they think I'm doing."

"And what is it they think you're doing? Other than writing badly."

Rising to the challenge of keeping my tone civil, I replied, "My guess is they want me to stop looking into the Jaylon Barnes case."

She slipped the note into a plastic evidence bag and handed it to Eric. "Why are you bothering with that, anyway? I was there. He's clearly guilty."

"Not according to him. And how would you know, anyway? You never worked the case."

Ignoring my last comment, she replied, "They all say they're innocent."

"And some of them are. How many wrongfully convicted people were let out of prison when DNA evidence came into play?"

She opened her mouth to respond, then closed it again without saying anything.

Behind her, Eric crossed his eyes. "All right, Jen. We'll

add this to the pile of things we're checking for fingerprints and DNA. I'm not holding out much hope, in any case. We haven't found anything so far. I think whoever did this was wearing gloves."

"No surprise there. Anyone who can pick a lock would know better than to risk leaving behind any evidence."

He nodded, tight-lipped.

"See you later?" I asked him, mainly to irritate Havermayer.

She grimaced, turned on her heel, then marched toward the door.

Eric winked at me and followed her out.

With all the extra hands onboard, it only took a few hours to put everything right again. When the last volunteer had gone and Angus had packed up the remains of his snack station, I stood at the front of the store and took in the amazing transformation. A few hours ago, the bookstore had been a total shipwreck. Now, we were ready to open tomorrow morning as if nothing had ever happened.

My body sagged, overwhelmed with gratitude for everyone who'd spent their afternoon cleaning up just because we needed the help. This was what small towns were all about. And this was what Simeon Kirby wanted to destroy with his development. Not necessarily what he intended, but it would be what happened if he got his way.

Why didn't anyone else see it the way I did? Blinded by dollar signs, I suspected. There was more to life than money, as the saying went. Friendship, fellowship, and a sense of community mattered too. I had to make people see that before it was too late.

Lacey and Charlie came out of the stockroom, chattering and laughing.

"All done?" I asked when they reached hearing distance.

"Yup," Charlie replied. "Just like new."

Lacey looked around the sales floor. "This place looks great!"

I smiled. "Yeah, they did a wonderful job. We're back in business."

"That we are." Lacey glanced at the clock, which read six fifteen. "Guess I'd better get home and feed the troops. My husband can't cook worth a lick, and the kids won't eat hard-boiled eggs."

"Have fun!"

When I entered my front door, Eric was in the kitchen laying out dinner, and Savannah was suspiciously not bouncing off the walls at my arrival. I suspected I'd find her at his feet, on crumb patrol. I dropped my things on the counter, walked around to his side, and kissed him.

"You know I could get used to this," I said, snatching a bite of Angus's meatloaf off the plate. "You're creating a monster."

He scooped out mashed potatoes and grinned. "I'm counting on it. And you're already a monster."

I ignored the comment, too tired to argue. Besides, he was probably right. I reached into the fridge for the wine, then looked over my shoulder. "Do you want a beer?"

He held up a bottle. "No thanks, I've got one."

I poured a full glass and sipped. "What can I do to help?"

"Nothing. I'm just about through." He handed me a plate full of meatloaf, mashed potatoes and gravy, and green beans. "The joys of takeout."

Accepting it gratefully, I relaxed on the couch and put my feet on the coffee table. Fatigue rippled through me. Hopefully, I could stay awake long enough to eat. "I think Angus would go out of business without us."

Eric came in carrying his plate and silverware for both of us. "Probably. Although, one of us will need to learn how to cook one of these days."

"Hmmm. I nominate you."

"We'll discuss it later." He dove into his meatloaf like he hadn't eaten in a week. After swallowing a large bite, he said, "How's the store looking?"

I washed down some potatoes with a gulp of wine. "Amazing! You'd never know anything had happened to look at it now."

"We dusted that note for prints and swabbed for DNA. Nothing came up. I'm sorry, Jen."

I drowned my disappointment with another sip of wine. "Not your fault. That's what we were expecting anyway."

"True, but I was hoping, for your sake."

"I know. It's too bad, though. If we could figure out who ransacked the store, we might know who killed Ewon Barnes. Or at least who's involved."

He massaged the back of my neck. "Don't worry. We'll get it figured out. Somehow. We always do, right?"

I wished I could share his confidence. At the moment, though, fatigue blocked any smidgen of enthusiasm. "Right."

We ate in silence until our plates were ready for the prewash cycle. Savannah happily obliged while I curled up next to Eric and laid my head on his shoulder. I let my eyelids close, drifting on the border of sleep.

A knock on the door, and Savannah's quick response catapulted my heart into my throat. I sat up in time to see Brittany poke her head in. "Hey, guys. You decent?"

I gave her our standard response. "No, but we're dressed. Come on in."

My German shepherd's deep-throated growls switched to demolition-style tail wags the instant Brittany stepped through the doorway, followed by Olinski. Brittany held up a bottle of wine, and Olinski carried a six-pack of beer.

Accepting the bottle, I said, "Yay! Greeks bearing gifts."

"I'm English and Irish, not Greek," she replied, tucking stray blond hair behind her ear.

"Close enough." I swapped the wine for the chilled bottle in the fridge and poured some into a glass for her.

She hugged me and took a sip. "How are you? I'm sorry I couldn't come over and help this afternoon."

"I know today's your long day, so I wasn't expecting you. We had plenty of help, though. Veronica sent an email to the whole town. I have more friends than I realized."

"Of course you do. You've done a lot for Riddleton, whether you know it or not."

Brittany and I got comfy on the couch while the boys chatted over their cold ones in the kitchen. Savannah squeezed between us, laying her head in Brittany's lap. Needless to say, I got the other end. Now I knew where *I* stood as far as my dog was concerned.

Stroking the dog between the eyes, Brittany said, "Any ideas on who might've vandalized the store?"

"A few, but none of them make too much sense. It almost has to be someone I haven't had any dealings with yet. Which leaves us nowhere as far as motive is concerned."

"Why do you say that?"

"One of the people I've spoken with is the detective who originally worked the Jaylon Barnes case. He wasn't too happy about me looking into it, but I can't imagine him reacting like this. The other is the developer, Simeon Kirby. He hates that we won't sell Ravenous Readers to him. Maybe he's trying to scare us out. But a note we found in a book said, 'Leave it alone,' which wouldn't make any sense coming from Kirby. I think that lets him out. Which leaves me with someone I haven't met in connection with the case yet."

Brittany studied me over the rims of her tiger-striped glasses. "Not necessarily. It could still be someone you've met but haven't considered. Who else do you know might be involved in the Barnes case?"

A swig of wine burned its way down my esophagus. "I've spoken with Jaylon himself, his parents, and one of the detectives who worked the case."

"What about the other detectives?"

"Only one. Larry Smith, who retired to Florida last year. That's a long drive for a twenty-minute conversation."

"You could call him. Don't they have phone service down there anymore?"

"No, they banned it. It's how the 'woke' communicate with each other, you know." I gave her a conspiratorial wink.

She sprayed me with the bit of wine left in her mouth when she started laughing.

"Hey, watch it!" I said, jumping out of the line of fire.

After wiping her face with a clean napkin left from dinner, she handed me one. "It's your own fault. You know better than to say something like that when I have my mouth full."

"You two all right in there?" Olinski asked over the half-wall divider.

"We're fine," Brittany replied. "I just gave Jen a wine shower, that's all."

"Did she wash behind her ears? She sometimes forgets," Eric chimed in.

"Not that I noticed. You want me to do it for her?"

I stared at them all, open-mouthed. "Uh, hello? I'm right here, people! If you're going to talk bad about me, at least have the decency to wait until I leave the room."

Eric showed his Opie grin. "But this is way more fun."

I stuck my tongue out at him.

He tipped his beer up to his mouth.

Olinski joined us in the living room, flopping into the recliner by the sliding glass doors. "How's the investigation going, Jen?"

"I feel like I'm treading water at the moment."

"What have you done so far?"

I sat at the end of the couch, facing him. "I've spoken with the parents and Jeremy Conway. I haven't accomplished much else, I'm afraid."

Olinski sighed and sipped his beer. "I got a call from a buddy of mine in Sutton today. Barnes isn't doing well. They don't think he has much time left."

Tension forced my shoulders up, and the wine soured in my stomach. Jaylon needed me more now than ever, and I floundered, unsure what to do next.

Olinski's voice pulled me out of myself. "What did you learn from the parents?"

"Not a whole lot. The mother repeated the same story she told five years ago. She struck me as angry, to be honest. Eric checked her out, and she's bipolar and didn't know it, which might explain the erratic behavior."

"Is she angry enough to kill her son and let her other son take the blame for it?"

I thought about it for a minute without coming up with a reasonable answer. "I don't know. Maybe. If she lashed out at Ewon during a manic episode. That still wouldn't explain why she allowed Jaylon to go to prison, though."

"What about the father?" Olinski retrieved another beer.

"He has a temper. I have an easier time believing he did it than the mother. Also, he has a walkie-talkie watch identical to the one found with the skeleton. When I asked him about it, he said it belonged to Jaylon when he was a kid. I'm not sure I believe him, though."

"What are you thinking?"

"According to the Blackburn police, three people were involved in a jewelry store robbery the day Ewon disappeared. They believe two of the three were Ewon Barnes and Lyle Pipkin. According to the father, Ewon and Lyle were close friends, and Lyle was a troublemaker. The third man is still unidentified."

Olinski leaned toward me with his elbows on his knees. "You think Ricky Barnes was the third man?"

183

"Could be, but that would be pure speculation. And the boys had another friend, Josh, who hung around with them sometimes. It could be him, too. And we don't even know that the skeleton I found is one of the thieves. And if he is, which one? Ewon or Lyle?"

"Ewon is the one who's missing."

"So is Lyle. And both their girlfriends haven't been seen since then, either. Plus, the jewelry never turned up anywhere."

Eric stood to get a refill for himself. "What if they all took off together to live happily ever after on the proceeds from the robbery?"

"That would make the skeleton the third man instead of one of the other two," Brittany said, draining her glass.

I shook my head. "The store owner described the third guy as short and stocky. According to the ME, the skeleton was tall. About the same height as Ewon and Lyle."

Brittany carried the wine bottle in to top us both off. "Maybe the skeleton had nothing to do with the robbery."

"But what about the watch?" I pulled up the skeleton picture on my phone and showed it to her. "See? He's wearing a walkie-talkie watch. I googled it, and it's a child's toy. Why would an adult male be wearing one?"

She shrugged. "Maybe he has . . . had a kid."

"Or maybe the range is perfect for thieves who want to communicate with each other during a robbery in a way that can't be tracked."

Olinski put his hands up to stop us. "Look, this is all speculation, and as interesting as it is, it's not getting us any closer to determining who killed Ewon Barnes or where he is if he's not dead. What's your next move, Jen?"

"I don't know. What would you do if it was your case?"

He looked at Eric. "What would you do next, Detective?"

Eric studied his fingernails as he wrangled the possibilities. When he finally looked up, he said, "I would start talking to friends and family, other than the parents. Maybe begin with the neighbors to find out if they saw or heard anything the day Ewon disappeared."

Olinski nodded and turned to me. "What do you think?"

"I'm not sure that's important right now, given what we've learned. If Ewon participated in the robbery the evening of the argument, isn't that proof Jaylon didn't kill him? I think tying Ewon to the robbery should be our priority. That would exonerate Jaylon in time to get his transplant. We can worry about what really happened to Ewon later."

"That's true, but if someone saw Ewon leave the house that day under his own steam, that would mean he was still alive, and, at the very least, the murder didn't go down the way everyone thought it did."

My brow pinched. "But if someone saw him leave, wouldn't they have told the police back then?"

"Maybe, maybe not. The truth doesn't always come out at the time, but five years later, whatever reasons the witness had for not revealing what they knew might not apply anymore. Sometimes stories change."

"I guess I know what I'm doing tomorrow. Visiting

Mrs. Barnes's neighborhood. I refuse to sing, though. She doesn't look anything like Mr. Rogers. Even in a sweater."

The chief of police tilted his beer bottle toward me as if in a toast. "Sounds like a plan."

CHAPTER EIGHTEEN

The flashing cursor on the screen mocked me, as always. Daniel Davenport stood in the tunnel, staring at the dead body of his classmate. I knew what he was thinking. What I wanted to say about it. I only needed to type the words on the page. Should be easy, right? Nope. Not for me. The towering writer's block stood firmly in my path, unmoving and unmovable.

All right. If I couldn't move or climb over it, I'd just go around it then. Time for the old standby: type whatever popped into my head and see what happened.

Daniel squatted beside his lifeless friend. Sightless, cloudy blue eyes looked past him as if he weren't even there. Eyes that had twinkled with laughter less than two hours ago when they'd joked about these silly escapades. And yet here they both were, participating in the ridiculous endeavor. Only one was dead, and the other had discovered him. Not so ridiculous after all.

Huh. Maybe there was something to this technique. I reread what I'd written. Not too bad for a rough first draft. Most of it would probably bite the dust in revisions, but at least it was a starting point. I couldn't rewrite what hadn't been written, could I?

But wasn't that what I tried to do with the Jaylon Barnes case? The story the detectives had created was more like something dashed off on the back of an envelope on the spur of the moment than a finished product ready for publication. They had an idea and ran with it, blinders on and truth be damned. I had to get to the real story. The one nobody had considered before. And it had little to do with the argument between Jaylon and his brother. Of that much, I was confident. Something else had to be going on.

My gut told me the real story had to do with the robbery. The one that ended in the tunnel under St. Mary's Catholic Church. If the skeleton was one of the thieves, why would they be there in the first place? I could think of only one reason. The stolen jewelry had to be hidden somewhere beneath the church. Nothing else made sense. I needed to get down there.

Leaving Daniel stewing over what to do with his dead friend, I donned jeans and a sweatshirt. When I retrieved my Nikes from under the coffee table, Savannah sat up to watch, tail thumping against the couch. Shoes meant out, and out meant petting and treats from all her friends. In her world, anyway. In mine, it usually meant work.

Since I didn't know how long I'd be gone, only that she couldn't come with me, I leashed her up for a trip around the block. She balked when I tried to lead her back up the steps but eventually gave in when she realized resistance was futile. After checking that she had fresh food and water, I tossed her a chew stick and headed out the door without looking back. Her disappointed expression always melted my heart, but she couldn't come this time. Although I imagined if anyone could sniff out the stolen loot, it would be my German shepherd.

I climbed into my silver Dart and turned over the engine. St. Mary's was close enough to walk, but I planned to follow through on my commitment to talk to Regina's neighbors when I'd finished searching the tunnel for clues. Maybe I'd find something to connect Ewon and Lyle to the robbery. Then everything else would fall into place.

The one-block drive down Oak Street took less than a minute. Then, I turned left on Riddleton Road and into the parking lot. St. Mary's Catholic Church was an imposing two-story structure that had once been a tiny shack at the original stagecoach rest stop.

A half-dozen marble steps stood between me and the hand-carved, wooden double doors. Above the doors, stained-glass eyes searched mine for my darkest secrets. I lowered my head and started up the steps. Sharing my secrets would mean acknowledging their existence. Not on my schedule today.

I pushed on the right-side door, which opened easily under my hand. The entrance was never locked. Father Hank believed a sanctuary should always be available to those who needed it. As far as I knew, nobody had ever abused the privilege.

Once inside, I was greeted by a life-sized crucifix, illuminated by a lamp, hanging on the tabernacle wall between two identical stained-glass windows depicting the Madonna and child. A table to one side held brass-and-glass candle holders with several lit candles, and a row of glistening, solid oak pews dominated either side of an aisle leading to the altar.

To my left, a staircase, guarded by a lustrous balustrade, led to the church offices on the second floor. I started up, carefully keeping to the protective runner in the middle. At the top of the stairs, I glanced at Father Hank Mathews's office to my left, but the closed door blocked my view. He either wasn't here or didn't want to be disturbed.

I heard a voice from the church secretary's office on the right and moved toward the doorway. A woman with dark hair long enough to be swirled into a bun sat with her back to me, talking on the phone. I waited until she ended the call before stepping into the room. We hadn't met yet, and I didn't want to startle her.

She replaced the receiver and turned to me with a wide smile. "Hi there. Can I help you?"

"I hope so." I extended a hand. "I'm Jen Dawson, and I was hoping to speak with Father Hank for a minute. Is he in by any chance?"

"Myra Sanderson." She accepted my handshake with a moist, limp grasp and shook her head. "I'm sorry, but he's with a homebound parishioner this morning. He'll be back this afternoon, though. Is there something I can help you with?"

I'd forgotten about the priest's standing Friday morning appointment with his hospitalized friend. I explained that I wanted to explore the tunnels but not why. Most people found the idea of investigating a murder disconcerting.

"You're the writer, aren't you? Father Hank has mentioned you."

"In a good way, I hope."

190

Her smile grew even wider, though I hadn't thought that possible. "Oh, of course. He's very impressed with you."

"I'm glad to hear that. He's quite impressive himself." I shuffled my feet, uncomfortable with what I was about to say. "Myra, I'm using the tunnels for the backdrop of the book I'm working on, and I'd like to take another peek if you don't mind." I quickly glanced up, looking for the lightning bolt. Nothing happened. Perhaps tiny fibs didn't count when there was an element of truth to them. I *was* using them as a backdrop, but that wasn't why I wanted to visit them today.

The grin diminished. "That sounds interesting. Unfortunately, while I'm sure Father Hank wouldn't mind, I don't feel comfortable allowing you to go down there without his permission. I'm new here and don't want to make a mistake. You understand, don't you?"

Drat! "Of course. I wouldn't want to get you in any trouble. When do you think he might be back this afternoon?"

"He should be here by one, I'd imagine. If not, he usually calls, so I can ask him then. Either way, you can call, and I'll let you know what he says. Do you have the number?"

"I do, thank you. I'll check back this afternoon. It was nice meeting you."

After she agreed with my sentiment, I headed back out the way I came in. When I reached the car, I sat with my hands on the wheel, looking out the windshield. I had three hours to kill. Might as well talk to some neighbors. I started the engine, backed out of my parking space, and returned to Main Street for the ride to Regina Barnes's house.

A twenty-minute drive later, the old two-story farmhouse appeared on my right, but despite Regina's car being in her carport, I didn't turn into the driveway. My goal was to pry information out of her neighbors, not her. However, I found knowing she'd be available should I need to speak with her comforting.

About a hundred yards down the road, a dirt drive led to what seemed like a brand-new double-wide mobile home set up in the middle of the lot. I turned in but suspected it would be a waste of time. These people had either traded their old place for a new one or just moved in. I hoped it was the former, but if I had to bet, it would be on the latter.

When I parked, a pack of dogs of all sizes sounded off inside the house. I placed my hand on the door handle but hesitated. Their security system deterred me quite effectively. I didn't imagine they had too many unwanted visitors. Should I risk getting out? Perhaps not. I wasn't particularly interested in being lunch.

My decision was made for me when a man in jeans and a blue-and-white checkered button-down came onto the three-foot-square landing that passed for a porch. I opened the car door, and he came down the steps toward me.

"Can I help you?" he asked.

"Quite an alarm system you've got there. How many dogs do you have?"

He glanced back toward the house. "Six, and nobody sneaks up on us. What can I do for you?"

I told him who I was, why I was there, and that I had a few questions.

He shook his head. "I'm sorry, but we only moved in a few weeks ago. I have no idea what went on back then. Have you tried the lady next door? From what I've been told, she's been here for a long time."

Well, that was one bet I didn't want to win. "I've already spoken to her. Thanks, anyway. Enjoy your new home."

I climbed into my car, and he watched me until I hit the end of the driveway before going back inside. I turned left onto the road and looked for the next driveway past Regina's. When I turned into it, a dilapidated double-wide as old as Riddleton itself waited for me at the end. No way these folks just moved in. They had to know something.

A different pack of dogs started up in the house, but this group didn't sound nearly as scary as the last. Well, not as big, anyway. Still, I waited in the car, hoping someone would come out. After a minute, somebody did. A woman this time, not a day under eighty, wearing an apron-covered sundress. She waved, and I got out of the car, watching to ensure she didn't reach for the handle on the storm door. The only thing separating me from that pack of dogs.

When I reached the bottom of the steps, I went through the spiel again: who I was, why I was there, and that I had questions.

She put a hand below her silver hairline to shield her eyes against the sun. "I'll help if I can. What do you want to know?"

"Ma'am, do you remember the day your neighbor's son disappeared and her other son was arrested? It would be about five years ago now."

"Call me Ida, honey. And I remember that day like it was yesterday. I was here all day baking cookies for the church bake sale that Sunday. I come outside to cool off a bit, and the older boy, the big one, came storming out of the house like he would bust from being so mad. He got in his car and drove away, spittin' dirt everywhere."

Ewon. "Do you remember seeing the younger son? Jaylon?"

"Sure do. He came out a little while later, totin' a rolled-up rug on his shoulder like he didn't have a care in the world."

On his shoulder? "Did the rug seem unusually heavy to you?"

She flashed a gap-toothed smile, showing teeth loaded down with eighty years of yellow. "Well, if it was, he's a lot stronger than he looks, I tell you. He just flipped that thing into the back of his truck and drove off."

Good-sized Oriental rugs were heavy enough by themselves. Throw a dead body into the mix, and there's no way Jaylon could've tossed it around by himself. "Ida, did you tell any of this to the police?"

"Ain't none of 'em ever asked me."

I stood there in stunned silence. Nobody ever asked her?

Great job, Detective Conway.

She peered at me from under penciled-on eyebrows. "Honey, are you all right?"

"Yes, ma'am. I mean, Ida. Are you sure the police never interviewed you? Is it possible they did, and you don't remember?"

She shook her head. "Honey, I can't tell you what I had for breakfast yestiddy mornin', but I remember everything from that day five years ago. That's what happens when you get old, you know."

She might be old, but she still did better than me. I

couldn't remember five years ago *or* what I had for breakfast yesterday. "Would you be willing to tell the police what you remember now?"

"Sure. All they gotta do is ask."

"Thank you, Ida. You've been very helpful."

She smiled again. "You come back any time, you hear? You're a nice young lady."

"Thank you. I will."

She waved as I got into my car and drove away. Ida had been very helpful indeed. Still, I suspected the recollections of an old woman might not be enough to convince the prosecutor to reopen Jaylon's case. But it might be enough to get the Palmetto Innocence Project to look into it. I headed back to town, more determined than ever to investigate the tunnels. There had to be something that tied Ewon and Lyle to the robbery.

CHAPTER NINETEEN

I called Eric on my way back to town since I still had an hour and a half before I could expect a response from Father Hank. Unfortunately, he was too busy for an early lunch, so I suppressed my disappointment and went to the bookstore instead. That should've been my first idea, but I had a ways to go before anyone would consider me a responsible business owner. One of the drawbacks of having a partner like Lacey around to take care of things. I never had to grow up.

When I entered the store, a sight I'd never dreamed I'd see greeted me. Charlie, in work boots, jeans, a red-and-black checkered flannel shirt, and a hat with ear flaps, carrying an ax.

My eye roll sent a clear message across the room. "What are you supposed to be this time?"

He held his arms out to the side. "A lumberjack, obviously. Don't I look tough?"

"Absolutely. I'm sure you'll sell a lot of paper towels."

He pulled his ear flaps down. "Nuh-uh. That guy doesn't wear this cool hat."

"Maybe he's so tough his ears don't get cold."

"Or . . ." He flashed an impish grin. "He's so weak he can only work in the summer."

I had to laugh. I couldn't help myself. "Could be. Either way, be careful with that ax, please."

Charlie held it up. "No worries." He grabbed the blade and bent it. "It's a prop, see? I bought it from a theater supply store online."

I gave him a thumbs up. "Sounds good. Have you had any luck with your research assignment?"

"A little. Still nothing on Ewon's girlfriend, Eliza Naismith. It's like aliens beamed her up to the mothership and whisked her away to their home planet five years ago. No phone, no Internet, no credit cards, nothing. But I did find Lyle Pipkin's girlfriend."

I filled my mug with coffee. "Go on."

"Her name is Abigail Adams and—"

My cup rocked as I almost knocked it over while stirring sugar into it. "Is she three hundred years old?"

"No, she's . . ." His eyes widened. "Oh, I knew that name sounded familiar! Maybe she's a descendant of the First Lady."

"Or her parents had a sense of humor. Anyway, tell me about her. This one, not John Adams's wife."

Charlie grabbed his notepad. "She's twenty-seven, unemployed, and lives alone in an apartment in Blackburn. She also has a juvie record, like Ewon and Lyle, but it's sealed, so I don't know what for." He flipped to the next page. "I tried calling her phone, but it went straight to voice mail, so I hunted down a neighbor, Edna Franklin, and called her. She said Abby's been out of town since last weekend and has no idea where she went or how long she'll be gone."

"Well, you've been a busy beaver. Great work!" I

sipped my well-doctored brew. "It's a shame we can't get into her juvenile record. I'd love to know if it had something to do with breaking and entering."

"You mean like picking locks, breaking and entering?"

"Yup. Somebody broke into our store, and I'm determined to find out who."

He tipped his cap back on his head, the flaps now covering his cheeks like a gladiator's. "But why would she break into the store? And why leave the note?"

"Maybe she's afraid I'll figure out she killed her boyfriend. Or, maybe she's after the jewelry that's supposedly hidden around here someplace, and she's afraid I'll find it first."

"Do you have any idea where it is?"

"None whatsoever. Although, if the skeleton is Ewon or Lyle, I suspect it's in those tunnels somewhere."

A tall, thin woman with medium-length brown hair entered the store and wandered to the Romance section. Charlie left his forest to help her.

"Where's Lacey?" I asked.

"In the back. I told her I'd cover the front for her."

I nodded and headed for the office to call the Innocence Project. If I could convince them to take Jaylon on, I might be able to focus on the robbery. Partly because I believed it was related to Jaylon's case but mostly because somebody didn't want me to.

When I reached my office, Lacey sat behind the desk sorting through papers. Why was she messing with stuff on my desk?

Because the desk didn't belong to me anymore. Neither did the office. As fifty-fifty partners, everything in the store belonged to both of us. My stomach churned at the thought, but I'd have to get used to it. My baby

198

wasn't my baby anymore. It was ours. Co-parenting stunk.

I perched on the chair on the wrong side of the desk.

Lacey looked up and smiled. "Look, you can see the blotter! I didn't even know there was one."

Forcing a smile, I said, "It looks great."

"Thanks. I figured cleaning up the last of what the vandals did might help us put the whole thing behind us."

My chest tightened. "Good thinking. Did you happen to run across a phone number written on the back of an envelope? I want to call the Innocence Project again."

She flipped through a pile on the corner, then held up an envelope. "Is this it?"

I recognized the Blackburn number and took it from her. "Yup, thanks."

"I thought you said they couldn't help. Did you find something new?"

"I did. A witness who saw Ewon leaving the house alive *after* the argument."

She clapped her hands. "Wow, that's terrific! They'll have to help now."

"Maybe." I punched the number into my phone and pressed the green button. "If it's significant enough for them."

Voice mail picked up on the second ring, announcing the office was closed. I hung up on the office-hours part of the automated speech. "They must close early on Friday for the weekend. I'll have to try again Monday."

"That's okay. It'll give you a couple of days to focus on your writing."

Interesting idea. Glad *somebody* remembered I had a book due in a few months. "True. I have one more

199

thing to do first. I want to look around the tunnels and see if there are any clues as to who killed that skeleton. Who knows? I might find the jewelry missing from the robbery."

She laughed. "Dibs on a Rolex. I want to give Ben something nice for Valentine's Day. It's our last one before the new baby comes."

"I guess I'll get one too. I've been so busy I still haven't gotten Eric anything."

"You'd better get to hunting then. We're both in trouble if you don't find it."

"The question is, who's in trouble if I do?"

Silence echoed off the church walls as I ascended the stairs to Myra's office. Guess she'd finally gotten a break from the incessantly ringing phone. When I tapped on the doorframe, Myra quickly shoved the paperback she'd been reading into a desk drawer and closed it. She was too quick for me to read the title, but the bare-chested man holding a scantily clad woman on the cover gave me a hint. Was she embarrassed about getting caught reading at work or because of what she was reading? Either way, I wasn't about to ask her.

I glanced at Father Hank's closed door, then asked, "Has he come back yet?"

She replied with a sheepish grin. "He has, but then he had to leave again. I asked him about the tunnel, though, and he said you could go down if you wanted. He said you knew how to find your way out."

No question, I did. "Have you been down there yet?"

She shook her head, then checked the security of her bun. "I have claustrophobia issues. If I can't see the sky through a window or something, I feel like I'm suffocating."

"Well, you'd better not go, then. Not a hint of sky to be seen." I checked the time: right at one. "What time do you leave for the day?"

"Around three on Fridays. But I'll wait for you if you want."

"Thanks, but I should be done long before then. I'm just going to look around a little."

"Have fun," she said with a smile. "If you're not back by the time I'm ready to leave, I'll consider you lost and call for help, okay?"

"Good idea."

I trotted down the stairs and moved down the aisle toward the kitchen in the right corner near the altar. The doorknob turned easily, and I stepped into the darkened room, feeling along the wall for a light switch. Flipping it on illuminated a countertop, sink, and dishwasher along one wall. A refrigerator and a small four-seat table took up the other. Clean, white four-inch tile covered the floor, with a blue, four-by-eight throw rug obscuring the center.

Hidden beneath the throw rug was the entrance to tunnels once used by the Underground Railroad in the 1840s and rumrunners in the 1920s. A swath of American history lay directly below my feet. Awe filled me as I lifted the ring over the two-by-two wooden trapdoor and peered into the darkness. The missing steps had been replaced since the last time I was here, and I started down, turning on the flashlight I'd collected from the stockroom before I left the bookstore.

By the time I reached the bottom, the square of light coming from the kitchen had shrunk to the size of the travel-size magnetic checkerboard I'd had as a child. I spent hours in my room playing against myself, ensuring I always won. I reached above my head for the hanging switch that controlled the lights the rumrunners had installed. Once the tunnel outside the doorway to the alcove lit up, I stepped into it, stashing the flashlight in my pocket. I'd definitely need it again in a few minutes.

I followed the low-wattage bulbs on wires tacked to the boards that shored up the hard-packed walls to the right, struggling to pull the thick, mildew-tainted air into my lungs. When the storage room full of folded tables and chairs holding cardboard boxes appeared on my left, I knew my first turn was coming up soon.

Damp dirt congealed in the treads of my Nikes by the time I reached the tunnel that I needed to use to reach my destination. This one had no lights, so I retrieved the flashlight and turned it on. The darkness ahead swallowed the light within twenty feet or so. No problem. I knew I had nothing to fear except for stray insects. Of course, I could always run into a brown recluse spider down here. They thrived in dark, undisturbed places. I immediately considered what I might find in the way of clues or jewelry to keep that thought from gaining any traction.

When I reached the end of the tunnel, I turned left toward the alcove where I'd discovered the skeleton. The likelihood I'd find anything useful in there was slim as the police had done a thorough search of the area. I was more interested in the area beyond, so I continued past the opening to where the wall had collapsed and the tunnel was blocked. The first time I'd encountered it, I'd assumed it resulted from structural failure.

Given what I now knew, I suspected the blockade might be man-made instead.

As I walked, I played the flashlight along the ground and around the walls, searching for any sign someone besides me had been there more recently than a hundred years ago. Other than minor scuffs in the dirt I could've made myself the last time I'd been here, I found nothing between the alcove and the deep pile of soil at the blocked section.

I shined the light around the edges, hoping to find tool marks or some other indication the wall had been deliberately pulled down to cover something. I saw nothing I recognized. And even if there were, how could I be sure the marks weren't left there when the tunnel was built? What in the world gave me the idea I could accomplish anything here? Still, I was already in the neighborhood, so I might as well keep looking.

The soil ahead was packed from floor to ceiling, making me wonder if this wasn't the end of the tunnel rather than a collapse, as I'd believed. But then, where did all the extra dirt come from? I'd wandered into several dead ends on my first tour, and none had piles of soil at their base. And none were inset into the end wall the way this one was.

Holding the flashlight in my teeth, I raked my hands through the loose dirt. I found no clues or jewelry, only clumps and small rocks. Of course, it couldn't be that easy, but it was worth a try. I sat against the side wall to regroup. There had to be some way to determine if someone had buried the loot from the jewelry store robbery here. I folded my arms across my knees and rested my head on them.

Come on, Jen. Think!

After a few minutes, I gave up. The only solution I could come up with was to break down the barrier to see what was behind it, and I hadn't come prepared for that. Not that I could do it by myself, anyway. I'd need a sledgehammer and someone to swing it, for starters. I didn't have the upper body strength for more than a few strikes at best.

Dejected, I clambered to my feet and headed back the way I came. When I reached the alcove where I'd found the skeleton, I stopped and flashed the light inside. The floor was covered with footprints left by techs and investigators. Running through it all were parallel tracks. Since I couldn't think of anything the police might've done to leave drag marks, I stepped inside and followed the tracks to the area behind the steps leading to the sealed exit above.

The light beam caught a flash of color where only disturbed soil was supposed to be. My heart froze, dread creeping up into my throat. The last time I'd seen color in here where there should be none was when I found the skeleton. I forced my legs forward until the design came into focus.

The orange muumuu adorned with pineapples hiked up to mid-thigh enclosed a bloated, lifeless form sprawled in the corner like a discarded marionette. Ring-covered fingers interlocked across the abdomen in an unnatural position, and a small tattoo of crossed knives adorned the inside of her left ankle.

Breathing shallowly through my mouth, I fought back the bile and covered my nose against the stench of decay. Playing the light up past the outsized peace-sign necklace, the blond-haired, open-mouthed face with eyes staring blankly into the darkness came into view. I dropped the flashlight and covered my mouth with my hands, not breathing at all now. The light rolled toward the wall, reflecting one lifeless blue eye. It was Madame Crystal Moon.

Beside her on the ground lay a hammer, covered with blood.

CHAPTER TWENTY

I squirmed on the hard wooden pew as Detective Havermayer straightened the creases in her black suit pants beside me. "Well, here we are again, Jen. Care to tell me how you managed to find *another* dead body?"

Her derisive tone made my skin itch, like when I fell into a patch of poison ivy while playing hide-and-seek with Brittany in the woods by her parents' lake house. "I went back to the tunnels to look for clues."

"Clues to what?" Havermayer asked, running a hand through her sandy blond hair. "We searched every inch of the area where you found the skeleton and unearthed nothing."

"I wasn't looking at the skeleton this time. I was . . ." Oh boy, was she going to hate this. Perhaps I shouldn't tell her why I really went down there. I had to, though. Otherwise, she'd jump on the chance to accuse me of killing Crystal Moon. Or, at the very least, withholding information to obstruct her investigation.

"You were what?" she prompted.

Here goes nothing. "I was searching for clues to the whereabouts of the jewelry taken in a jewelry store

206

robbery five years ago. The day Ewon Barnes disappeared."

She trained her shamrock eyes on me with one eyebrow cocked. "Why?"

I told her my theory about the jewelry store robbery and the disappearance of Ewon and Lyle being connected. And how the skeleton might be one of them. To my surprise, she listened without interruption, giving me the impression she actually cared about what I had to say.

"And you think the unidentified third man got rid of the other two to keep the stolen property for himself?"

"It's possible. All I know for sure is Jaylon Barnes didn't murder his brother. I found a witness who saw Ewon leave the house after the argument. She also saw Jaylon carrying the rug Ewon was supposedly transported in slung over his shoulder. There's no way he could've done that with a dead body in it."

"Who's this witness?"

I gave her Ida's name and address. "She's old but completely coherent. Very credible."

"Why didn't she tell us this back when we were investigating the initial disappearance?"

"She said nobody spoke with her."

For once, Havermayer didn't direct her frown toward me. "All right, Jen, that's it for now, but I might have more questions later."

Of course, she would. She always did. "You know where to find me."

"Yeah, sticking your nose where it doesn't belong."

"If I hadn't, you'd have another disappearance on your hands."

Ignoring her eye roll, I went to search for Eric. He

207

was chatting with one of the crime scene techs in the kitchen, so I stood in the doorway, waiting for him to finish. When he noticed me, his smile lifted some of the tension from my shoulders, but Crystal Moon's unseeing eyes in my mind froze the bulk of it in place. My stomach twisted, making me glad I'd skipped lunch.

After the tech began her descent down the steps to the tunnel, Eric came over and hugged me. "How are you?" he asked, squeezing me close.

"Tired, sad, scared, confused." I lifted my head off his chest to look at him. "Why would anyone kill Crystal Moon? She seemed weird, a little creepy even, but harmless. No threat to anyone, unless you count her message to me. And I didn't kill her."

"I don't know, but I'm sure we'll find out."

I snuggled into the security of his arms, my head rocking with his breaths. "Do you think it has anything to do with the robbery?"

"Could be. It's hard to say at this point."

Blowing out a lungful of air, I said, "You're no help."

He chuckled. "I know. I'm absolutely useless."

"Guess I'd better let you find something useful to do then." I reluctantly let him go.

"I'll call you later, but I probably won't have time for dinner with you. A murder has a way of taking up all my time."

"Rather inconsiderate if you ask me. Make sure you eat something, though. You know how you are when you get caught up in an investigation."

"I will. Talk to you later."

Since I could do nothing more at the church than get in the way or incur Havermayer's wrath, I drove to the library to talk to Brittany. Somehow, she always helped me make sense out of things nobody else could. Given how long we'd known each other, that didn't surprise me at all. What did surprise me was how well she understood the inner workings of my mind. Something I didn't comprehend myself most of the time.

The Riddleton Public Library sat on the corner of Main and Pine, next to the Piggly Wiggly, Riddleton's only grocery store. I made a right on Pine to enter the parking lot, and Detective Conway's black Bronco went by in my rearview mirror. Apparently, Eric's warning had worn off. Still had no idea why he wanted to follow me, but as long as he left me alone, I had more important things to worry about.

My tires crunched over cones fallen from the ancient pine tree, standing guard over a listing picnic table on the edge of the lot. I eased into one of the four spaces and cut the engine. Conway came up Pine Street from the other direction without stopping, but I suspected he'd be lurking somewhere when I came out. Whatever.

I climbed the half-dozen steps to the door and entered the library, stopping just inside to let my eyes adjust to the dimmer light of the hall leading to the reading room. After a moment, I strolled into the room and encountered a Valentine's Day extravaganza.

Brittany had strung pink bunting with red hearts all around the walls by the ceiling, and pink hearts with people's—mostly girls'—names on them covered every inch of unoccupied wall space. Romance novels were propped anywhere they would stand, surrounded by children's homemade Valentines. No doubt about it, Brittany was in love.

I repeated my mantra—*I know nothing!*—in my head, as I wandered through the stacks searching for my besotted friend. I would *not* tell her about Olinski's proposal plans. I wouldn't. Olinski would kill me, and Eric would never speak to me again. But most importantly, it would spoil the surprise for Brittany. And what if Olinski changed his mind? She'd be devastated. I couldn't do that to her.

I found her pushing a trolley along the back wall, shelving books. "Hey, Britt, how's it going?"

She pushed a book into its slot and turned. "Hi, what are you doing here?"

"What? I'm not allowed to visit my best friend when I want to?"

"Of course you are. You just haven't in a while. What's wrong?"

Get out of my head, Brittany! "I guess you haven't heard."

"No, what?"

"Crystal Moon is dead. I discovered her body in the tunnel where I found the skeleton."

Her mouth squeezed into an "O." "Oh! I'm so sorry. What happened to her?"

"Somebody hit her with a hammer."

"I assume you don't know who or why."

"Correct. Who would want to do that? As far as I could tell, she was a harmless nut job."

Brittany wheeled the cart forward a few feet and grabbed another book. "Apparently not. What were you doing down there, anyway?"

I gave her the standard story about my theories and searching for clues, almost exactly as I'd said to Havermayer. "You think Crystal was involved in the robbery somehow?"

"I don't know what to think. Do you?"

210

"At this point, anything's possible. This whole thing has my mind spinning around like a gyroscope. One good thing is I have the proof I need to exonerate Jaylon." I told her about my conversation with Ida and what it meant.

She clapped her hands together. "That's wonderful! Do you think it'll be enough?"

"I hope so. My only concern is it only proves Jaylon didn't kill Ewon how and when the prosecutor thinks he did. It doesn't prove he didn't kill him."

"But the how and when was what the jury convicted him on. This new information should be grounds for a new trial at least."

"Maybe, but will it be soon enough? Olinski told us Jaylon's not doing well. He might not have much time left."

Brittany studied me, wearing her thinking cap. "You know, if Crystal *was* involved in the robbery, finding her killer might also lead to Ewon's. You find that person, and they have to let Jaylon out."

"I should assume the psychic was a part of it all, to begin with? I don't have any evidence of that."

"Do you have any better ideas?"

"No, I'm stumped."

"Then what do you have to lose?"

If I moved on Brittany's suggestion, it would be reasonable to assume that whoever killed Crystal Moon was also part of the robbery. There were three men in the store. Two had disappeared so that only left the unidentified third man. "Britt, it has to be the third man, but how was Crystal involved to begin with? She wasn't in the store during the robbery."

She stopped with the next book in her hand. "Could

211

she have been the getaway driver or a lookout? Maybe the girlfriends handled those jobs so they didn't have to go in the store."

"We have names for the girlfriends now. Eliza Naismith and Abigail Adams. No Crystal Moon, Madame or otherwise."

Brittany responded with a long look at me over the top of her tiger-striped glasses.

"Crystal Moon is a made-up name, isn't it." *Duh*.

"Obviously. Now you just have to figure out which one of them she is. Was."

For once, that shouldn't be too difficult. "Forensics will help us with that one. If her fingerprints are on file anywhere, they'll come up when the police run Crystal's through the system. Then we'll know who she really is."

"Actually," Brittany began, "we could try a social media search on both of them."

Leave it to my research guru to find an easier way. "Great thinking. Let's give it a try. Do you have time?"

"I always have time for you." She blew me a kiss and headed for her computer station.

After a Mount Everest-sized eye roll, I followed.

She entered the two names into her search engine, one at a time. Nothing came up for either one. Charlie had been able to find information on them, so something had recently changed. They'd both gone off the grid.

Brittany looked at me and shrugged. "Well, I guess that idea was a bust. Sorry."

"Not a complete bust. Now we know we're on the right track or all the information on them wouldn't have been scrubbed. It'll just take a little longer, that's all. We'll find what we need, don't worry."

212

"Excellent. What're you going to do until then?"

"I'm going to figure out who the third man is. It has to be someone both Ewon and Lyle knew. We have his stocky body type to go on." I shrugged and chuckled. "How hard can it be?"

She laughed along with me. "Exactly. You should know something by this time tomorrow, right?"

"Well, maybe the day after."

"Okay, we got that settled." We returned to her shelving cart. "What else do you need?"

I thought briefly, then said, "I think that's it."

"Good. Now get out of here and let me go back to work."

"Yes, ma'am."

When I reached my Dodge, Jeremy Conway sat in his Ford in the post office parking lot across the street. What did he want? Why was he following me? Only one way to find out. I marched over to talk to him. Time to settle this one way or the other.

When I approached the Bronco, he lowered his window. "Good afternoon, Ms. Dawson. What can I do for you?"

Cut the friendly crap, for starters. "Why are you following me?"

"Who says I'm following you? I'm just sitting here, enjoying a pleasant afternoon."

"At the post office? Baloney. What do you want?"

He placed both hands on the steering wheel as if to show me he was unarmed. "I should be asking *you* that. You're the one who came over here."

Unarmed, maybe, but not innocent. "Simple. I want to know why I see this car every time I look in the rearview mirror."

"It's a small town. We're bound to run into each other now and then."

"We never have before."

"That you noticed. Maybe you're seeing my car because you're looking for it. Did you ever think of that?"

Nonsense. "No, because it's ridiculous. Leave me alone, and stay away from my home and my store."

I turned and strode away before he could respond. I felt him watching me, and the hair on my neck bristled. Just because he didn't have a gun in his hand didn't mean he didn't have one. As an ex-cop, it was almost guaranteed he did. I refused to look back, though. It would be suicide to show fear to a predator like him. I would, however, tell Eric about our encounter the first chance I got.

When I pulled up in front of Ravenous Readers, Simeon Kirby was peering in the front door. Terrific. Ring the bell for round two. I stepped out of the car. "Is the door locked or something, Mr. Kirby?"

He jerked around, cheeks the color of a fresh-picked American Beauty rose. "Uh . . . no. I was checking to see if you were busy before going in. I didn't want to interrupt anything."

At the rate things were going today, I'd soon have enough baloney to feed me for a week. "Since I'm out here and not busy, what did you need?"

"I wanted to see if you'd come to your senses yet. I heard about your little mishap the other day and thought you might be ready to cash in. My offer still stands. It's double what the place is worth."

A flare of anger rushed from my brain to my mouth. "My little mishap? You mean when you vandalized my store to bully me into selling?"

214

He sighed and regarded me like I was a wayward child. "Now, really, Ms. Dawson, you know I had nothing to do with that."

I knew the note left behind made it unlikely that Kirby had anything to do with it, but I couldn't help myself. "Do I?"

"I think you do. The police haven't questioned me yet, so I'm reasonably certain they know it, too."

He was right, and deep down, I knew it, even if I didn't want to admit it. Now I had to convince my temper. I took a few deep breaths before attempting a more civilized tone. "All right, you've done what you came for. I haven't come to my senses, as you put it, so is there anything else you need?"

Kirby gave me a tiny headshake. "I'll take my leave. Have a good day, Ms. Dawson. Call me when something happens to make you change your mind." He slid past me and sauntered down the sidewalk toward the diner with his hands in his trouser pockets.

I watched him go. The guy had more than his share of nerve; I'd give him that. But I'd never give him my bookstore.

CHAPTER TWENTY-ONE

When Savannah and I reached the Riddleton Park gate three minutes late for our Saturday morning run, only Angus and Lacey greeted us. Eric told me he had to work the homicide, which explained his absence. Ingrid, however, remained a question mark.

"Just the three of us this morning?" I asked as my German shepherd scampered between the two of them, collecting her chest rubs and chin scratches. "I know Eric's working. Anyone heard from Ingrid?"

"She came by the diner for breakfast this morning," Angus replied. "Crystal Moon's autopsy is on her schedule for today."

"Looks like you're stuck with us, Lacey. I hope we don't drag you down too much."

She laughed. "Are you kidding? I'd love a chance to relax and chat with you for a change. Eric is so competitive, he brings out that side in me. Which is great because we both get the most out of our run. But occasionally, it's nice to enjoy the scenery, so to speak."

Angus patted her shoulder. "Well, come on then. You'll have every leaf memorized by the time *we're* done. Spoiler alert: most of them are pine needles, so they all pretty much look alike."

Lacey led us through our stretches, but my muscles had knotted into steel balls after the tension of finding another dead body and once again having to explain myself to Havermayer. It would take a bulldozer to budge them, and I'd left mine in the parking lot at home. I settled for the ability to turn my head far enough to avoid large obstacles and set off with the others down the mile-long path that circumnavigated the park.

This time of year, we had the park to ourselves, the ball fields and picnic areas abandoned for activities more suited to the weather. The solitude in the morning was the only thing about winter I enjoyed. My mind wandered unencumbered, and the silence connected me to the world around me. The low temperatures and icy rains from November to March, I could happily live without.

Angus, Savannah, and I settled into our usual rhythm, and Lacey matched us like a gazelle trying to keep pace with sloths. I took pity on her. "Lacey, would you consider taking Savannah for a sprint around the track? I'm sure she'd love to stretch her legs a bit. She hardly gets any exercise running with me."

She glanced at the dog, who wasn't even panting yet. "I'd be happy to, but don't think I don't know what you're doing."

I painted on my best "innocent" expression. "Why, whatever do you mean?"

Lacey rolled her eyes and shook her head. We all burst out laughing.

When Angus could breathe again, he asked, "How

are you doing, Jen? I heard about your little adventure yesterday."

"Of course you did." The engineer of Riddleton's gossip train was on top of everything. "I'm all right. A little shaken but coping. Discovering dead people is becoming a way of life for me. Just what I needed. Another bad habit to break."

"You *do* seem to have bad luck when it comes to that sort of thing."

"No kidding," Lacey added. "Did you know the woman?"

"Not really." I switched Savannah's leash to my other hand. "I only spoke to her a couple of times. When she gave me that ridiculous message."

Lacey sped up so she could turn and face me, running backward. "What message?"

Show-off. "Beware the golden bones."

"What's that mean?"

"Beats me. That's all she would say, and now she's dead, so I'll never know."

She dropped back in line with us. "That's nuts."

"Tell me about it." I shuffled my feet to match strides with Angus. "Eric told me she came into the police station talking about a vision related to the skeleton I found. They pretty much laughed her out of the building."

"She came in the diner a few times," Angus said. "Spent most of her time talking to Marcus and Penelope, though. I guess, after seeing me with you, she figured I wouldn't believe her nonsense any more than you did."

"Did they?"

"Can't say for certain. I think Marcus humored her

until he could get away, but I saw her with Penelope several times."

"Maybe Penelope's tired of being a waitress." Lacey grinned. "Now she's taking 'psychic' lessons." She shook her head. "Was taking lessons, I mean."

We ran silently for a few minutes, absorbing the reality of Crystal's death. Even though none of us knew her, someone dying deserved our respect. Even a woman we all laughed at while she was still alive.

I tried for a subject change. "Angus, did you ever decide whether to sell the diner to Simeon Kirby?"

Lacey's jaw dropped. "You too?" she asked him, then turned toward me. "Why didn't you tell me?"

I shrugged. "It wasn't my story to tell. I figured Angus would fill you in when he was ready." Touching Angus's arm, I said, "I shouldn't have mentioned it. I wasn't thinking. I'm sorry, Angus."

Angus nodded, then glanced at Lacey. "I was going to tell you, I just never got around to it. I don't see you as often as Jen. You know how to cook." He grinned at his joke. "Kirby made a terrific offer. Much more than the place is worth, but I'm happy here. I love what I'm doing, and I love Riddleton. What would I do with myself if I sold?"

"You could travel. See the world. What's on your bucket list?"

"I don't have one. I've never thought about retiring."

"Well, Angus," I said. "Maybe that's your answer."

"Could be."

We reached the one-mile mark, and Lacey took off with Savannah frolicking beside her. Angus and I plodded along until they caught up again. My dog's sides heaved, and her tongue hung out the side of her mouth. I envisioned her crashing on the couch when we got home. Fine with me. A tired dog is a happy dog, as the saying goes.

Showered and dressed, I stared at a picture of Madame Crystal Moon on my laptop screen while sipping fresh coffee. I'd found a rudimentary website for her by typing her name and the word *psychic* into my search engine. If she had a business address, it wasn't listed on the site, and when I dialed the phone number on the screen, I got a barbershop in Blackburn. I didn't ask about her, despite the remote possibility she might've had a second career as a men's hairstylist. My gut told me the website was more than likely a sham. As was Madame Crystal.

As far as I could tell, she had no other online presence. How could she drum up business if nobody knew she existed? There must be at least one group for psychics on Facebook. They had groups for everything else. Although, maybe the psychics didn't need the Internet to communicate. They could just intuit each other's thoughts. But she'd certainly want a page advertising her services. Especially if she didn't have a storefront or office people could visit. Of course, there *was* the barbershop.

I packed up for a trip to the bookstore. It was time for a Charlie-style deep dive into Crystal Moon. If she was out there, he'd find her. Meanwhile, I had to figure out my next move. If my assumption was correct and all these deaths and disappearances were related, finding the connection had to be first on my list. All I had right now was assumption and supposition; the prosecutor would never go for it.

Savannah was sacked out on the couch, ears and eyebrows wiggling and paws twitching. Best to let her sleep. She'd had more exercise running one lap with Lacey this morning than she got in a whole week hanging around with me. That said nothing good about my exercise routines. Perhaps I should run more often than once a week.

Hah! Who was I kidding? That would never happen.

I slid a chew stick out of the package for Savannah, and she lifted her head for a second. I laid it on the couch beside her and headed for the door. She made no move to follow. How hard did Lacey run her? I went back to check her out. Her eyes were clear, nose cold and wet, and ears normal temperature. Okay, she wasn't sick, just a really pooped pup. My wallet and I both sighed in relief.

Eric called on my way to the bookstore. After a brief exchange of pleasantries, he said, "I thought you might like to know we have an ID on Crystal Moon."

"You mean Madame Crystal Moon isn't her real name? Imagine that! I'd never have guessed, even after I couldn't find anything besides an obviously phony website online."

He chuckled. "Well, in that case, you're going to love this. We ran her prints, and she has a record for breaking and entering. Crystal Moon is none other than Abigail Adams. And no, I don't mean the First Lady."

"Lyle Pipkin's girlfriend?"

"We think so, yes. I can't imagine too many other people with that name in this area."

My heart skipped a beat. "You think she's the one who broke into the bookstore?"

"Could be. She has the skills for it, but we haven't been able to tie her to the break-in yet. She must've worn gloves."

"We figured that, but her being the culprit makes sense. Abigail tried to scare me off the investigation with her ridiculous message. When that didn't work, she trashed the bookstore and left the note."

"It's possible. We still don't have a motive, though."

I switched the phone to my other hand to open the door to Ravenous Readers. "Unless I'm correct and the jewelry from the robbery is buried near where the skeleton was hidden."

"But how would the thieves have known about the tunnels? Very few people in town even knew they existed. I didn't until you told me."

When the door closed behind me, I looked out on the sales floor and froze. The bookstore was packed with people. "Eric, I have to call you back."

I hung up on his "okay" and searched for Lacey. I found her coming out of the stockroom with an armload of books. "What's going on?"

She carried her wares to a customer near the Biography section, then headed for the cash register where three people stood waiting to check out. "I'm not sure," she said, pushing hair that had escaped from her ponytail behind her ear. "I think many of them are just looking for information about Crystal Moon. It's all over town that you found the body."

"You're kidding me."

"Nope." She glanced at the crowd milling around the coffee bar. "Would you mind giving Charlie a hand, please? I have this covered."

I scurried over there, doled out pastries, and handled

the register while Charlie took care of the specialty coffees. To nobody's surprise, I still hadn't mastered the complexities of the espresso machine.

People began peppering me with questions as I worked.

"Is it true you found Crystal Moon's body?"

"Yes."

"How did she die?"

"I don't know," I replied, though I suspected that bloody hammer beside her might've had something to do with it.

"Was she murdered?"

Probably. "They don't know yet."

"Do the police have any suspects?"

Not that I'll tell you about. "I really can't say."

"Did you kill her?"

I jerked my head up at that one. The speaker was Simeon Kirby. "No, Mr. Kirby, I did not. And I'd appreciate it if you wouldn't start rumors about me that might hurt my business."

He grinned, sipped his coffee, and walked away.

Terrific. It wouldn't do him any good, however. Even if he somehow convinced all our customers to stop coming in overnight, we'd close the store before selling to him. And I was comfortable believing that Lacey would back me on that decision.

When the mongers finally figured out I wouldn't supply any grist for the rumor mill, the crowd dispersed, but the boost in our daily sales was undeniable. Once again, Ravenous Readers would benefit from an unexpected death in Riddleton. There had to be a better way for us to stay afloat. I was beginning to feel like the Grim Reaper in drag.

Charlie and I cleaned up and restocked while Lacey helped the remaining customers, who were actually here to buy books. The store finally emptied, and the three of us occupied a table to enjoy the momentary respite. I suspected our afternoon would be taken up with the gossip lovers who liked to sleep late on Saturday.

"Well, that was fun," I said, sipping my fresh-brewed coffee.

"Just think," Charlie said. "It could be like that every day if Kirby is right about his resort bringing more people to town. Wouldn't that be great?"

Everyone knew how I felt, so I didn't respond. Strangely, Lacey also remained silent. When I thought about it, I realized I had no idea how she felt about the new development. She'd never said, even when I railed against it. She didn't want to sell the bookstore. That much she'd made clear. But the resort? Nothing.

"What do you think, Lacey?"

She studied the coffee in her cup as if searching for the answer. "I don't know. I can't make up my mind." She took a fortifying sip. "On the one hand, it would be great for business. On the other . . ."

I waited for a minute, then finished for her. "It would destroy our town as we know it."

She nodded. "Does it really matter, though? The resort is a done deal. There's nothing we can do about it."

Charlie examined me over the rim of his cup. "As long as Kirby's in charge, anyway."

"Good grief, Charlie, don't say that! The way things are going around here, somebody will kill him, and I'll find the body."

224

His eyes twinkled. "And wouldn't that be good for business?"

Lacey and I groaned and exchanged a glance. Good thing we had no cameras with audio in here. We'd be in big trouble if anything ever happened to Simeon Kirby.

CHAPTER TWENTY-TWO

A middle-aged woman wrangled two teenage girls and an elementary-school-aged boy through the doorway into the store, declaring our coffee break over. Lacey rushed over to offer assistance, and Charlie and I moved back to the coffee bar to ensure we hadn't missed anything. Charlie offered the boy a chocolate chip cookie when he passed us on his way to the kids' section. He smiled and stuffed the whole thing in his mouth.

Charlie looked at me. "Well, he's either not allowed to have cookies and wanted to get rid of the evidence before his mother caught him, or he hasn't eaten this week."

"Nah, I'm thinking typical ten-year-old boy."

He laughed, then sobered. "I never got the chance to ask how you're doing. Finding another body had to be traumatic."

"I could've lived without it." I sighed. "I didn't know her very well, so it hasn't hit me as hard as it might have, but I'm more determined than ever to know whether it has anything to do with the jewelry store robbery."

"What makes you think it might?"

"Eric told me Crystal Moon was actually Abigail Adams. It would be too much of a coincidence if the two aren't related, and as far as I'm concerned, there's no such thing as a coincidence in a murder investigation."

His mouth popped open. "Wow! No wonder I couldn't find anything other than a simple website about Crystal online. She doesn't exist."

"Exactly. Can you work your magic on Abigail Adams? We need to know more about her other than she's Lyle's girlfriend. Like where she was the night of the robbery."

"I'll do my best. It should be easier now that I know what to look for."

"While you're doing that, I'll talk to Jaylon's parents again."

I waited a while to see if the expected afternoon coffee klatch materialized. When our business flow seemed typical for a Saturday, I went to Regina Barnes's house. Guess the rumormongers were all early risers.

Regina, wearing the same ruffled yellow apron over a different floral-print dress, opened the door with a smile that quickly disappeared. "What do *you* want?"

"I just want to talk for a minute. I have a few more questions."

"About what?"

"May I please come in?"

She stepped aside. I moved past her into the living room and waited for her to take me where she wanted me to go. We went back to the kitchen, only instead of the mouth-watering aroma of baking cookies, the metallic odor of tarnished jewelry spread out on the table greeted me. Beside the bottle of cleaner sat a cherry jewelry box with a rose carved into the top.

227

"Excuse the mess," she said. "I'm cleaning up some of my old stuff to sell. I never wear it anymore and don't have a daughter to leave it to."

Or a son who'd ever get married the way things stood. I gazed at the assortment of rings, bracelets, and necklaces and selected a sapphire pendant on a large-link chain, holding it up to the light. "You have some lovely pieces here."

"Thank you. My grandmother left me that one. I'd hoped to pass it down to my daughter-in-law or granddaughter someday, but . . ." Her gaze drifted to a spot somewhere above my head. When she returned from wherever she'd gone, she said, "It's yours if you want it. Make me an offer."

"I appreciate that, but I never wear jewelry, either, and I couldn't begin to know what something like that might be worth. Whatever it is, I'm sure I can't afford it."

She shrugged and picked up a gold wedding band with a matching diamond engagement ring. "How about these? I'm sure you'll need *them* someday. I certainly don't anymore."

Odd. Didn't Ricky tell me she'd returned her engagement ring to him? "Maybe someday, but not anytime soon, I suspect. I'm not quite ready to get married yet."

"If you change your mind, let me know." Regina moved toward the refrigerator. "Would you like some tea? I made it fresh this morning."

"That would be great, thanks."

She filled two glasses and carried them back to the table, gesturing for me to sit. "What did you want to ask me this time?"

I settled into a chair and sipped from the glass she

228

handed me. "How well did you know Lyle Pipkin and Abigail Adams?"

She held her tea with both hands. "I've known Lyle since he was a teenager. He and Ewon were almost inseparable in high school. I met Abigail once or twice when they came over to see Ewon after he got out of jail. I didn't like her much, though. I can't say why for sure. She seemed to bring out the worst in Lyle."

"I understand Lyle was a troublemaker of sorts. Always dragging Ewon down with him."

"Lyle was a lost soul. His father abandoned the family when he was a baby, and he never had anyone to show him the way."

"When was the last time you saw him?"

"A few days before Ewon disappeared and Jaylon . . . well, you know."

I nodded my understanding. "Do you think Lyle was capable of robbing a jewelry store?"

She pinched her eyebrows together. "I don't know. He was troubled, but I didn't think he'd go that far. Why do you ask?"

"There was a robbery in Blackburn the night Ewon disappeared. The police think he and Lyle participated. I believe that might be why they both haven't been heard from since that night."

"What do you mean? Why would the two be related?"

"I think either the two of them took off after the robbery to avoid prosecution, or it's possible someone else involved killed them to keep all the proceeds for himself."

"Someone else like Abigail?" she asked, rubbing her temples.

"Possibly, although she wasn't actually seen in the

229

store. She might've been a lookout or the getaway driver. Of course, that's pure speculation on my part. There's no evidence she had anything to do with it that I'm aware of."

"What makes you so sure she was, then?"

I inhaled, then released the air slowly. "I'm not, but it's the only thing that makes sense. Abigail has been in town for the past week, masquerading as a psychic who had a vision about the robbery. I found her dead yesterday. She was murdered."

Regina's eyes widened. "Oh! That's terrible. Who would do something like that?"

"I was hoping you could help me figure that out. There was an unidentified third man who participated in the robbery that night. Do you have any idea who he might've been? Another friend of Ewon and Lyle's, perhaps?"

"Ewon didn't bring his friends around. Lyle was the only one I met, but I know there were others. I'd overhear the boys talking about them."

I took a swallow of my drink, the syrupy sweetness of southern iced tea sliding easily down my throat. "The shop owner described the man as stockier than the other two. Does that ring any bells?"

She hesitated, studying her manicure. "I'm sorry, I can't help you."

Can't or won't? Her body language screamed there was more to this story than she was telling. Now I had to pry it out of her.

"Regina, I think you know something." I leaned forward on the table. "I think the third man might've murdered your son. Two of the three thieves disappeared that night. Don't you find that strange?"

230

Her hands once again drew her full attention. "I don't know anything about it."

"The stolen jewelry was never found. I think they hid it somewhere, argued about it, and that unidentified man murdered the two boys to keep it all for himself."

She stood, her chair scraping the polished linoleum. "I told you I can't help you. I don't know anything about a robbery, and I don't know who that man is. Now, please go!"

I had to work on my social skills. Getting thrown out of places was becoming another bad habit for me. "All right, I'll leave. If you think of anything that might help, please call me. Remember, finding out the truth about Ewon may be the only way to save Jaylon's life." I dropped one of Eric's business cards on the table in front of her. "If you won't tell me, at least tell the police."

A tear dripped from the corner of her eye and rolled down her cheek.

"I'm sorry I upset you."

Regina pulled a tissue from her apron pocket and blew her nose.

I turned and left with a sick feeling in my belly. She knew more than she let on. Or, at a minimum, suspected something she didn't want to share with me. Did she know who killed her son? Who was she protecting? And why?

My only option now was to ask Ricky Barnes the same questions I'd asked his wife. Ex-wife. Would he stonewall the same way? At this point, I didn't believe for a minute nobody in the Barnes family knew anything about the events surrounding Ewon's disappearance.

When I turned on the road to Sutton, a black Ford

appeared in my rearview mirror. Detective Conway was back on the case, it seemed. Too bad he wasn't this dedicated when it was *his* turn to investigate. I might not be having to do his job for him now.

I negotiated Saturday afternoon traffic into Sutton, then asked Robot Woman for help navigating the maze that led to Ricky's house. The Bronco behind me had disappeared, but I had no doubt he'd be somewhere near Ricky's, waiting for me. Perhaps he knew a shortcut. Next time, I'd let him lead.

No vehicle occupied the driveway of Ricky's ranch-style house, but I gave it a shot anyway. I knocked on the peeling brown door and waited. No answer. I tried again with the same result. My shoulders sagged with disappointment. I'd have to come back tomorrow.

The February sun edged toward the horizon as I trudged back to my Dodge, feeling as ineffectual as the winter sun tended to be. When I opened the driver's side door, shouting pierced the air in the backyard. I slammed the door closed and headed in that direction, stopping at the corner of the house where I could hear but not be seen. My mother's constant reminders about the rudeness of eavesdropping bounced through my brain.

Sorry, Mom, but sometimes it's necessary.

Besides, Ricky's gravelly voice was impossible to ignore. "I don't care what she said. I had nothing to do with that."

Who was he talking to? And who was "she?" My gut told me Regina spoke on the other end of the line, and they were referring to me. However, that could also be my ego talking. But if my instincts were correct, Ricky was claiming not to be the third man in the robbery. I'd never said he was. Perhaps Regina was hiding her suspicions about him, and that's why she reacted so strangely. Olinski would tell me my overactive imagination was getting the best of me. This time, he might be right, but I didn't think so.

After listening to a lengthy response, Ricky replied, "Whatever you do, don't talk to her again. She's a nosy nobody who's filling your head with lies about me."

Not true. I hadn't told a single lie. All I did was lay out the facts as I knew them. If Regina jumped to conclusions, that wasn't my responsibility.

I stepped out of my hiding place, wiping sweaty palms on my jeans.

Ricky sat at a picnic table with his phone beside him, drinking a beer. When he saw me, he slammed the can down. "What are you doing here? I just got off the phone with my wife. She's very upset. Talking nonsense. All because of you!"

Raising my hands, I replied, "All I did was ask her a few questions. It's not my fault she interpreted them in a way you didn't like."

He stood and stepped toward me. "You need to leave me and my family alone."

"All I want to do is help your son. Don't you care that he's sitting in jail for something he didn't do? That he might even die there?"

"You and my wife seem to be the only ones who consistently believe he's innocent. Even I'm not so sure at times."

"Not anymore. I spoke with a witness who saw Ewon leaving the house alive after he argued with Jaylon. He *is* innocent."

Ricky took another step closer, his eyebrows straining to touch the bridge of his nose. "What witness?"

Did I dare tell him? If he was involved, he might do something to Ida. "I'm not at liberty to say. The police want to speak with her before making it public." His icy brown eyes had me shifting my feet in discomfort. I shouldn't have let it slip that the witness was a woman. "I don't understand why you're so angry. You should be happy that Jaylon might be freed."

His face relaxed a bit. "Of course I'm happy. But I'm angry that she didn't come forward to begin with. He's wasted five years of his life rotting in that prison."

Why don't I believe him? Was I so desperate to imagine he took part in his son's disappearance? What did that say about me? Nothing I wanted to hear. "Look, I only want to ask you a few questions about Lyle Pipkin and his girlfriend."

"I think I've answered enough of your questions. Thank you for telling me about the witness. The police know about it, so let them take it from here."

"But—"

"Goodbye, Ms. Dawson. Please leave and don't come back."

"Just one more question, please. Now that we know Ewon wasn't killed in the afternoon while you were at work, where were you that evening?"

His face donned a mask of fury. The force of it pushed me back a step.

Never mind. I didn't really want to know. I turned and headed back to my car, forcing myself to walk, though my vibrating legs were determined to run.

I drove home, periodically checking my rearview mirror. No sign of Detective Conway's black Bronco. Perhaps he'd finally given up. My life was way too boring for anyone to remain interested in for long. And

234

if his goal was to intimidate me into dropping the investigation, I clearly refused to cooperate. It just took him a while to get the message.

Only one parking spot remained in front of my building, and I slipped into it, fatigue creeping through my bones. This afternoon's travels had been a waste of time. I was no closer to making a connection between the robbery and Ewon's disappearance than I'd been when the now-setting sun had risen this morning. And to make matters worse, I'd given out more information than I'd received in return. Pretty sure that wasn't how it was supposed to work.

I lumbered up the steps to my apartment, slipped the key into the lock, and opened the door. Savannah greeted me, tail waving with excitement. The best part of my day so far. I shared her joy at our reunion until I looked up and noticed Detective Conway sitting on the couch, smiling and holding a beer.

"Cute dog, you got there."

CHAPTER TWENTY-THREE

I stood with my mouth open, staring at the detective who did his best James Dean imitation by wearing jeans, a white T-shirt, and a black leather jacket and made himself at home in my living room without an invitation. And helped himself to one of Eric's beers. "What are you doing here? How did you get in?"

Conway gave me a one-sided smile. "You really should have a deadbolt lock on your door. They're much harder to pick."

"Are you kidding me?" I took a deep breath to settle myself. "Do the words 'breaking and entering' mean anything to you?"

He laughed and set his beer bottle on the coffee table. "What're you gonna do? Call the police? I worked with most of those guys. They won't do anything to me." He stood and showed me his empty hands. "Look, all I want to do is talk."

"Next time, use the telephone." I eased past my too-friendly German shepherd and sat in the recliner by the double glass doors. "What do you want? Are you the one who broke into my store and trashed it?"

"No, that would be illegal."

Ironic much? "Like breaking into my apartment, isn't?"

"I haven't done any damage, have I?" Conway pulled two dollars from his pocket and dropped them on the table. "Here, I'll even pay you for the beer."

I stared at the rumpled bills on the coffee table but didn't reach for them. "I don't want your money. I want you to leave me alone."

"And I want you to stop trampling on my investigation. I did good work, and you're damaging my reputation. Jaylon Barnes was guilty. A jury of his peers agreed with me. What more proof do you need?"

I leaned forward with my elbows on my knees. "You know as well as I do that juries don't always get it right. Even when they have all the information, which, in this case, they didn't. A crucial witness never testified in the trial."

He sat up straight and peered at me. "What witness?"

"The one who saw Ewon Barnes leaving the house after you claimed he was already dead. We've found no evidence Jaylon did anything to his brother but argue with him."

"Who's the witness?"

"I'm not telling you. If you'd done your job properly in the first place, you'd know because you'd have heard it for yourself. But you never interviewed this person. You dropped the ball, and an innocent man went to jail." I took a deep breath to dissipate my growing anger. Nothing would be gained from bickering with the detective.

"How sure are you this witness is credible?"

"One hundred percent. There's no doubt in my mind."

Conway took a long swallow of beer. "Is this true?

You're not just saying it because you're upset I broke in?"

Savannah sat on my feet, watching him. I scratched behind her ears. "It's true. Jaylon didn't murder Ewon the day they fought."

"That doesn't mean he didn't kill him."

"Maybe, but he definitely didn't do it like you said he did. And that's grounds for a new trial, at the very least. But, honestly, the case falls apart without your theory of the crime. There's still no proof that Ewon is dead. He might be lying on a beach in Florida, for all we know. Or skiing in Colorado."

He deflated like a tire with a nail in it. Deep in thought, he rolled the beer bottle between his hands, seeming genuinely disturbed by the new revelation. Perhaps I'd misjudged him. Although, he *had* broken into my apartment, and he'd never let me see anything but his indignation at his integrity being questioned. Still, it might be better to work with him than against him.

Conway poured the last of the beer down his throat. "I don't believe Ewon Barnes is lying on the beach or skiing. I think he's dead. Maybe he didn't die the way I thought he did, but I'm sure he died around the same time."

"What makes you so sure?"

"Cop's gut instinct, I guess. I mean, why would he disappear without telling anyone? He had a life here. Plans for the future. A girlfriend and family. It just doesn't make sense that he'd take off and leave everything behind."

I agreed with him but played devil's advocate. "Perhaps he ran because he knew he could be tied to

238

the jewelry store robbery in Blackburn and the jewelry couldn't be sold here. He might've gone somewhere else to cash in and stayed to open his shop."

"Possibly, but how would he have known how to dispose of the jewelry? He was a kid, not Al Capone. He didn't have a network for that kind of thing."

How could I even be having a conversation like this? I didn't know anything about trafficking in stolen jewelry. "Then how was he going to dispose of the stuff here?"

"He couldn't. That's why they had to hide it until the investigation went cold."

"Let's say I agree with you, and he's dead. Will you help me tie his disappearance to the robbery? If we can do that, we might be able to find his killer."

Conway picked up the beer bottle as if forgetting he'd emptied it, then put it down and said, "Let me see what I can find out. If nothing else, I owe it to Jaylon." He met my gaze. "I honestly believed he was guilty."

"I know you did. Now help me fix it."

He left, promising to call if he learned anything helpful. I locked the door and picked up my phone to call Eric. But Conway and I had ended our conversation on a positive note. If Eric knew the former detective had broken into my apartment, he'd feel obligated to do something about it. That would destroy my new working relationship with him. I should wait until the next time I saw him. He'd react better when he saw for himself I'd survived the ordeal unharmed.

I stretched out on the couch, desperate for a nap. Savannah squeezed in behind me, and we jockeyed for position. She'd grown too big for both of us to fit comfortably. I turned on my side, which barely created enough room if she curled her paws against my back. The voice in my head told me to shoo her down onto the floor, but as usual, I didn't listen. Some things would never change.

When I closed my eyes, my brain spun a whirligig. The few bits I'd learned in the past week swirled around in my skull but refused to come together. I felt no closer to understanding what had happened to Ewon today than when I started. And Jaylon sat in jail, getting sicker every day. I had to help him, but other than finding Ida, I'd accomplished nothing so far.

I wanted to believe the new witness alone would be enough to have him released, but somehow, I didn't think it would. The only thing that might convince a judge Jaylon hadn't killed Ewon would be figuring out who did. The one thing I hadn't yet been able to do.

I finally dozed off, only to be awakened by my ringing phone. With one eye still closed, I picked it up and looked at the screen. Eric. I swiped.

"Hey, do you want to meet me at the diner for a quick dinner?"

A time check showed 4:30. "It's a little early, don't you think?"

"It's now or never, babe. We've got a lot going on right now. And I have some info you might be interested in."

"All right. I'll be there in a few minutes."

After hanging up, I hoisted myself off the couch and went into the bathroom to splash water on my face. The spiky-haired, sleep-creased face looking back at me from the mirror told me I needed much more than that to be presentable. The only way to tame my hair in its current condition would be to wet it, so I did. No time for a blow-dry. Eric would just have to deal with it slicked down. Nothing else I could do. And, though the cold water on my face had helped some, the remaining wrinkles would have to fall out on their own.

I took Savannah for a business-only walk, fed her, and trotted down the stairs to the diner. Angus greeted me at the door, wiping his hands on his apron. He pointed toward Eric, who was sitting in a booth other than ours, which was occupied by a couple with two kids. Guess it had to happen sooner or later.

I kissed Eric and sat across from him. New lines around his mouth and purple swaths accentuated his bloodshot emerald eyes. Nothing like a homicide to wear out a small-town detective in a hurry. I took his hand. "You look tired."

"I am. It's been a long day. And it's not over yet."

"Sorry. What're you working on?"

"Well, we got fingerprints off the hammer you found next to the body, but no match in the system. Whoever the killer is, they've never been arrested. When I get back, I'll compare them to the ones we took from your bookstore, and maybe something will pop up."

"But you still won't know who it is, though." I reached for a menu.

"No, but it'll tell us if the same person is likely responsible for both crimes. That should narrow down the field a little." Eric took the menu from my hand. "I went ahead and ordered for us. I really don't have much time."

If Eric was correct, and the same person who broke into Ravenous Readers also killed Abigail, that might be the connection we needed to find Ewon's killer. "Okay, do we know anything else?"

"Ingrid confirmed the hammer was the murder weapon. That's about it for now. We're having trouble finding anyone with a motive to kill Abigail Adams. Everyone we've spoken with claims they only knew her as Crystal Moon, and not well at that."

"Somebody had to know her unless the killer came in from out of town. Charlie told me Abigail lives . . . lived in Blackburn. Maybe she made some enemies there."

"I spoke with a detective from BPD this morning, and he's going to nose around a little for me. Talk to her neighbors. Find where she worked and talk to her coworkers."

"Charlie told me her neighbor told him she was unemployed."

"Hopefully the detective will ferret out her former employer then, which might turn out even better for us. They'll be less likely to sugarcoat their responses if she didn't work there anymore, anyway."

Penelope came up carrying two dinner plates in one hand and a drink for me in the other. How did she do that? I couldn't handle four drinks on a tray without spilling them. She set the glass and one plate in front of me. I unrolled the napkin containing my silverware, and the fork bounced off the table onto the floor.

Way to go, Jen.

I leaned over to pick it up and noticed a tattoo on the inside of Penelope's left ankle, just above her no-show sock. The familiar crossed knives jumped out at me. The same tattoo I'd seen in the exact same place on Abigail Adams's body. Possibly a stock tattoo you could find in any artist's portfolio, but what were the odds they'd pick the same one and put it in the same place? Astronomical. They had to know each other. My heart rate moved into the staccato range.

Deep breath in, slow breath out.

Calmer now, I said, "That's an interesting tattoo, Penelope. What does it mean?"

She glanced at her ankle. "It's silly. A bunch of us girls got one in high school. The knives represent how we felt at the time. We thought we were tough. Stupid kids."

"It's not so bad. At least you didn't get it on your face, right?"

"That was never an option. My parents would've killed me." She glanced from me to Eric. "Ya'll need anything else?"

"Nothing else for me, thanks."

Eric had a mouth full of potatoes, so he shook his head.

When Penelope walked away, I leaned over the table and asked, "Eric, do you have any pictures of Crystal Moon's body?

"No, why?"

"I think she has the same tattoo as Penelope. What if they went to high school together?"

He dropped his chicken leg onto his plate. "What if they did?"

"Penelope might be involved in Abigail's murder. That's a distinctive tattoo, and I don't think she told us the truth about it."

Eric thought while he chewed. After swallowing, he said, "Okay, but where would we begin to look? Neither one of them is from Riddleton. And what does it matter, anyway?"

"Maybe Penelope knew Abigail from high school and

was going to out Crystal as an impostor. They fought, and Penelope killed her."

He cocked an eyebrow. "Come on. You've known Penelope for years. Do you really think she might be involved in a mess like this? You're starting to sound like Havermayer."

"That was a low blow, Detective O'Malley. Just talk to Penelope. Find out where she went to high school and if she knew Abigail. If she does, I think it's strange she didn't mention it since now everybody knows Abigail was Crystal Moon."

He wiped his mouth on a napkin and slid out of the booth. "Fine. I'll go talk to her."

I chomped on my chicken breast while Eric chatted with Penelope by the counter. After a few minutes, he returned to the table.

"She said she went to Blackburn High and never met Abigail Adams. Now, can I finish my dinner?"

"Absolutely. I love you."

He forked mashed potatoes into his mouth and flashed a goofy closed-lipped grin, his emerald eyes glittering in the fluorescent light.

CHAPTER TWENTY-FOUR

Eric finished his dinner and went back to work. With nothing to do on a Saturday night for the first time in months, I went home feeling lost. How had he ingratiated himself into my daily life so easily? I was the one who never needed anybody. The kid who sat alone in her room every night, listening to music and reading. Sometimes, writing when an idea popped into my head, and I couldn't get it out any other way. Content to write more and more as the years passed, and I realized I might actually have something to say. What happened to me? I wasn't a kid anymore. And I loved him.

Savannah twirled in circles at my arrival, wagging and leaping. I was the center of her universe. Did she feel empty when I left her? Probably, if dogs had feelings like that. If she did, she couldn't tell me about them, though. I sat on the floor and scratched her neck while she scoured my face as if it were coated with bacon grease. True love at its simplest.

When she finally calmed down, she ran and got her monkey. I threw the stuffed toy down the hall, and she charged, grabbing it for a few trips around the apartment. I wondered again how my downstairs neighbor felt about her running the Riddleton 500 every time she got excited. I had no idea. He never complained. Maybe he was a dog lover, too.

I'd never much cared about dogs until a woman in Savannah gave me a puppy to keep me out of trouble. It didn't work, but the baby German shepherd somehow opened a place in my heart I hadn't even known existed. I couldn't imagine my life without her, and Eric loving her the way I did made life that much better.

I grabbed a bottle of wine from the fridge and poured a glass. Savannah had exhausted herself and lay on the couch, panting. I dropped in beside her and hugged her neck. "So, little girl, what should we do tonight? Uncle Eric has abandoned us for his silly job." Of course, I didn't find his job silly in the least, but she didn't know that.

She responded with a sloppy kiss I interpreted as, "How about a movie, Mom?"

My scroll through Netflix was interrupted by a knock on the door. Savannah leaped off the couch, barking and growling as if she'd rip the face off anyone who entered. I knew better. So did Detective Conway. "Come in!" I called, knowing no stranger would dare.

Brittany came through the doorway, hand out to control Savannah, whose growls had changed to excited yips the instant the door opened. "Hi. I had nothing to do tonight, so I thought I'd come over and bother you for a while. We haven't had a girls' night in weeks."

"Olinski ditch you? Eric's working, too."

"Yeah. I hate it when someone dies over the weekend. The police have to work the case, and no time off for good behavior." She carried the bottle of wine she'd

246

brought into the kitchen and swapped it for the cold one in the fridge and an empty glass.

"I know. You'd think the victims would be a little more considerate and wait 'til Monday. I just don't understand some people."

Brittany laughed and said, "We shouldn't be joking about it. Crystal Moon is dead. We should show more respect." She sat beside me and filled her glass. Savannah squeezed between us like the Berlin Wall, forcing us to talk around her. "Does she do this with you and Eric? Must be fun when you're trying to get cozy."

"Yup. My dog is nothing if not consistent. She's the center of the universe and makes sure everybody knows it." I pulled on her collar, but she didn't budge. "You want me to make her get down?"

"She's fine. Besides, I don't think you could if you wanted to."

"Oh, I could, but she'd only bounce back up again."

Brittany turned sideways, curled her knees under her, and rested an arm on the back of the couch. "Don't worry about it. I can see you from here."

"Works for me. And by the way, Crystal Moon isn't Crystal Moon. She's Abigail Adams, Lyle Pipkin's girlfriend."

"No kidding? Well, that changes things. What did she want? And why the charade?"

I shrugged. "I can only guess, but I think she was after the jewelry from the robbery. And I have no idea why she faked being a psychic. Maybe she thought she'd get more information if she pretended to be helping with the investigation."

"I doubt it worked, though. Olinski thought she was

a joke. Pretty sure nobody told her anything. Nothing useful, anyway."

"Angus said she spent more time with Penelope than anyone else at his place. I wonder what the connection is. Did Penelope know she was Abigail Adams?"

After a sip of wine, Brittany said, "Maybe she was just humoring her. Letting Crystal tell her fortune or something."

"Maybe." I told Brittany about the tattoos. "I think it's a huge coincidence that Penelope and Abigail had the same tattoo if they didn't know each other. And they each had it on the inside of their left ankle."

"You think Penelope's involved? If so, in what?"

"The murder? The robbery? Both?"

She shook her head. "I don't know, Jen. Penelope's been around for a long time. Years. I've never heard anyone say a bad word about her."

"True. Maybe you're right, and it's a coincidence she got the same tattoo Abigail had."

She cocked a golden eyebrow. "Since when do you believe in coincidences?"

"Since I don't have any proof otherwise, I guess." I scratched Savannah's chest absently, then stopped with my fingers entangled in her fur. "I don't have to like it, though."

Brittany swirled the wine in her glass, holding it up to the light. "Well, for once, I agree with you. I don't like this coincidence either. We should go talk to her."

"And say what? It's not like she'll volunteer that she killed Abigail."

"We can tell her we want to have a memorial and include Abigail's high school friends. She doesn't know

248

we recognized her tattoo as the same one Abigail had. Eric already told you she said she didn't know Abigail."

"But we don't know Abigail went to the same high school as Penelope."

"This might be a good way to find out. Penelope might not realize Eric told you she said she didn't know Abigail. If we approach her with the assumption she did, she might forget and confirm it for us."

"Not a bad idea, Watson. If we get her talking, she might let something else slip, too."

"Watson? Uh-uh. I'm the brains in this outfit. I should be Sherlock Holmes."

"No way, I'm the detective in the family. But we'd better fight this out in the car. I don't know what time she gets off work." I untangled myself from the dog and stood. "You drive. I've had more wine than you."

"And my car is cleaner."

I blew her a sarcastic kiss for her to interpret however she chose, grabbed a chew stick from the bag on the counter for Savannah, and we bolted out the door.

I climbed into the passenger side of Brittany's immaculate blue Chevy Cruze. She was right, of course. Her car was much cleaner than mine.

Brittany cranked up the engine. "I feel silly driving a block and a half."

"I know, but we're in a hurry. If we take the time to walk, we might miss her."

Sure enough, when we arrived, Penelope was already seated in her red 1970 Mustang convertible parked on Pine Street beside the diner. She pulled out of the spot as we approached.

I turned to Brittany. "Let's follow her. We can catch her at home, instead."

249

Brittany made a U-turn on the empty street and waited for Penelope to turn at the corner.

Penelope made a right on Main, then again on Oak, which ended on Riddleton Road. I told Brittany to continue past our apartment building, then turn on Park instead so we wouldn't be noticed. We'd have no trouble spotting Penelope's tail lights in the dark when we caught up. With no traffic, we could see a clear path for several blocks in either direction.

When we rolled up to the stop sign at Riddleton Road, though, I saw no sign of Penelope's Mustang. Brittany and I looked at each other. "Where'd she go?" I asked.

"I don't know," Brittany replied. "She's just gone."

"Okay, let's see if we can find her. Make a right and cruise slowly. She has to be parked somewhere on this street. None of the houses have garages."

I checked the vehicles on the right side of the street and Brittany the left as we rolled slowly past. No sign of Penelope. When we hit the end of the road at Walnut, we turned around and went back the other way.

"She has to be here someplace," I said.

"Unless she figured out we were following her."

"But how could she? That's why I had you turn on Park instead of Oak. As far as she knew, we went home."

Brittany stopped and put the car in park. "What if she circled back around and saw we hadn't parked in front of our building?"

"We'd have seen her. She would've had to drive right past us."

"Not if she turned right and went down Pine to the diner, then back on Main. In that case, we would've passed each other on parallel streets."

As usual, Brittany was right. "Let's stick to the plan and hope that's not what happened. Otherwise, we've lost her."

"We might've lost her anyway. Riddleton Road becomes the back road to Sutton when it crosses the town limits. Maybe she was headed there and likes to take the scenic route."

"Can't see much on that road in the dark. But you have a point. How about we go as far as the town limit and then give up if we don't see her."

"Sounds good."

She shifted back into drive, and we sped down the road at ten miles per hour. We'd already checked this section, but I kept watch anyway in case we missed something the first time through. As we approached Oak Street, a glint of light from behind the rectory of St. Mary's Catholic Church caught my eye.

I poked Brittany. "Hey, did you see that?"

"No, what?"

"I thought I saw something. Turn down Oak and stop behind the rectory."

She did as I asked, and I got out of the car. I could see nothing in the dark. The light was gone, but I crept forward for a closer look. About fifteen steps in, a vehicle appeared ghost-like before me. A few more strides, and I recognized the Mustang convertible. It had to belong to Penelope. Our headlights must've reflected off the chrome bumper.

I ran back to Brittany's Chevy. "Swing around into the parking lot. That's Penelope's car. She must be in the church."

Brittany made another U-turn and parked in front of the church. "It's a little late for confession, isn't it?"

"That depends on what she's confessing."

We bolted up the steps and entered through the door that always remained unlocked. I didn't see Penelope anywhere. I looked at Brittany. "Let's keep looking. She has to be here."

"Unless she only parked her car here and caught a ride with someone else."

"Will you please stop doing that!"

"What?"

"Finding logical reasons for illogical actions. It's getting annoying."

She laughed. "You're mad because you hate being wrong."

"That's true, but I don't think I am this time. If she was looking for a safe place to leave her car, wouldn't she have parked it in the lot under the lights? It can be stolen or vandalized where it is, and nobody would see a thing."

"You're right."

My jaw dropped. She almost never said those words to me, probably because they were almost never true. "If we weren't in such a hurry to find Penelope, I'd make you say that again so I could record it."

"Good thing we're in a hurry then." She took my arm. "Let's go."

We stepped into the aisle between the rows of pews, and I listened for any sound from above. If Penelope had gone up to the offices, she wasn't doing anything I could hear. When I scanned the altar area, I spotted a light under the kitchen door. Father Hank making a midnight snack? Possibly, but not likely since I didn't see his car parked anywhere. He must be sitting with a parishioner.

I tapped Brittany's arm, put one forefinger to my lips, and pointed toward the kitchen with the other. In the tiniest whisper I could manage, I said, "She's in there."

We crept down the aisle to the kitchen door. I laid my ear against it, heard nothing, and shook my head. I opened the door, hoping Father Hank had kept up with the WD-40 and the hinges wouldn't squeal. They didn't, and I allowed myself to breathe again. I stepped into the room. The rug had been moved, and the hatch lay open against the floor.

Penelope was in the tunnels.

CHAPTER TWENTY-FIVE

"What is that?" Brittany asked, pointing to the hole in the church kitchen floor.

Something I hadn't expected to see again so soon. "It's the hatch leading to the Underground Railroad tunnels I told you about."

Her eyebrows shot up. "You mean the ones you got lost in?"

"I found my way out, remember?"

"Obviously. But what's Penelope doing down in that place?"

I shook my head. "I don't know, but I'm about to find out."

"Are you crazy? You can't go after her. What if she's the one who killed Abigail?"

Here we go again. "No, I'm not crazy. I think she's down there looking for the jewelry from the robbery."

"What makes you think that? We still don't know she was even involved in the robbery. Or anything other than taking orders and serving meals in the diner for that matter."

"She didn't have to be involved to be aware of it. She and Abigail seemed pretty friendly with each other.

They certainly spent more time together than Abigail spent with anyone else in town. Maybe Abigail told her about it, and now that Abigail is gone, she wants the money all to herself. Or maybe they were both involved, and nobody could identify them because they never entered the store during the robbery."

Brittany crossed her arms. "Well, if that's the case, you're definitely not going down those steps. Let's call the police and let them handle it."

A knot of irritation appeared in my throat. I struggled to keep it out of my voice. She was only trying to protect me. "And tell them what? Those tunnels run under the whole town and beyond, which makes them public property. She's not even trespassing. And besides, until we actually see her down there, we don't have anything to report. What're we going to say? Penelope parked her car behind the rectory, come quick?"

"First of all, the entrance is in the church. That's not public property. And the rug didn't move itself. Neither did the door. Any reasonable person would conclude she's in the tunnels."

"The church is left open twenty-four seven for anyone to use whenever they want. Maybe somebody came in for a snack and discovered the access hatch. They didn't necessarily go down the steps, though. We have to know for sure."

She sighed out her frustration. "Fine. Then I'm going with you."

"I don't think that's a good idea. You don't know your way around like I do. You could lose your way and end up under the lake or something."

"I'll be with you." She gave me a lopsided grin. "You said yourself, you know the way out, right?"

255

She had a point, but anxiety prickled my chest. Our adventures didn't always go as planned. In fact, they almost never went as planned. "What if we're separated?"

"Honey, I'll be like gum on your shoe. You could scrape for a year and never get rid of me. Not that you'd ever try." She smiled and gestured for me to lead the way.

That much she was right about. She'd been stuck to me since kindergarten, and I'd never once tried to get rid of her. "Be careful on these steps. They're kind of steep."

I lowered myself into the void, with Brittany right behind me. When we reached the bottom, I pointed at the tiny square of light from the kitchen. "Look, a Chiclet!"

"Ha-ha. Let's move out before I change my mind."

Penelope had left the rumrunner's lights on, so I led Brittany into the first tunnel. She wrinkled her nose and waved away a cobweb. "It's musty in here. This place gives me the creeps." She shivered.

I laughed. "You think this is bad? Wait 'til the lights run out, and it's so dark you can't see the end of your nose."

"Goody. Something to look forward to." She stopped to check out the storage room. "You think we should be quiet? Penelope might hear us."

"If she's where I think she is, she's a good ways away. I'll worry about that when we shorten the distance some."

"I assume you'll tell me when we're close enough?"

"Count on it."

At the first turn, I pulled out my phone. "It's flashlight time. The lights don't go where we're going."

"Uh-oh. I left my phone in the car."

"No problem. One should be fine." I checked my phone battery. Three-quarters full. "I'm good for a few hours, at least."

Brittany shuddered. "I hope we're not down here that long. I'm feeling a little claustrophobic, which is strange because I don't have claustrophobia."

"This place'll give it to you, that's for sure. Just follow me. You'll be fine."

"I'll take your word for it."

I made the left into the crossover tunnel. The light from my phone penetrated about ten feet of the darkness ahead of us until it was swallowed up as if we were walking into the black hole in the center of our galaxy. At least I knew we'd be coming out the other side.

We shuffled over the packed dirt floor beneath our feet for ten minutes before Brittany asked, "How long is this tunnel? It feels like we've been walking for hours."

"Are you kidding? This is the short one. Wait'll we hit the next one. You'll think time has stopped altogether." I took a few more steps, then looked back at Brittany. "When did you become so whiny, anyway? You don't usually complain about anything."

"There's something about this place. It's like I can feel the spirits of all the people who passed through before us."

To lighten the mood, I waved my hands and said, "Ooh. Spooky!"

She slapped my arm. "Cut it out! You're such a pain in the butt."

"Maybe, but I'm a lovable pain in the butt."

"Yeah, keep telling yourself that. Can we just get this over with, please?"

257

A few minutes later, we reached the end of the tunnel, where we had to make our final left. I turned to Brittany and said, "Okay, this is where we need to be quiet. She's at the end of this tunnel, and our voices may carry. I don't want her to know we're coming."

Brittany nodded, her eyes wide, enlarged pupils so black the irises were nearly invisible.

I took her hand and whispered, "Relax. You have nothing to be afraid of. No boogeyman down here."

She cupped her hand around her mouth and leaned close to my ear. "You mean besides Penelope?"

I smiled and shot her an eye roll she couldn't possibly see in the dark. We plodded ahead until the ground rose beneath our feet. We'd entered the danger zone. The alcove where I found Abigail was just ahead, and a couple hundred feet past that, we'd find Penelope digging for buried treasure. Although, we'd probably hear her before getting that far.

Brittany tightened her grip on my hand as if sensing something was about to change. Perhaps *she* should've pretended to be a psychic instead of Abigail Adams. She might not've completely been acting. How had I never noticed her sensitivity before? Probably too stuck in my own head. I'd been a selfish friend most of our lives, taking much more than I ever gave. I needed to change that, and would, but I had more important things to worry about right now. Like confronting Penelope and surviving it without anything happening to me or Brittany.

The ground leveled out as we reached the alcove. I looked ahead, and a light appeared at the end of the tunnel. Literally. From the look of it, Penelope had brought a lantern with her. I turned off my flashlight and pulled Brittany into the recess. "We're in the dark from here on out," I whispered. "We can't risk Penelope seeing our light."

"Jen, I'm having a bad feeling about this."

I couldn't blame her. The moment I turned out the light, the darkness closed on us as if it'd been waiting for the opportunity. The air seemed thicker and heavier, and my lungs strained to pull in enough to keep me alive. I shook the thought out of my head. I was being ridiculous. Nothing had changed other than I'd turned the light out.

"It's all right, Britt. It's just our minds playing tricks on us."

"Maybe, but what are we trying to accomplish here? So, we find Penelope hunting for the jewelry. What then?"

A chill passed over me, and I shivered. "Then we go to the police."

"That's it? No confrontation that leads to one of us getting killed?"

I chuckled. "No, of course not. I have to confirm my suspicions before calling it in. Otherwise, Havermayer will write it off as my writer's imagination. You know how she is."

"Okay, so we go down there, verify she's digging around for the hidden jewelry, then slip away into the darkness. That's what you're saying, right?"

"That's what I'm saying." Unfortunately, my words hardly ever manifested into reality.

"Great, but how do we prove what she's digging for?"

"That's not our problem. Just the fact that she's down here will make her a person of interest in Abigail's murder."

Brittany took a deep breath. "All right. Let's go."

I took her hand and inched into the passageway. As I'd warned earlier, we could see only the tiny point of light thrown off by Penelope's lamp. I focused on it and trailed one hand along the wall to my right. At some point, rocks and debris littered the path, which would make our journey treacherous without light to guide us, but I hoped we'd be able to catch Penelope in action before we reached that place.

We covered half the distance in about fifteen agonizing minutes. Sweat covered me like a second skin, and my heart pounded. Brittany's hand was slick in mine, but I couldn't tell if the accumulated perspiration was my own, hers, or a combination of both. I suspected both. The light from Penelope's lamp had grown from a pinprick to the size of a watermelon. Still not enough to see by at this distance. We crept into the darkness, following the digging sounds growing louder with each step.

Around twenty-five feet from the end, I saw Penelope wearing jeans and a sweatshirt she must've changed into between the diner and here, standing beside the lantern, leaning on a shovel. Streaks of dirt covered her cheeks and forehead, where she'd wiped the sweat away. Loose soil covered the mound left by the original wall collapse, and a two-foot opening had appeared at the base of the wall at the end of the tunnel. We'd seen what we needed.

I grabbed Brittany's arm and turned her back toward the way we came. Our feet tangled in the dark, and we went down. A grunt followed by a rush of air escaped me when my ribs hit the ground, and Brittany landed on top of me, planting an elbow in my gut. Pain flashed through my midsection.

"Who's there?" Penelope called, and the light bounced in our direction, her feet crunching on loose dirt and rocks. Another minute and we'd be in full view.

As we no longer had any reason to maintain our silence, I squeezed out from under Brittany, who hadn't moved yet. "Are you all right, Britt?"

She rolled over onto her back. "I'm fine. Just got the wind knocked out of me."

I guarded my aching ribcage with my arm. "I know what you mean. Anything else? Did you hit your head?"

"Nope. You made a nice, cushy crash mat."

"Glad I could help," I said, smiling, though I knew it wouldn't be visible in the black. "I live to serve." Now I just had to make sure we stayed alive. Penelope might've murdered Abigail. She likely wouldn't hesitate to do the same to us if we got in her way.

"That'll be the day." Brittany sat up as Penelope reached us with the light.

"What are you two doing here?" she asked, her blue eyes snapping in the lantern's glow.

Using Brittany's shoulder for support, I pushed myself upright and then helped her. "Oh, nothing much. Just out for an after-dinner stroll."

Penelope stepped forward, brandishing the shovel. "Knock it off. Why are you here?"

I opened my mouth, but Brittany spoke first. "We noticed your car and came in to make sure you were all right."

Great save, Britt!

"Why wouldn't I be?"

"No reason," I said. "We wanted to make sure, that's all. Now we're sure, and we'll take off. I'm sorry if we disturbed you."

261

"What're you doing anyway?" Brittany asked.

"That's none of your concern, and you two aren't going anywhere." Penelope grabbed Brittany's arm and pulled her toward the end of the tunnel.

Oh, crap! I leaped forward to squeeze between them, but Penelope swung the shovel at my head. I ducked, tripped over Brittany's feet, and brought us all down in a heap with Brittany on top.

The electric lantern skittered away. I reached for the shovel. Penelope struggled, but Brittany had her pinned. I squirmed out from the bottom of the pile and ripped the weapon from Penelope's hand, holding it poised over her head while Brittany stood. Penelope rolled over onto her back, covering her face with her hands.

Brittany retrieved the lantern. "What are we going to do with her?" she asked.

"We're going to take her back and turn her in to the police."

"For what? I didn't do anything wrong," Penelope said.

I held up the shovel. "You attacked us with this. Last I heard, that counted as assault with a deadly weapon."

"I never touched you."

"True. We'll make it attempted assault, then. And attempted kidnapping since you tried to keep us here against our wills. Either way, we're taking you to the police. We'll let them sort it out."

I gestured for Brittany to take the lead with the lantern, and we walked single file through the tunnel, with Penelope in the middle and me bringing up the rear, shovel at the ready.

CHAPTER TWENTY-SIX

I called Eric as soon as I had bars and told him to meet us in the kitchen. No way I'd try to control Penelope in the back seat while Brittany drove us to the police station. Her fury radiated off her like pavement on a hot summer day when we trapped her on the steps right below the kitchen. I didn't trust her enough to let her loose in the church. This way, if she tried anything, she risked falling onto the hard-packed dirt floor below.

Within minutes of our arrival at the top of the steps, Eric's face appeared in the opening on the floor. "Whatcha doin'?" he asked, grinning.

"Oh, just hanging around, enjoying the view," Brittany replied, raising a hand for him to help her up.

When Brittany cleared the hatch, Eric called down to me. "Okay, let her go."

I released my grip on Penelope's pant leg, but she refused to move.

Eric laughed and shook his head. "You might as well come on up. There's nowhere for you to go."

Penelope wrapped her arms around the staircase. "I'm being held against my will. You need to arrest these two for kidnapping."

"We'll sort it all out when you come out of there."

"You'll arrest them?"

"If it's warranted, absolutely. You have my word."

What? Would Eric really arrest me for helping him out? Nah, that's crazy. I peeked around Penelope and caught his serious expression. Maybe not so crazy.

After a moment's thought, Penelope conceded and climbed out the hatch.

Eric handcuffed her. "Penelope Ulrich, you're being detained for questioning."

"About what?"

"The murder of Abigail Adams, also known as Crystal Moon."

Penelope pressed her lips together. "I want a lawyer."

"You're not under arrest, but you can have one if you insist. It'll only make you look guilty of something, though. I'd rather we just talk for a while and hash some things out. Give you a chance to tell your side of the story. However, you can call a lawyer from the station if you'd like."

Eric handed her off to Zach Vick, who was waiting outside the door for transport back to RPD. We followed them through the church and watched as he loaded her into the back of his patrol car. I'd half expected her to try to escape and felt a twinge of disappointment when she didn't. I'd never seen Eric chase a suspect; it would've been fun to watch.

When Zach drove off, we gathered at Eric's official vehicle: a Chevy Suburban just like Havermayer's. He leaned against the driver's door and crossed his arms. "What's this all about?"

I told him how we'd followed Penelope to the church and what we'd discovered her doing in the tunnel. Then

I explained how I believed she fit into the situation I'd been investigating. How she might've been involved in the jewelry store robbery along with Abigail and killed her to have the spoils all to herself.

He listened intently and, when I finished, asked, "What makes you think she was one of the thieves?"

"How else would she have known the jewelry was hidden in the tunnel?"

He pursed his lips. "That's it? That's all you got?"

My cheeks burned. It wasn't much to go on. "What about how she reacted when we caught her digging? She threatened us with a shovel and tried to hold us so we couldn't tell anyone what we'd seen."

He rested one elbow on the other forearm and stroked his chin. "We can detain her on that, I suppose. But she'll probably claim you snuck up and scared her." He stood and opened the car door. "Let's go talk to her and hear what she has to say."

Brittany linked her arm through mine. "We'll meet you at the station." We walked to Brittany's car and climbed in.

As she started the Cruze, she said, "Eric doesn't seem convinced Penelope's done anything wrong."

"Honestly, neither am I. I've found no connection between her and the robbery, but my gut tells me there has to be one."

She drove us down Oak and made the left on Main toward the police department. "I hope you're right, and they find it before they have to release her. Otherwise, our visits to the diner will be pretty awkward from now on."

"No kidding. I might even have to learn how to cook."

Brittany laughed and glanced at me. "Let's not go getting all crazy, now." She parked in front of the bookstore, and we climbed the steps into the station. "If anyone's going to learn how to cook in your family, it'll be Eric, I'm sure."

When we entered, I spotted Eric chatting with the duty sergeant at his desk. I waved, and he came over.

"What's going on?" I asked.

"She's refusing to volunteer her fingerprints, so we're being creative."

Brittany smiled. "Meaning?"

"I gave her a warm bottle of water and left her sitting in the interview room with the thermostat turned up. With luck, that'll give us both fingerprints and DNA."

A guffaw escaped before I could stop it. "That's brilliant! You think she'll fall for it?"

"She's not exactly a career criminal, so I suspect she will. Besides, she was digging in hard-packed dirt when you found her. That's thirsty work. I imagine that bottle will be empty by the time I go in to speak with her, and she'll be asking for another."

"What about the lawyer?"

"If she mentions it again, I'll let her make the call. But I think she wanted a public defender, who probably wouldn't be here before morning at the earliest. They usually don't even meet their clients until the arraignment. Most people break down and talk instead when they hear that. Especially when they think there might be a deal to be had."

I hoped he turned out to be correct. If my theory held, one accidental word from Penelope could crack two cases, possibly even three. I mentally crossed my fingers.

He glanced at his watch. "She should be ready for more water by now, so I'm going to head on in. You two should go home. I'll call you in the morning."

I shook my head. "I'd rather wait and see what she says. I've got a lot riding on this, and so does Jaylon Barnes."

"Me, too," Brittany said. "I want to see how this plays out."

Eric considered it for a minute. "This might take a while, but if you insist, you can wait in the break room. There's coffee, but I can't guarantee how long it's been cooking."

Brittany opened the break room door. "No problem. We'll make a fresh pot."

While Brittany made the coffee, I rifled through the refrigerator, searching for something with Eric's name on it. No luck. We mostly ate out, and his man-sized appetite didn't lead to a lot of leftovers. It was worth a shot, though.

"If you're hungry, we can order a pizza or something." Brittany filled the pot at the sink.

"Nah, then one of us would have to go pick it up. I'm not really hungry, just scavenging because I'm stressed."

She poured the water into the coffeemaker and turned it on. "Stress eating isn't healthy for you. That's how people get fat."

"Chocolate chip muffins are how I get fat. And I eat those whether I'm stressed or not."

"I don't blame you. Bob makes a mean muffin."

Bob Underwood had learned to bake from his grandmother, spending much of his free time as a boy in her kitchen. With financial help from her and a box of old family recipes, he launched Bob's Bakery right after high school graduation.

When Ravenous Readers opened, he provided the baked goods for the store to sell, even though it could've cut into his business, in the hope it would expand his customer base. Good thing I didn't work at the bakery instead of the bookstore, though. I'd be big as a house by now.

Brittany set a cup of coffee on the table and sat across from me. "How are things going with you and Eric? Will I be hearing wedding bells anytime soon?"

I almost spit a mouthful of coffee back into my cup. Why did she have to bring that subject up? I'd done an excellent job keeping Olinski's secret to this point but didn't know how much longer I could hold out. We'd told each other everything all our lives. Did she suspect me of keeping secrets and brought up the subject of marriage to draw me out? I sealed my lips.

"Hey! Earth to Jen. Where'd you go?"

"Nowhere. I'm right here. What was the question?"

"Is there going to be a wedding soon?"

Maybe, but it won't be mine. "We haven't even talked about it. Neither one of us is ready for that kind of commitment."

"Neither one of you or just you? I'm sure I've heard him mention it once or twice."

Sometimes, I found it irritating how well she knew me. She never let me get away with anything. "Fine. It's me. Whenever I hear the word 'marriage,' it sends me into a panic. My chest tightens up. I can't breathe. It feels like I'm gonna die. There, you happy now?"

"No, but I want you to be. Eric is perfect for you. He's the one, even if you're not ready to see it. And at this rate, you may never be ready."

268

"Says you. What about you and Olinski? When are you going to take the plunge?"

Careful, Jen. Don't say anything stupid.

Brittany gave me a coy smile and twirled blond hair around her finger. "He hasn't proposed. Yet."

Okay, what was happening here? Did she know, or was she fishing for information? I had to play it cool. "Do you think he's going to?"

"I don't know, but he's been secretive lately. Something's going on he won't tell me about." She sipped her coffee. "Of course, it might be wishful thinking on my part."

"You could always propose to him."

"I never thought about that. I guess I've always pictured a guy down on one knee, singing my praises and telling me how much he loves me before popping the question."

"Okay, that explains it. He's probably still trying to come up with some praises to sing."

She balled up a napkin and threw it at me. "I thought you were my friend."

"You know I am. I'm only teasing. He's probably trying to narrow it down to a few so it doesn't take all night for you to answer."

"Yeah, that's it. You figured it out."

"Don't fret. He'll propose when the time is right. He's crazy about you."

"I feel the same way about him. Does it still bother you?"

I had my chance to marry Olinski after graduation. But I turned him down and never had a single regret. I'd made the right decision. "No, not at all. He didn't look at me the way he looks at you. We were never right for each other the way the two of you are. Deep down, I think we both knew that. It just took him a little longer to see it."

"Good, because if we ever do have a wedding, I want you to be my maid of honor."

"I'll be happy to, but I get to pick out the dress." Did I just volunteer to wear a dress? No question, I loved my best friend if I'd do *that* for her.

"Deal."

The door to the break room opened, and Eric strode in. He poured a cup of coffee and joined us at the table. "You seem awfully serious. What have you been talking about?"

Brittany turned red, and from the skyrocketing heat in my face, I suspected I had too. "Nothing. Just girl stuff. You wouldn't be interested."

His glance ping-ponged between us as he sipped from his cup. "I'll take your word for it. I have something *you* might be interested in, though."

"What's that?"

"Penelope fell for it. She's still not talking, but we got her fingerprints. They're not in the system, but we're comparing them to the ones we pulled off the hammer now."

"You think they'll match?"

He shrugged. "Could be. I never got to tell you we matched Abigail Adams's fingerprints to one we collected off the bookstore doorknob. Was she ever in the store that you know of?"

"Not that I remember. I spoke with her outside after the store was ransacked, but I don't think she ever came in."

"She might be the one who trashed the place, then."

270

"I thought we decided whoever did it had to be wearing gloves?"

"Maybe she couldn't manipulate the lock picks with gloves on. Either way, we got something, at least."

Before I could respond, the door opened again. Havermayer poked her head in and nodded at Eric.

A broad smile covered his face. "We got a match. Penelope handled the hammer that killed Abigail. I think we have our killer."

CHAPTER TWENTY-SEVEN

My third cup of coffee cooled beside me on my desk in the home office I called the living room as I struggled to get Daniel Davenport out of the tunnel so he could call for help. Luckily, I had my own experiences to guide me, but keeping my focus turned out to be a more significant challenge. Pictures from last night flashed through my mind, pushing the words away.

Penelope had murdered Abigail Adams. Why? And how did they even know each other? Did Abigail tell Penelope about the hidden jewelry, or were they both part of the robbery? Actually, I had no proof the jewelry was what they were looking for. It made sense, however. What else could be hidden in those tunnels worth killing over?

Perhaps, when confronted by the fingerprint evidence, Penelope had confessed. Eric might already have the answers to all my questions. I picked up my phone and called him. He answered on the first ring.

"Good morning! I didn't expect you to be up so early today."

"It's ten o'clock. That's not early."

"It is when you didn't leave the station until almost two. And it's Sunday. The perfect day to sleep in."

I explained how I'd woken up thinking about the Penelope situation and couldn't go back to sleep. I didn't tell him about the nightmares featuring her and Abigail and the skeleton dancing around like kindergarteners in a bad Halloween recital. If I'd been completely honest, I'd have mentioned the cold sweat drenching me and the soaked sheets, too. No need to worry him about that.

Instead, I asked him about his interview with Penelope. "How did Penelope react when you confronted her with the fingerprint evidence?"

"She shut down and demanded a lawyer, so we arrested her. Refused to tell us anything after that. Guess she'll get her public defender after all."

"Too bad. I was hoping she'd tell you something about why she was in the tunnel to begin with. I've been assuming it was to hunt for the hidden jewelry, but I'd love to have some confirmation to back up my theories."

"Sorry, I can't help with that. I can tell you I haven't been able to find anything on her from before she moved to Riddleton. It's like she was born on that day."

Odd. I didn't know exactly how old she was, but she had to be in her twenties. If I had to guess, I'd say a few years younger than me, at most. "Huh. Maybe she was. Penelope Ulrich is obviously a fake name. Nobody that young could live completely off the grid for their entire lives. Where's her high school Facebook page?"

"Good question. We have to figure out who she really is first. I might have to go back to the missing persons reports."

Not necessarily. I knew another person who'd disappeared shortly after Ewon and Lyle did. Someone else who might've been involved in the robbery.

Ewon's girlfriend, Eliza Naismith.

"Didn't you tell me Penelope had been here around five years?"

"Something like that, yes."

"Ewon's girlfriend disappeared right after Jaylon's trial. Could Penelope Ulrich be Eliza Naismith?"

Silence.

"Eric?"

"I was thinking. It's possible, but how would we prove it? Eliza was never fingerprinted that we know of."

"I think I know a way. Can you send me a copy of Penelope's mug shot?"

"Sure, but what would that accomplish?"

"There's no way Ewon's parents didn't meet his live-in girlfriend at least once. One of them might recognize her from the picture." But would they speak with me long enough to show it to them? That was the million-dollar question. I'd have to try Regina first.

"You should let us handle it, Jen. I'll interview his parents."

"But you need to go through the missing persons reports. What if I'm wrong and it's not her? This way, we're covering everything at once. I'm only showing them a picture. How much trouble can I possibly get into?"

"You?"

His ensuing laughter was all the answer I needed.

A few minutes after we completed the call, my phone dinged with his text. Penelope's photo. Dirt and fatigue covered her face, but that shouldn't interfere with an identification. For the first time since I heard Jaylon's story, I felt I had a real chance to unravel this complicated knot. And maybe solve two more cases in the process.

Savannah lifted her head off the couch and watched with interest when I jumped up to take a shower. As I massaged shampoo into my scalp, I tried to remember any religious memorabilia in Regina's house. I'd never make it before she had to leave for church, and if she was a pious worshiper who participated in all the church activities, I might not have the opportunity to see her all day.

Nothing came to mind, however. I'd spent most of my time in the kitchen but passed through the living room several times, spotting nothing with a religious theme. Not that I'd been looking for anything in particular. Still, not having a solid foundation in any religion tended to make me notice things like that.

After soaping, rinsing, and drying, I collected clean jeans and a Gamecocks sweatshirt from the bedroom. Savannah had moved to the bed while I showered as if she knew that would be where I landed next. My little girl was no dummy. In her mind, if she constantly reminded me she was there as I prepared to go, I wouldn't leave her behind. Unfortunately, her reasoning didn't account for weather conditions or places she wasn't welcome. I suspected Regina's house would be one of those places.

My German shepherd pranced around the living room carrying her leash while I tied my Nikes, forcing me to address the situation. "I'm sorry, kid. You can't go this time. You'd have to wait in the car, and you know how much you hate that."

She dropped the leash at my feet and sat, ears pricked and the end of her tail flipping back and forth like a windshield wiper in a thunderstorm.

"I'll take you for a walk. That's the best I can do."

Savannah grabbed her leash and ran to the door. I took her out, and she dawdled all the way around the block as if she'd understood every word I'd said earlier and thought she could wear me down. Nope, not this time.

We finally made it back to the apartment, and I tossed her a chew stick, gathered my necessities, and trudged down the steps, struggling with warring emotions, as usual. Half of me was excited at the prospect of finding Penelope's true identity. The other half dreaded the possibility of another confrontation with a member of the Barnes family. However, I had to know the truth, so my choice was clear.

I started up my Dodge and drove to Regina's house. When I approached the two-story farmhouse, a black SUV stopped at the end of Ida's driveway, waiting to turn onto the road. It was a Chevy, but I couldn't tell what model. However, Detective Havermayer sat behind the wheel, frowning at me as I passed, so it had to be a Suburban like Eric's. She'd followed up on the tip I'd given him. I waved, but her facial expression remained frozen in her usual scowl. I could only hope she was angry that I'd turned up again, not upset about the information Ida had given her.

Either way, I had a mission of my own to accomplish. I turned down Regina's drive and was pleased to see her Nissan in the carport. She came out the front door before I reached the house and stood with her arms crossed, watching me. Her facial expression, though somewhat indecipherable, clearly wasn't joy.

I cut the engine and pulled Penelope's picture up on my phone to have it handy if she tried to throw me out. I climbed out of the car and shut the door, leaving it unlocked for a quick getaway. At least she didn't have a half-dozen dogs to sic on me.

"Ricky told me not to talk to you anymore."

"Do you always do everything your ex-husband tells you?"

Confusion flashed across her face, quickly changing to determination. "I do when there's a threat to my family."

"I'm no threat to your family. In fact, I'm trying to give you your family back. Can't you see that?"

"Just go away."

"Okay. Let me show you a picture, and I'll leave." She said nothing, so I took a chance and stepped closer, holding up my phone. "Do you know who this woman is?"

She looked, then looked away.

"Please, Regina. This is very important. Have you seen this woman before?"

Her face crumpled into despair. "That looks like Ewon's girlfriend. Eliza, only her hair was blond, not red like this lady's. Now, please leave me alone." She went back into the house and slammed the door.

Blond like Penelope's roots? I kept my expression neutral as I turned and walked back to the car. I wanted to jump up and down, but not if she would believe her misery made me happy. Sitting in the driver's seat, I gripped the steering wheel and allowed the satisfaction of knowing I'd finally made the connection between the jewelry store robbery and Ewon's disappearance bring a smile to my face.

277

When the living room curtain moved, I turned the car around and headed back down the driveway. I sat at the end, unsure what to do next. Should I go to Sutton and show the photo to Ricky to make sure I had the right person, or go home? Right to Sutton, left to Riddleton. Regina seemed certain that Penelope was Eliza. Showing up at Ricky's for a second opinion would only risk stirring up trouble. And Ricky was much more volatile than Regina.

It'd been a week since I'd seen Jaylon. Perhaps I should stop by the jail and give him an update. I hesitated to get his hopes up prematurely, but he deserved to know I'd been making progress. And I'd yet to ask him about the walkie-talkie watch in Ricky's cigar box under the couch. Besides, he might have an idea about who the third man might be. Decision made, I turned right toward Sutton.

I spent the entire drive formulating the words I'd say to Jaylon when I got there. By the time I pulled into the parking lot, I thought I had it down. I'd be positive but not give away too much. If I told him about Ida and the prosecutor refused to act on the new evidence, Jaylon would be devastated. In his current condition, staying upbeat and hopeful might be the only thing keeping him alive.

Plodding up to the brick building, I suddenly regretted my decision to visit Jaylon. What if I said too much or not enough? But as it stood, he might believe I'd abandoned him. The despair that came along with that might be worse than false hope. I had to go inside.

On the other side of the double doors, I unloaded my pockets into the deputy's bowl and stepped through the scanner. After receiving the all-clear and retrieving my belongings, I went straight to the door at the end of the lobby, where I knew two deputies waited for me to turn my things over again and pat me down. Through the doorway into the dining hall or whatever the room was, I took a seat near the front and waited for them to bring Jaylon out.

When his escort guided him into the room, I struggled to mask the shock and horror determined to cover my face. His short-sleeved orange jumpsuit hung on his skeletal frame like living room drapes on a bathroom window. When he smiled, the skin stretched so tight I thought sure it would split.

He eased into the chair, adjusting himself for comfort. "I was hoping it was you," he said, the simple act of talking seeming painful. "I thought maybe you changed your mind about helping me."

"No, not at all. I didn't see any point in bothering you when I had nothing to report."

"You're not bothering me. You're the only visitor I've had."

How could his parents not visit? "I'm sorry to hear that. I don't have much to tell you at this point, but I have been working on it. Things are looking a little better, though. Please don't get your hopes up until I have something more concrete to share with you."

"Thank you, but can you tell me anything at all? I need to know."

Jaylon's pleading brown eyes drilled into my heart. I had to reveal something. Perhaps not knowing might be worse than false hope after all. "All I'll say is there may be a witness who saw Ewon leave the house alive that afternoon. No guarantee it means much, though. Without corroboration or some other evidence, the prosecutor might not do anything about it." I reached for his cool, dry hand. "I promise we're working hard to find what we need to get you out. That's why I'm here. I need to ask you some questions."

His chest rose and fell rapidly, and he squeezed his fingers into fists. "Okay, shoot."

"There was a robbery in Blackburn the night Ewon disappeared. The police believe Ewon and his friend Lyle were involved. A third man—quiet with a stocky build—was also involved. Do you have any idea who that man might be? Your father mentioned a guy named Josh they were friends with."

"I never met this guy Josh, so I have no idea." He absently scratched a dry patch on his forearm. "Ewon didn't have too many other friends that I remember. The only person I can think of who fits that description is my father. And he wouldn't rob anybody. Why would he?"

My heart hammered in my ears, trying to drown out my thoughts. Interesting that Regina Barnes also seemed to jump to the conclusion that Ricky might be the third man. Had I missed something? "Ewon asked him for money, but he didn't have any because he was paying your tuition. Could Ewon have pressured him into it?"

"You don't know my father. Nobody pressures him into doing anything he doesn't want to do. If anything, I'd say it was the other way around."

I sat back in my chair. "You're saying your father made Ewon do it?"

He shook his head. "No, I'm saying my father couldn't be involved. Certainly not the way you're describing it."

Hoping for his sake he was right, I said, "Okay, well,

let me ask you this. Did you ever have a walkie-talkie watch when you were a kid?"

"A what?" His eyes widened. "Oh yeah, me and Ewon both had one of those. Mine broke, and I had to throw it away."

"You're sure you threw it away? You couldn't have saved it as a souvenir or something?"

"No, I remember throwing it in the trash and asking my mom for a new one. She said we couldn't afford it, and I should've taken better care of the one I had to begin with."

I reached for my phone to show him Penelope's picture, then remembered the deputy had confiscated it. "Jaylon, can you describe Ewon's girlfriend for me?"

"Not really. It was a long time ago, and I only met her once or twice."

"Anything at all you can remember might help."

"All that comes to mind is she had long, blond hair she used to twirl around her finger whenever she was upset." He chuckled. "She and Ewon fought one time, and I thought her hair was going to break off in her hand, she twisted it so tight."

Just like Penelope did when I commented about wanting to get to know her better.

CHAPTER TWENTY-EIGHT

When I finished recounting my visit with Jaylon to Eric, he remained silent momentarily, then said, "What you're telling me is half the Barnes family might've been involved in a jewelry store robbery in Blackburn?"

An instant of doubt crept in, but I banished it to obscurity where it belonged. "When you put it like that, it does seem a little out there. But facts don't lie, unlike Ricky. He lied about the watch and ring I found in his hidden cigar box. And I find it very hard to believe the Blackburn police never interviewed him when they decided Ewon was involved in the robbery, so I'm pretty sure he lied about that, too."

He sighed into the phone. "People lie for all sorts of reasons, Jen. Most of them aren't killers or jewel thieves. Usually, they lie about one thing because they're hiding something else."

"True, but if he's not involved, we're talking about a heckuva lot of coincidences. And you know how I feel about coincidences."

"Everyone knows how you feel about coincidences."

"And I'm usually right. There's no such thing as a coincidence when it comes to murder. I think you should be looking at Ricky Barnes for Ewon's murder and the robbery."

"The trouble with that is, we still don't know for a fact Ewon is dead, and the robbery's not in our jurisdiction. What do you expect me to do?"

A touch of irritation danced through my skull. I waited for it to dissipate before speaking. "Eric, they convicted Jaylon on less evidence than we have here. Nobody knew if Ewon was dead or alive back then, and it didn't matter. All I'm asking is that you look into the possibility."

"I'll discuss it with Havermayer and Olinski. That's the best I can do."

I'd have to take it. "Speaking of Havermayer, what did Ida tell her?"

"The witness? Basically, the same thing she told you."

"And?"

"And, what?"

I tightened my grip on the steering wheel. He could be so dense sometimes. Or, more likely, I unreasonably expected him to read my mind. *I* barely understood my mind. "And what's Havermayer going to do about it?"

"She called the prosecutor, and he wasn't thrilled about her bothering him on a Sunday. He's not buying it. He thinks the lady's making it up for some reason, like someone's paying her to say these things so Jaylon can get his transplant."

"That's ridiculous."

He chuckled. "Is it? How would you know? It's not like she'd tell you if someone bribed her to lie."

He was right. I couldn't know for sure if Ida told the truth, but she struck me as someone who'd go straight to the police if someone tried to bribe her to lie. "I don't know, except she said she never told anyone what she'd seen before because nobody ever asked her, and I believe her. Detective Conway doesn't remember interviewing her and left no notes on it in the case file. Plus, I went to her, she didn't come to you. If they were paying her to lie, wouldn't she have been more proactive?"

"I don't know what to tell you, Jen. It's out of my hands."

"I'm sorry. I don't blame you. I'm frustrated, that's all."

"I know. How about we talk over lunch?"

That sounded wonderful, but I was running out of time to help Jaylon. "There's someone else I need to talk to. How about dinner instead?"

"Dinner it is. I'll call you later."

When the call ended, I pressed the icon next to Detective Conway's name.

He picked up. "Who is this?"

"It's Jen Dawson, Detective. I have a few questions for you if you have a minute."

"Okay, what's up?"

I wiped my sweaty palms on my pants legs, one at a time. "If you'd known someone had seen Ewon alive that afternoon after the argument with his brother, would you still have arrested Jaylon for his murder?"

He hesitated so long I checked to see if the call had dropped.

Eventually, he said, "No, probably not. We would most likely have turned the case over to missing persons."

"Then, why won't the prosecutor let him go? He thinks Ida is lying."

"It's hard to say. Once you have a conviction, it's a lot more difficult to overturn. Particularly if you don't want to. This case gave his career a huge boost."

I struggled to control my anger. Jaylon would die in jail so that guy could run for office someday. I told Conway what I'd learned and my belief that Ewon died because of the robbery, as Abigail Adams did. "I have bits and pieces to back me up, but not enough to convince anyone with the power to do something about it."

"All right, well, let me ask you this . . . Do you believe Ricky Barnes murdered Ewon?"

Great question. Did I? Maybe. "I'm not convinced he did it himself, but my gut is adamant that he had something to do with it or knows who did."

"Then let's go see him together. If I'm with you, he won't make any threats."

Maybe not, but that wouldn't stop him from coming after me later. But if I found the missing piece I needed, he'd go to jail. He'd never be able to bother me again, which made him a lot more dangerous right now. "Okay. Let's give it a try. Besides, you're a professional. You might notice something I missed."

He chuckled. "Somehow, I doubt that. Meet me at the coffee shop in Sutton at three. Does that work for you?"

I glanced at the clock. A little after one. I was almost to Riddleton, so that would give me time to eat something and walk Savannah before heading back out again. "That works. I'll see you at three."

Customers occupied every seat in the Dandy Diner when I stopped to order lunch to take home. Angus scrambled to keep up with the order-taking while

Marcus handled the register and Jacob manned the grill. I knew better than to offer assistance, given my last disastrous attempt to help out my friend. The floor still seemed sticky in spots from all the drinks I spilled, though it couldn't possibly be. Angus kept a spotless place.

"Hey, Jen," Marcus said between customers. "Were you looking for a table? We should have one available in a few minutes."

"No, I was going to get something to go, but you look awfully busy."

"Not having Penelope is hurting us. Now I know how Angus felt when it was me in jail."

A couple of months ago, Marcus had been arrested for a murder he didn't commit. It was during his stay in the Sutton County Detention Center he met Jaylon. "Maybe, but at least you weren't guilty. I'm positive Penelope can't say the same."

A strange look flitted across his face, like a mix of anger and confusion.

"Are you all right?"

He smiled. "Yeah, just remembering things I'd be better off forgetting." He grabbed an order pad. "What did you want for lunch?"

I returned his grin. "You have to ask?"

"Nope. Coming right up. It'll be about fifteen minutes."

"Thanks."

The hum of chattering voices weaved around the one in my head, reviewing every bit of information I had on Ewon's disappearance and the robbery. I knew, somehow, Ricky Barnes was the key to solving both cases, but had no idea how. Had he murdered his son?

286

Helped him run away? If so, why did he let Jaylon be convicted? And what about the jewelry store robbery? Was he the mastermind, a participant, or did he have no role at all?

I sipped on my drink and watched Jacob expertly flip burgers and lay out bacon as if he'd been a grill cook all his life rather than only a few weeks. Some people had a knack for those kinds of activities. I'd never be one of them. Cooking was second only to performing my own appendectomy on my list of least favorite things to do. And it was almost a tie. I might enjoy the process more if the results were any good, but nothing edible ever came of my efforts.

Marcus interrupted my musings by setting a paper bag on the counter next to me. "Did you need anything else? Dessert maybe? Angus baked a fresh batch of chocolate chip cookies this morning."

Tempting as that sounded, my stomach rejected the offer. I'd be lucky to finish what I'd already ordered, given the queasiness that increased with every minute the hands on the clock moved closer to three. "No, thanks. I'm not very hungry." I handed him a twenty-dollar bill.

Marcus returned my change. "Are you all right? You've never turned down fresh cookies before. You must be getting sick."

"No," I said with a laugh. "I have an important meeting this afternoon, and my stomach's letting me know how it feels about it. It could be good for Jaylon, though, so keep your lucky charm handy."

"I will."

I arrived home a few minutes later, and Savannah greeted my lunch enthusiastically. Her only acknowledgment of

287

my presence came when she poked my hand with her nose to encourage me to give her the bag. I might as well have since I only ate a bite of burger and a few fries before my stomach threatened to send it back. She ended up with it anyway.

When she'd licked the wrapper clean and gulped down half a bowl of water, I took her for a walk around the block. Marshmallow clouds dotted the pale-blue winter sky, and a chill permeated the air as the sun began sinking toward the horizon. Another winter day gone. Soon, it would be spring.

Savannah sniffed her way to the church, then stopped with her hackles up and her nose in the air as if she knew what'd happened there last night. She couldn't possibly, of course, but her behavior was strange just the same. I coaxed her on, unwilling to relive the experience myself. I'd once found those tunnels fascinating enough to make them the backdrop of my novel, but now I decided that I'd done all the research I needed. I'd wander back down there again someday to explore the avenues I hadn't yet taken, but not anytime soon.

By the time we returned home, I needed to leave if I was to make it to Sutton on time. Savannah hung her head when she saw me reaching for the bag of chew sticks, knowing that the only time those came out was when she was being left behind. I scratched her neck, kissed her between the eyes, and promised I'd make it up to her when this was all over.

The main road to Sutton seemed more congested than the back road I'd taken this morning, and the trip took about ten minutes longer. I entered the coffee shop at five minutes to three and looked around. No sign of

Conway, so I ventured up to the counter and ordered a double espresso. I suspected my stomach might balk, but my brain needed the boost.

I sat at a window table and watched more traffic go by in ten minutes than passed through Riddleton in a whole day, which was why I lived in Riddleton instead of here. How much longer would it last, though? When Simeon Kirby completed his resort, the same amount of traffic would flow past the bookstore every day from March to September. Could I live with it? Probably, but did I want to? No.

Detective Conway walked in wearing jeans, a blue and gold flannel shirt, and a baseball cap with an insignia I didn't recognize. I drained my cup and stood to throw it in the trash.

"Sorry I'm late," he said. "I had an errand that took longer than I expected."

"No problem. I needed a cup of energy, anyway."

He gestured toward the door. "Shall we go?"

I followed him to his Bronco and climbed into the passenger side. We drove in silence, and he negotiated the maze as if he'd last been there yesterday rather than five years ago. Perhaps he had.

"You have a good memory," I said when he parked in front of Ricky's house.

"Some things you never forget." He took a deep breath and got out.

A curtain twitched on the left side of the living room. I suspected Ricky watched our approach, although I hoped my imagination had something to do with it. No telling how he'd react if he had time to prepare. I hadn't noticed any guns during my visit, but that didn't mean he didn't have any.

289

Conway lifted his hand to knock on the door, and Ricky opened it. "What do you want?" He turned to me. "I told you I didn't want to see you on my property again."

"I asked her to come," Conway said. "We'd like to ask you a few questions."

"About what?"

"May we come in?"

Ricky crossed his arms. "I'm fine right here."

"This might take a while. You sure you won't be more comfortable inside?"

"It won't take long at all." Ricky lifted his lip into a sneer. "I don't have to answer any of your questions. You're not a cop anymore." He jutted his chin toward me. "And she never was."

Conway shrugged. "You have one son missing and another in jail for killing him. I'd think you'd want to help any way you can, but that's just me. Of course, my friends at RPD might also find your reluctance interesting. And they *are* cops."

"Fine," Ricky said, stepping aside. "But don't get too comfortable."

Somehow, I doubted I could get comfortable in his house, no matter what. I trailed Conway into the living room and perched beside him on the couch. Ricky dropped into the armchair opposite us, legs crossed, ankle on knee, and arms folded over his chest.

"Well?" he asked.

Conway considered me. "This is your show."

I swallowed, forcing saliva down my dry-as-a-desert throat. "I spoke with Jaylon this morning. He says he threw away his walkie-talkie watch when he was a kid. Why did you tell me the one I found in the box was his?"

"It is. He must be remembering wrong." Ricky glared at Conway. "Is that what this is all about? A silly kid's toy?"

Drawing his attention back, I said, "Not a silly kid's toy. A way for thieves to communicate with each other while robbing a jewelry store, which is exactly what I think you did five years ago."

"That's ridiculous. I'm an engineer. A law-abiding citizen. Why would I do something that stupid?"

"To help Ewon get the money to open his auto repair shop. Only you didn't consider how you would sell the stuff you took while the police were still investigating."

"Hah. I didn't even know about that robbery until you told me."

Conway broke in. "That's not true. The Blackburn police asked you about it because they thought Ewon was involved. I spoke with one of the detectives this morning."

Ricky glowered at him but said nothing.

I continued. "And that's not the only thing you lied about. Regina still has her engagement ring. I saw it myself. That ring I found with the watch came from the robbery, right? You kept something for yourself and hid the rest in the tunnel under the church."

"Bull. I bought that ring at a pawnshop. I was gonna give it to Regina for our anniversary, but she filed for divorce, so I kept it."

"I assume you have the sales receipt to prove it?"

"I threw it away."

"Why would she need two engagement rings?" I shook my head. "Never mind. How did you know about those tunnels, anyway? Very few people do."

"Ewon and Lyle used to hang out in the woods,

smoking dope and drinking. One day, they found an entrance in an abandoned shack they ran into when it rained. They told me about it, but I've never been down there."

Why did I think he'd ever admit to anything? Especially to me. This was a waste of time. All I'd accomplished was telling him everything I knew. Foolish and dangerous. I laid a hand on Conway's arm. "Let's get out of here. He's not going to tell us anything."

"In a minute. I have a question." He met Ricky's gaze head-on. "What do *you* think happened to Ewon?"

Ricky squirmed in his seat. "Regina won't agree, but I think he's dead. He wouldn't have disappeared for no reason."

"Who do you think killed him?"

"I don't know, but it wasn't me."

"Come on, you must have some idea. Who do you suspect?"

"Lyle. They probably got drunk, had a fight, and Ewon died. Lyle panicked. Hid the body and took off. That's my theory."

Conway and I stood, and the former detective said, "Thanks for your time."

Ricky escorted us out and slammed the door behind us.

CHAPTER TWENTY-NINE

I climbed into the passenger seat of the Bronco while Conway did the same on the other side. As I buckled my seat belt, I said, "Well, that was pointless."

"Not necessarily. When animals are cornered, they come out fighting. When people are cornered, they do stupid things. They make mistakes."

"Like what?"

"That depends. In this case, he could try to move Ewon's body or dig up the jewelry. We'll have to wait and see. I'm going back to watch the house after I drop you off."

"I should go with you. It'll be safer with two of us."

He adamantly shook his head. "No way. I won't be responsible for a detective's girlfriend's safety. If anything happened to you, every cop in the state would come after me."

"That's not true."

"Doesn't matter. I'm taking you to your car, and you're going home."

I fumed, weighing my need to help with the knowledge that if Eric discovered what I did, he'd kill me himself. "Fine."

He deposited me beside my Dodge and blocked traffic, waiting for me to climb in and start the engine before heading back to Ricky's house.

I pulled away from the coffee shop, feeding carefully into the heavy Sunday evening traffic. The horizon split the sun, leaving a fading orange glow in my rearview mirror. The taillights in front of me required my full attention, so I took the back road instead of the main one to Riddleton. I needed time to think, and being surrounded by motorized humanity wouldn't give me any.

The light disappeared as the sun fell out of sight, and I flipped on my high beams. Darkness enveloped everything around me except for the small stretch illuminated by my headlights. The road had its share of twists and turns, with deep drop-offs in places on either side. Nothing to worry about, though, as long as I maintained a safe speed.

It would take longer to make the trip home this way, but my irritation level would be much lower when I arrived. I was already annoyed by my stupidity at confronting Ricky Barnes. I should've handled the situation better. Perhaps not gone to see him at all.

Either way, there was no need to add to my foul mood. I'd only take it out on Eric when we met for dinner. He didn't deserve to be penalized because I'd acted like an idiot. Headlights from passing cars appeared before me occasionally, but nothing from behind. I felt like I had the road all to myself, which was fine with me.

I'd been mentally kicking myself for about fifteen minutes when lights appeared in the mirror. I glanced at the speedometer and found I was doing the speed limit, so the only way the driver behind would catch up was if they were in a hurry.

It turned out they were. Within a minute or two, the headlights filled the car's cabin, and I couldn't see. I flipped up the rearview to change the angle and slowed, allowing the vehicle to pass, but they stayed on my bumper. I braked and rolled down the window to wave them around. No good. They came closer, giving me the sensation their grill sat in my back seat.

I sped up. Forty-five. Fifty. Fifty-five. I dared not go any faster. One of the drop-off points on a sharp curve was coming up soon. The vehicle—an SUV or maybe a pickup truck—swerved into the oncoming lane and stayed beside me, matching my speed. I slammed on the brake, hoping they'd lose interest and move on. It was too dark to glimpse the driver through the lightly tinted windows. I had no idea what or who I was dealing with. I only knew whoever it was had a death wish. But for themselves or me?

The vehicle alongside slowed until their passenger-side door aligned with my fender. I sped up again. They stayed with me. I thought about calling 911 but didn't dare take my hand off the wheel. The drop-off was just ahead on my right. I could only keep going and, with luck, ride it out. It had to be some teenager playing a prank.

When I slowed for the curve, the vehicle suddenly swerved into my lane, pushing me toward the guard rail. The front end hit.

The car flipped.

Glass shattered, and the world outside spun. Time slowed as I floated in the cabin, restrained only by my seat belt. My Dodge landed on its passenger side, slid into a tree, and settled on all fours. I slammed back into the seat like a ragdoll with no control over my arms and legs.

Chest heaving and heart pounding, I froze to get my bearings, then did the limb test—legs, arms, neck—all intact and moving. No pain, but I had adrenaline and shock to thank for that. I had to get out of here before it wore off.

Turning my spinning head slightly, I noticed a figure standing on the road where the guardrail used to be out of the corner of my eye. I couldn't make out any features or even gender. Was it a bystander here to help or the person who did this, ensuring the job was successful?

In the hope they couldn't see me any better than I could see them, I closed my eyes and remained still. If I put on a good enough act, the perpetrator would declare victory and go away. A bystander would've certainly already called 911, so I had nothing to lose either way. I held my position for as long as I could stand, then risked another peek. The figure had gone.

A rush of fear paralyzed my brain. I struggled to think. I'd been in a similar position before. What did I do? To begin with, I had to find a way out of my seat. I pressed the red seat belt release button. To my surprise, the belt released easily. First problem solved. My next step was to find my phone and call 911. I reached toward the cup holder beneath the dashboard where my phone clip stayed, but it must've flown out while the car was upside down. The only way to find it would be to escape the damaged vehicle.

The roof had caved during the roll and now sat only an inch above my head. I suspected opening the driver's side door might be impossible, but I tried anyway. It didn't budge. The frame had bent. I saw a new car in my future but had more pressing problems at the moment. I had to get out of the vehicle.

Maybe I could squeeze out the window. I pressed the power button to roll it down. No dice. Either the bent frame held the glass in place, or the electrical system had failed. I'd have to break it. However, after the last time I was run off the road and trapped in my car, I heeded Eric's advice and bought a multi-purpose tool for occasions like this. It had a seat belt cutter and a spring-loaded window-glass breaker. Now, I only had to reach it.

I shifted toward the glove compartment. A twinge of pain shot up my side. The adrenaline was wearing off.

I had to move.

I grabbed the handle on the compartment door and pulled up. It moved, but the door didn't open. It was stuck. I cleared the clutter that had escaped the floorboard during the roll, scooted into the passenger seat, butt first, then legs, and tried to open the passenger-side door. No luck with that one, either. Back to the glove compartment and the magic tool.

Trying the compartment door again, I used both hands this time. Still stuck. I slammed my palm against it in anger, then sat for a moment, letting the frustration drain away. I'd never free myself if I let my emotions take charge. Then I realized I was doing all this to escape the car to look for my phone. From the passenger seat, I had free access to both floorboards. Why didn't I just find my phone? *Duh*.

My chest and ribs ached, so I slowly reached toward the driver's side floorboard and felt around, grateful I hadn't replaced the airbag after it had deployed in the last accident. No broken nose to deal with this time. I couldn't quite reach the floor, so I lay on my belly, knees bent against the door, and shifted forward. Nothing on the floor or under the seat. The phone holder must've landed on the other side.

I sat up, bent over with my cheek against the glove compartment door, and pushed my hands through the discarded receipts, junk mail, and paper bags, looking for anything solid. My thumb bumped against an unidentified rolling object. Using both hands, I swept debris away from the URO, eventually achieving a good grip.

It was evident in the dim light my phone screen had shattered into a spiderweb. Fingers crossed, I pressed the side button to light up the screen. Nothing happened. I wiped my hand on my jeans and tried again. It flickered on, then off again. All right. Progress. One more time. My lock-screen photo of Savannah holding her stuffed monkey appeared, emergency calls only scrawled across the bottom.

No problem. Pretty sure this qualified as an emergency. I swiped the screen, tapped the phone icon, and dialed 911.

An operator answered on the second ring: "911, what's your emergency?"

I told her who and where I was and what had happened. She promised help was on the way and asked me to stay on the line until they came.

"Should I try to get out of the car? The doors are stuck, but I have something to break the window if I have to."

"Do you see any fire or smell smoke?"

298

"No, nothing like that."

"Then just stay put until the fire department arrives. They'll pry you out safely. You might have injuries you aren't aware of. We don't want to make them worse."

She asked me questions about friends and family to keep me distracted, and my breathing and heart rate returned to a level near normal. "Is there anyone you'd like me to call for you?"

I gave her Eric's number, which I'd studiously memorized after discovering it'd hurt his feelings that I didn't know it. She promised to notify him as soon as we disconnected. The first red-and-blue lights flashed against the pitch-black sky a few minutes later.

When a firefighter in full turnout gear slid down the hillside toward me, I told the 911 operator help had come. She wished me luck and hung up. I hoped she'd remember to call Eric.

The firefighter pulled on the door handle, but even with his strength and better leverage, it didn't budge. He barked instructions into the radio attached to his jacket, the light clipped beside it blinding me. Two more firefighters negotiated their way down the hill, peeled open my car with a giant hydraulic can opener, and turned me over to the EMTs carrying a backboard.

After I correctly answered a series of questions, they fixed a padded plastic collar around my neck, strapped me onto the backboard, and carried me back up the hill to the ambulance. The adrenaline pain-killing effect had begun to wear off, and every jouncing step shot through me like a lightning bolt.

When we arrived at the hospital, the emergency room staff greeted me like a long-lost friend. Not surprising since it'd only been a few weeks since my last visit. A few more punches on my card, and I'd receive the next trip free.

A doctor's examination and full-body X-rays later, Eric and Brittany came barreling in. They took turns alternately fawning over and chastising me for putting myself in danger again.

I put my hands up. "It wasn't my fault this time! All I did was drive home from Sutton."

Eric leaned down and gently kissed my forehead. "I'm sorry. I'm worried about you. The good news is, we caught the guy."

My eyebrows shot up, sending a flash of pain through my scalp. "How?"

"Jeremy Conway called me. He said you two had visited Ricky Barnes, and Conway was supposed to be watching him after you left but lost him in traffic. When your 911 call came in, we knew who to look for. We caught up to him in Sutton and found a big dent in his right fender. He admitted running someone off the road but claimed it was an accident."

"Baloney," I replied. "It was no accident. He even got out of his car to check out the damage. And probably to make sure I was dead."

"Don't worry. After hearing what Conway had to say, we're getting a warrant to search Barnes's house. If anything incriminating is there, we'll find it. And I'm sure we can match paint transfer on his vehicle to your car."

I attempted a deep breath, cut short by rib pain. Finally, I had real hope for Jaylon.

CHAPTER THIRTY

Brittany held her left hand in front of her, unable to take her eyes off the two-carat filigree engagement ring Olinski had presented her at their Valentine's Day dinner last night. "Isn't it gorgeous?" she said, her eyes glittering more than the diamonds.

I swallowed my bite of bacon cheeseburger. "It's beautiful. Even prettier than when you showed it to me two minutes ago."

She stuck her tongue out at me. "You're just upset that Eric didn't give *you* one yet."

"Absolutely untrue! Eric and I are nowhere near ready to get married. The best thing about that ring is I don't have to keep the secret anymore."

"I think that was the biggest surprise of all." Brittany reached over and took my hand. "Finding out you knew about it and didn't tell me."

"I'm sorry, Britt, but I couldn't betray Eric's confidence. He'd never trust me again."

Her smile was almost as brilliant as the shimmering stone on her finger. "I know that. I'm not upset. I'm proud of you for not telling me. You understood how important it was for me to enjoy the surprise Olinski had planned. You're growing, and I think it's wonderful."

I wasn't quite sure how to respond to that. Was she complimenting the person I'd become or condemning the person I used to be? Maybe a little of both. Luckily, I didn't have to answer because Olinski and Eric entered the diner and headed straight for us. Brittany and I slid over in the booth to make room for them.

"Hi, guys!" I said.

"Have you seen my ring?" Brittany held it out to Eric.

He laughed. "I have. Congratulations!"

"Thank you," Brittany replied.

I slipped my arm through Eric's. "What've you been up to?"

"Debriefing Ricky Barnes. He confessed to everything. The robbery, killing Ewon so he wouldn't try to sell the jewelry too soon, putting his body in the car and dumping it in the lake. All of it. He didn't want to put his family through another trial, so he cut a deal."

"You mean he didn't want the whole world to know he murdered his own son and let his other son take the rap for it."

"Probably."

"Have the divers found the car yet?"

"Not yet, but I'm sure they will."

Brittany sipped her drink. "Has anyone spoken with Jaylon? How did he take it?"

"I went up to see him," Olinski said. "He has mixed feelings. He's thrilled that his conviction will be overturned, but it's like he lost his brother all over again and now his father, too. And he has to live with the fact that his father allowed him to go to prison for

302

something *he* did. It's tough." He turned to me. "I spoke with his mother, too. She asked me to thank you for helping get her son out of prison."

"I imagine she's having a hard time with the way things worked out, also."

Olinski nodded. "She is, but she didn't seem entirely surprised to me. Almost as if she expected that her husband was involved somehow."

Eric caught Angus's eye and waved. "Do we have time for lunch?" he asked Olinski. "I'm starved."

"Yeah, go ahead and eat. I'll probably get something, too." He glanced at his watch. "I have a meeting with the prosecutor in an hour. He wants all the evidence to present to the judge. Jaylon should be out in a week or two at most."

I stirred the ice around my drink with the straw. "That's wonderful. I'm so happy for him. I hope that lady on the donor list will give him her kidney now."

Brittany nodded. "I'm sure she will. She said Jaylon's conviction was the only thing standing in the way, right?"

I tapped my head with my fist. "Knock on wood," I said. "People have a way of changing their minds." I touched Olinski's hand. "What about Lyle Pipkin? Did Ricky tell you what happened to him?"

"He said Ewon shot Lyle in the back of the head when he refused to let Ewon have any jewelry to sell. Then Ricky showed up, he and Ewon struggled for the gun, it went off, and Ewon died. But we may never know what *really* happened since Ewon and Lyle are dead. Either way, Ricky's going away for a long, long time."

As far as I was concerned, they couldn't make a cell

small enough for him. What he did to Jaylon was unforgivable. "Is it safe to assume Lyle's body is at the bottom of the lake with Ewon's?"

Olinski grimaced. "As much as I hate to say it, you've been right all along. Lyle Pipkin is your skeleton. Ricky didn't think he could get away with carrying two bodies out of the church, so he left Lyle in the alcove where you discovered him. Of course, he was never supposed to be found. You messed everything up that day."

"No wonder he was angry with me from the start." I sipped my drink, then turned to Eric. "Hey, did Penelope ever talk?"

"Her lawyer worked out a deal with the district attorney. She agreed to twenty-five to life for both the robbery and the murder. And she *is* Eliza Naismith. She came to Riddleton after the trial to find the stolen jewelry. But she didn't know about the tunnels until Abigail told her."

"Why did she kill Abigail?"

"She said it was self-defense. Abigail came after her because she wanted all the money for herself. Eliza grabbed the hammer Abigail had been using to break up the rock and hit her to get away but killed her instead."

"It's crazy what people'll do for money."

"I feel sorry for Regina," Brittany said. "She's lost her whole family except for Jaylon because of it."

We sat silently for a moment, none of us knowing what to say. By discovering the truth, we'd ripped the scab off her partially healed wound. Now, she had to begin the healing process all over again. At least she had Jaylon to help her through it this time.

Brittany held her left hand up again. "Let's talk about something happy. Have you seen my gorgeous ring?"

We all busted out laughing. Good thing I knew Brittany wasn't this excited about the ring itself, but more about what it represented. Otherwise, I'd suspect her gold-digging instincts had failed her. Olinski would never be rich, but he'd always be a good man. I was thrilled for my friend and not the least bit jealous. We were both exactly where we wanted to be in our respective relationships.

She flashed the ring again, this time in Eric's direction. "Well, Eric? When are you going to make an honest woman out of Jen?"

I dropped my hands on my hips and lifted my chin. "Hey! I'm as honest as they come. Mostly."

Eric took my hand. "As soon as we're *both* ready."

"What did Jen end up giving you for Valentine's Day?"

His grin stretched across three states. "A key to her apartment! I think she might want me to stick around a while. Finally!"

Heat spread through my cheeks to my ears. My brain scrambled for a way to change the subject. I rolled the paper from my straw between my fingers, feeling like I'd forgotten something. Then, I remembered. "Have you found the jewelry from the robbery?"

Olinski shook his head. "When they brought the wall down to bury it, they covered it with rock. It's going to take a lot of work to get to it. We don't have the manpower."

"I imagine the insurance company might be willing to help with that. They probably laid out a bundle after that robbery."

"We think we might be better off trying to get to it from the other side of the barricade. As soon as we figure out how to get to the other side."

I grinned. "I'll be happy to help with that. You know how I love a challenge."

He gave me his "don't you dare stick your nose in my business" stare. "No, thanks. We can handle it."

"If you say so."

Olinski looked at me over the top of his glasses. "Hold on a minute. I see those wheels turning in your head. You're planning another wild-goose chase, aren't you?"

Who me? Never!

ACKNOWLEDGMENTS

I'd like to express my never-ending gratitude to:

My agent, Dawn Dowdle, for taking a chance on me and providing her constant support. This series wouldn't exist without her.

My editor, Amy Mae Baxter, and the entire Avon team for all their hard work bringing Jen and the gang to life.

The dynamic duo: Julie Golden and Ann Dudzinski, for helping turn my indecipherable drivel into something people want to read.

And, as always, Sadie, for never leaving my side, no matter what.

**She can write the perfect murder mystery...
But can she solve one in real life?**

Crime writer **Jen** returns to her small hometown with a
bestselling book behind her and a bad case of writer's
block. Finding sanctuary in the local bookstore, with an
endless supply of coffee, Jen waits impatiently for
inspiration to strike.

But when the owner of the bookstore dies suddenly in
mysterious circumstances, Jen has a real-life murder to solve.

The stakes are suddenly higher when evidence places Jen
at the scene of the crime and the reading of the will names
her as the new owner of the bookstore ...

Can she crack the case and clear her name, before the
killer strikes again?

Don't miss Sue Minix's debut cosy mystery – available now!

I wrote murder mysteries. I didn't investigate them. Until now...

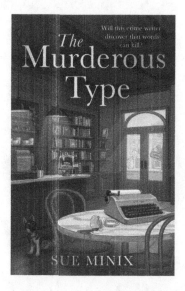

Crime writer turned amateur sleuth, Jen, has taken over the running of the local bookstore in her hometown of Riddleton.

But balancing the books at Ravenous Readers is nothing compared to meeting the deadline for her new novel.

Dodging phone calls from her editor takes a back seat, however, when the local police chief is poisoned. To solve the murder, Jen must dust off her detective hat once more.

With everyone in town seemingly a suspect, and evidence planted to incriminate local police officer and close friend Eric, Jen is working against the clock. Can she find the killer and beat her own writer's block before it's too late?

Don't miss the second instalment in this cosy mystery series – available now!